QUEEN OF DREAMS

BOOKS BY KATHRYN ANN KINGSLEY

For a full list, visit www.kathrynkingsley.com

KATHRYN ANN KINGSLEY

QUEEN OF DREAMS

SECOND SKY

Published by Second Sky in 2024

An imprint of Storyfire Ltd.
Carmelite House
50 Victoria Embankment
London EC4Y 0DZ
United Kingdom

www.secondskybooks.com

First published by Limitless Publishing in 2019.

ISBN: 978-1-83618-291-7
eBook ISBN: 978-1-83618-290-0

ONE

Lydia was dreaming.

Or was she dead?

Was there even a difference now?

I don't want to die.

What was a person, really, when it came down to it? What did it mean, the sense of self? What defined a person? The limits of their mind? Their soul? Voices rang in her head, each speaking over the other, demanding she choose. *Choose now!* But she didn't understand. Choose what?

Please, don't let this happen…

Where did we begin and end with ourselves? What created that endless list of ones and zeroes that became an individual? Were we only a product of our memories? A collective string of choices that turned us into who we were? Or was it defined earlier on, at the moment of our birth? Were we steel tempered by our lives, or were we a whisper of smoke, given form instead?

Or was it not about lives lived at all? Were we merely what we chose to do in those bare few moments where we were not given the option to think? Where instinct alone may rule? In the split second that primal rule took hold, was that truly the judge of who a soul may be?

Questions crashed through her mind, a million at once, tangling with memories. Over it all, she heard the voices demanding she choose.

Choose now!

A soldier in the trenches, sweat mixing with blood and rain alike, was soaked in the ever-present mud around him. Who thought digging ditches and fighting in them was ever a goddamn good idea?

A flash of a memory that wasn't hers. Or was it? It was so hard to tell where things began and ended. Where she started and stopped.

An object, no bigger than his fist, fell in the mud next to him with a thick plop. There was shouting and panic and the scramble to save their own lives. The scamper of limbs as men tried to escape what should honestly have no business being so dangerous; it was so small. They had no chance to get away.

In that moment of instinct, did you save your life or others? Did you leap upon that grenade or use their bodies to climb to safety?

The swerve of a car. That hair's breadth to avoid the vehicle in front of you. Instinct. Reaction. Primal desires. Was that what defined us? Was that what we were when boiled down to nothing? That made us who we were?

To live or die.

To be or not to be, wasn't that the age-old question?

Dying was simpler. Easier. Hamlet said it himself. And he wasn't wrong. Her situation might be different, but the question was the same. Live or die, knowing accepting death would spare herself more pain and suffering.

Voices rang out in her mind, deafening and wrong. Whispers as much as they were shouting, filling her very soul with their presence. Seven voices, speaking in turn. Each ghastly and horrible.

> *"You will suffer, Child. You will die.*
> *Once more and again, as all must do.*
> *What will you decide?*
> *Do you wish to live, or to die, knowing what waits for you?*
> *For He waits for you. Our Favorite Son. His heart is yours.*
> *His love will bring you nothing but pain.*
> *It is your choice to make. It will always be."*

Fire licked up her flesh, turning her skin black. Her nerves were dead, and now she could only watch as the fire curled up her skin that darkened, bubbled, and flaked away. The roar of the inferno around her had taken the air from her lungs, and as darkness took her, she could only pray for her soul and the souls of those who did this.

These weren't her memories! The voices were doing this. Why?

It is the decision they're giving you. You have to choose whether you wanna live or die.

A rope tangled around her neck as the men pulled the chair out from under her. She spasmed as she was denied the quick drop of a hanging and instead felt her throat crushed by the cinch of the biting hemp against her flesh. Her eyes bulged as they screamed at her.

It's a warning. This is what's waiting for you. Pain, and death, and pain, and death.

Tied to the tree. Her hands were tied to the tree. *Oh God. No, please!* Struggling, she screamed in pain as she realized her legs wouldn't move. They hurt.

Looking down, she screamed again as she saw why. A man was hunched over her, sawing away at her skin with a serrated army knife. Blood soaked his hands, his clothes, his face, as he sliced off a piece of her skin and... and ate it. Slurped it between bloody lips, savoring it like the finest delicacy. He moaned in pleasure as he wiped her blood along his lips, returning for more.

He looked at her, mad eyes wide with glee as the knife suddenly entered her throat.

Seen enough?

Whose memories were those? Not hers. She hadn't died like that. She had died with a man's hand burning holes in her heart. Setting her blood on fire in her chest.

Her name was Lydia. She was *Lydia*. And she had died. Edu had killed her.

She was herself.

Nobody could take that away.

Decide. Now.

In that split second, she had her answer.

Her hand pressed against a stone surface. Crawling. On her stomach, she inched forward. Water was in her lungs. She had to climb out. She had to. She wanted to live.

She was already dead, though. Wasn't she?

Pressing herself up onto her hands and knees, she felt the water pour off her. She hacked and coughed, retched, and finally felt air fill her lungs. Oh, that felt like heaven. She wheezed, trying to fill her burning body with more of that blessed and vastly underrated substance.

At this rate, she might as well learn to breathe water, with the sheer number of times she'd been nearly drowned lately.

Funny. I'll work on that.

Who was speaking? What'd just happened to her? Had Edu messed up? Had he not managed to kill her and Aon saved her at the last minute?

No. She had been dead. She *knew* it. Just simply felt it to the core of her body. Was she even alive now? What happened?

Lydia raised a shaking hand to her face and placed her palm

against her cheek, tried to rub her eyes. Something blocked her path. Something hard and strange. She ripped it from her face and, for the first time, opened her eyes.

She was kneeling on a stone floor in a dark room. The air was wet and damp like a cave.

In her lap was a full mask, made of bits of stone, glued together in a mosaic. It was grotesque and made to terrify. It looked almost Aztec but twisted in a nightmare, arranged into the face of a feathered snake's skull. Empty-eyed and horrible.

And it was made of turquoise.

"No!" She hurled the mask away from herself. It sailed into the waters of a pool of glowing crimson liquid, over which loomed the carved faces of demons and monsters. It quickly sank beneath the ripples it created. "No... no, that's not me! That will never be me..."

She was back here at the Pool of the Ancients, looking up at that waterfall, at that glowing red liquid like blood pouring from the enormous stone faces and from their eyes and mouths.

Pulling in a shaky, wavering breath, she did the only thing she could think of that made any sense.

She screamed.

* * *

The panic and bickering between the lords and ladies of Under was beginning to grow nigh insufferable, even for Lyon's considerable patience. Keenly in this moment, he had no greater desire than to go home with his wife and enjoy what little calm they had before the storm.

Before Aon made good on his threat to destroy them all.

Instead, he had been ordered to attend Edu here in his home with all the others. And so he stood in the keep of the King of Flames and watched the fire burn in the great pit in the center of the main hall. Everyone was on edge. Even the king in question paced back in forth in front of the perpetual blaze that illuminated the carved dragon heads and monsters that decorated the arches and posts of his home.

Burned into his thoughts like a brand, Aon's threat echoed in Lyon's mind. *"For millennia I have had to listen to you all whimper and whine like simpering children over how I seek to destroy this world. Heed me now, Priest, and know that you have not once seen me try."*

When Lyon relayed the message to the others, it had sent them into an excited jabbering of panic and fear. For good reason. If the warlock meant to end the world, none of them were certain he could not easily do so.

He knew the words the warlock had said were true. Aon was correct in his assertion that never once had the warlock ever *truly* desired to destroy Under in its entirety. Now he had no reason to let it linger for the last hundred years before the void claimed them all.

The din that raged around him was nearly unnavigable. Too many were attempting to speak, and it made the thread of conversation barely discernible.

"He means to do it!"

"Of course, he does."

"But why? Over the girl?"

"Does he even need a reason?"

"This is asinine! She was only a human."

"Perhaps he only needed an excuse."

Lyon knew the truth. He knew it by the way Aon had carried himself in his grief. The magnitude of the suffering he had felt coming from the warlock had been palpable. That the King of Shadows had chosen to bury her in the Pool of the Ancients alone, and by his own hand, meant only one thing.

Aon had loved the young woman.

Lyon was the only one present who knew the truth of

Aon's Great War. The *real* reason behind the death of King Qta made the tragedy of Lydia's death far more poignant and tragic.

Indeed, it made him wonder if they did not, in fact, deserve whatever revenge Aon was about to pay them.

To be denied love was one thing. To be robbed was another. And to be robbed of the woman he loved by Edu, Aon's greatest beacon of hatred in this world... Yes. This would spell their ruin. Perhaps rightfully so.

He held his tongue and did not offer the truth he knew or his observations of the warlock's behavior, for reasons twofold. First, he still felt some manner of desire to protect the dread king's dignity in his grief. And second, it would do no good to say it.

No one would believe him.

It was the mindset of all the others in the room that Aon was not capable of love. That it was either a feeling long since removed from him by the ravages of time or madness or that he never had the capacity for such things in the first place.

That would be the straightforward opinion to hold, after all. The notion that Aon had no heart beating in his chest made him effortless to despise. They would dismiss Lyon for being the soft-souled creature he was if he said his mind.

"You said she had to die to save this world," Kamira snarled at Ziza.

The Oracle was not fazed. Through all the shouting in the room, she stood silently with her eyes shut. She was placid as the frozen lake her countenance resembled. "And so she did. And so she has."

Lyon furrowed his brow at the Oracle's words but said nothing.

"This world will be burned to a cinder by the warlock! We have little hope of stopping him, if all six kings and queens of old could not stand against him. You—" Kamira's shouting was broken off as a sound interrupted her. The noise silenced all the rumble of the group assembled at once.

Thunder.

Rolling, booming, and echoing in the distance. At first, Lyon thought perhaps he had mistaken it, but a second low rumble followed.

It may have been the arrival of the warlock himself, heralding his approach, if not for another strange sound. This new sound even stilled Edu's pacing.

"What is that?" Maverick was wary as he stood from his chair.

Whatever it was was small and persistent. It was a noise Lyon had not heard in a very, very long time.

Lyon moved from where he stood against a column and quickly headed for the door that led outside. He knew by the flurry of steps behind him that he was not alone.

He burst through the door, tossing it open in front of him and hearing it smash into the entryway, careless for how quickly he moved. As his feet touched the landing outside the entrance to King Edu's home, something tapped him in the face. Cold and strange. Familiar yet as foreign as a dream.

The sound of thunder was not Aon's doing.

Lyon looked up and saw the clouds that had covered the skies overhead, blanketing the abyss of the night sky in a dark gray, only highlighted by the faint glow of the moons beyond. Kamira moved to stand beside him, holding her palms up before her, looking at them in confusion. The others slowed to a stop upon the landing, each experiencing this new truth in their own way.

It was raining in Under.

TWO

Lydia had screamed until she had lost her voice and dissolved instead into sobbing. She knelt there, doubled over, pressing her arms against the stone of the platform that overlooked the lake of blood. But, like screaming, her tears wound down after a time. Breaking down into a fit could only last her so many minutes before she had to scrape herself up off the floor and go on.

But go on with what? I died. What happened?

Damn them. Damn them all to hell for doing this to her. She didn't deserve any of this. She didn't deserve to be dragged into this nightmare world. Hunted, nearly drowned, rejected as an outcast, chased and tormented, and *then* murdered. And then nearly drowned *again*.

And now what, she was resurrected from the dead? For what? More suffering? More of this bullshit?

Are you done yet? I'm bored. We should go.

Maybe if she ignored the voice, it would leave her alone.

It snickered. **Unlikely.**

The voice sounded vaguely male. It was a "he," whatever he was.

Lydia sat back on her heels and ran both her hands through her hair. She was soaking wet. Again. From nearly drowning. Again. Yeah, she was going to be bitter about that for a long while.

Technically, you were already dead when you went in this time.

Sighing, she looked around. Here, on the shores of the Pool of the Ancients, surrounded by the creepy staring statues and piles of ghastly skulls with their exaggerated features, and eerie, glowing, red light from the blood of the pond. But nobody else to be seen. "Who are you, anyway?" The voice sounded strange, as though it wasn't coming from anywhere in particular.

You.

"Excuse me?"

I'm you.

"No, you're not. Try again."

Yes, I am. I think I'd know.

Shutting her eyes, she tried not to lose her temper. *Great, another crazy asshole speaking in riddles. That's all I need.* Climbing to her feet, she wavered. She felt like jelly or like she'd just been squeezed through a wringer. Walking toward the altar in the middle of the platform with the statues, she leaned on it with both hands. They were still her hands. She was still her. Maybe. Mostly.

Lydia had a few memories of dying she didn't think she had gone in with. Flashes of those memories—dreams of dying in the trenches, or in frozen water, or dying in a fire—came back to her, and she cringed, lowering her head. Even without the subject matter, it was giving her a headache.

The Ancients wanted to show you what it meant to suffer. They wanted to make sure you wanted to do this.

"Do what, exactly?"

Live. You could've said no.

"I didn't really get a chance to think about it."

But they still gave you the choice, even if you weren't smart enough to understand it at the time.

"Listen, jackass." Now she was being taunted by a wiseass disembodied voice. "I thought you said you were me. And now you're calling me stupid? Which is it, Skippy?"

Temper, temper.

"I think I have a right to be upset. I just died!"

Yesterday. Get over it.

"I... what? I've been dead for a day?"

Did you have something better to be doing?

Okay, now she was pissed. "I don't know who you are, but fuck you."

They say masturbation is a sin, y'know. The voice had an odd hiss to it, drawing out the *S*s strangely.

Laughing, weak and exhausted, she was at her wits' end. "Okay, asshole. Explain to me how exactly you're 'me,' then." Coughing, she groaned. It was wet and painful. The feeling of water still lingered in her lungs.

I'm all the power gifted to you by the Ancients. I'm all that you should be. But cramming that much strength into a dead girl's soul was going to drive you insane. *Soooo,* you had a choice. Die, go bonkers, or... compartmentalize.

"Look, buddy, I—" She lifted her head to yell at the disembodied voice. She came face-to-face with a creature that was curled up on top of the altar she was leaning on. The sight of him made her yelp and flail, falling backward and landing hard on her ass with a painful *unf.*

He was a snake, or a ghost, or a weird snake made from smoke. No, he was a ghost snake, she decided. He seemed to flicker in and out of existence in waves, like a fire might lick in and out. The creature took up the whole of the altar and was reared up like a cobra, maybe ten feet long total. He had huge wings, but unlike the black smoke of its body, the wings were cast in a myriad of glowing turquoise and teal.

His head was like a cartoonish, exaggerated skull of a snake missing its lower jaw. Jagged teeth and pointed upper maw were all that was left. He had gaping black holes for eyes. The end of his tail and the back of its head had tufts of the glowing turquoise feathers.

The peaks of his wings were like the claws of a dragon, and he folded them in front of him like arms, claw on claw like a cat. He was looking down at her with what felt like amusement. She certainly couldn't read any expression on his ghastly features, but weirdly, she could... sense it.

"Holy fuck." She wondered for a moment if this thing was going to kill her a second time.

Kill you? Why would I do that? I'm you, remember?

And he could read her mind.

I'm in your mind. I *am* your mind. C'mon, Cupcake, pay attention.

She just stared in silence. His forked tongue flickered out of his mouth, turquoise and glowing. But as ghastly and weird as he was, he felt familiar. Like something she would have doodled in her notebook in college.

As bizarre as it was... she knew he wasn't lying. Looking at this creature, she just... trusted him. He felt like a friend, even if he was being an abject smartass. This eerie and weird creature seemed connected to her. Like recognizing something from a dream. "Am I hallucinating you?" That would also be perfect form for her life right now, going from one bizarre thing to another, and now to seeing an imaginary ghost snake.

He seemed to think it over for half a second. **Hmmm... no.**

The way he hesitated made her suspect. "I'll rephrase. Could other people see you?"

Well, yeah, of course. I'm perfectly real. Unless you don't want people to see me, and then I'll hide.

How he was somehow real, and yet also inside her head, made no sense. But nothing in Under made sense, and she had to start learning to roll with the impossible. She had a pounding headache. She was exhausted. At least now that she'd seen the ghost-snake-monster-thing, she understood the lisp it had.

It's not a lisp! I'm a snake. There's a difference.

"Uh-huh."

There is!

"Just keep telling yourself that." Standing, she winced as she wiped herself off. Her shirt was soaked and burned to pieces, and she had a char mark on her chest. No, correction, she had five char marks in the shape of fingertips. Fear jabbed at her as the memory of Edu killing her flashed through her mind.

He was trying his best.

"At what, exactly?" Touching one of the marks on her skin, she discovered they wiped off like soot. She wiped the rest of the marks off as fast as she could, eager to get the proof of what had happened off her. There were no other wounds underneath, no mark left behind from what he'd done.

At making it quick. It's not really his strong suit. Edu really didn't want you to suffer, you know.

"Good for him. I'm still fucking pissed." Rubbing her hands over her face, she let out a long, overwhelmed breath. "I died. I really died."

Yeah. I'm sorry, Cupcake. You did.

"I don't get what's happening. Why did the Ancients bring me back? I was dead. I should have stayed that way. Why did they bring me back and put that thing on my face—" She broke off as she suddenly remembered. Everything was still too much all at once, and all at once she recalled what had been on her face when she crawled out of the pool of blood.

The snake on the altar curled his tail around himself with a flick like that of a cat.

There you go. Now you're getting to the important part.

The mask. She had come out of the lake with a *mask*. A mask made of *turquoise*. She had yanked it from her face and hurled it back into the glowing pond. It had been a full mask. Just like Aon's or Edu's.

She might not understand a great deal about this world, but she wasn't that stupid. Only kings and queens had full face masks like those. And the House that wore turquoise was dead. Aon had called them the House of Dreams and told her that he had killed its king out of wrath after attempting to control them.

Terror washed over her in a wave of realization. She covered her mouth with her hand and felt her heart quicken. *No. No, please. Anything but that.*

Are you going to start screaming again?

"Shut up, asshole."

Oh, take a seat before you fall over. All I need is you cracking your head open and dying again.

She was dizzy, that much was true. Her heart was racing, and she needed to calm down. Walking to the altar the snake was perched on, she sat on the ground and pressed her back up against the stone. She wasn't afraid of the snake. Resting her head on her knees, she tried to breathe. She felt the drape of a tail against her shoulder and knew the snake had reached down with it, to try to comfort her.

"I'm a dreamer."

Yup.

"But they're all dead."

Not anymore. Now there's one. You.

"Are you Qta?" She looked up at the snake. He was peering down over the edge at her, upside down from her point of view.

Nah. But you saw a painting and a carving of him once, and poof, here I am. I'm what you made me. You

didn't want to be the **Queen of Dreams. Not really. Not yet. So you made me to soften the blow. Otherwise, you'd probably wind up being crazier than a bag of cats. Or Aon. Or Aon as a cat.** The creature snickered.

He tilted his head to look at her, upside down. He was freakish and strange and horrifying and... okay, kinda cute.

Thanks, Cupcake. You ain't so bad yourself.

"Stop that."

Stop what?

"Reading my goddamn—" *mind,* she finished silently as she realized it was pointless. This thing was in her head. He already knew what she was thinking. She sighed. "Never mind."

At least you catch on eventually.

"What do I do now?"

The snake wrapped his tail around her arm, and she knew he was trying to be a friend.

If you stay here, they'll come for you. They already know something's happened.

"Who'll come for me?" She'd already been murdered once this week. She didn't want to make a second go at it.

He tilted his head to the side, a perfect ninety-degree angle on his neck. The glowing turquoise tufts of feathers dangled to one side.

Why, all of them, of course!

* * *

Aon had retreated to his home, to sit in his library and think. He had been here for a day, if his clock was any indication.

Time for him was a broken, lurching thing.

His mind was reeling with the loss of Lydia. His ill-fated mortal. She kept him in a regular tempo—suddenly, time mattered for an outside reason. Now, without her there, he was once more caught in the shattered mirrors of his mind.

This room carried so many new bittersweet memories for him now. The thoughts of her standing by his table, wide-eyed and beautiful as her curiosity and fear of him warred for supremacy, would haunt him.

Her laughter, her smile, the touch of her hand. There was no doubt in his mind that this pain in his heart was the result of a love taken away. The memories burned in him as if they were real knives in his flesh.

But they would not do so for long.

Unlike all his other memories that would fade in time, these would have no opportunity to do so. He would destroy this world before they had a chance to lose their recent pain.

Perhaps after finally killing Edu, he would let the others kill him. Perhaps he would let Lyon do the honors.

He changed his mind as soon as the thought came to him. No. If this world were to end, it would be by his hand. Let him greet the void alone.

Pulling the glass chrysalis out from underneath his shirt, he studied the little blinking orb of magic. It had been fashioned to resemble an insect, but it was merely a creation of skilled magic. It was a facsimile of a creature long since dead from this world. None of the little fireflies of Under had existed since he had crushed Qta's life in his wrath. It was merely a lie of hope.

Just like Lydia had been.

He traced his fingers along the surface of the glass and had a sudden urge to smash it in his hand. To shatter it to pieces. To feel the glass bite into his flesh and scatter the magic within. The merchant who had given it to Lydia had insisted that the little ball of energy had "moods." That it had a mind. What an absurd sentiment.

A lie of hope.

It had no life. No soul. No heart within it. It blinked and flashed, oblivious to him within its little glass cage. He should destroy it. He had done far worse in his day. Far more careless acts of violence he had wrought, unheeding of the cost it may carry.

Why, now, would he hesitate to smash this little lie into oblivion?

For her?

For it was her memory that he held in his hand. It was all he had left of her brief time. She had been false, a blink of an already dead insect in the darkness. And as soon she had come, she had gone.

He closed the chrysalis in his palm and rested his fist against his chin. Resisting the temptation of his rage, he did not smash the item in his hand. Instead, he let his eyes slide shut behind his mask.

Oh, Lydia...

A boom in the distance broke him of his reverie. The fire had grown low. He must have been here hours without realizing. Damn his faltering mind!

What was the sound that had raised him? Slipping the glass pendant back beneath his shirt, he stood. *Perhaps those idiots are finally smart enough to be the ones to strike first. Finally, they try to outclass me.*

A flash on the horizon caught his attention. Another boom followed moments later. Thunder? The sound of tapping against the windows of his library drew him to the glass and inspired him to undo the latch and swing the large glass panes open.

A wind blew into his home, billowing the long curtains into the chamber. They whipped in the wind before calming as the gust receded.

Rain. A storm. Clouds hung low in the air. There was wind.

How? How is this possible? Could it be...?

More false hope. More illusions cast into his failing mind by the imperfections within. He pounded his fist into the railing of the window until his knuckles began to bleed. He only found the reason to stop as he watched the rain droplets begin to mix with the marks of his blood upon the wood surface.

Pausing, he traced his fingers along the drops of water, smearing them in a lazy and heedless pattern. It was damp against his skin.

This could only mean but one thing.

But how?

The truth would be his. And he knew where to begin looking for it.

Pushing through the fabric of space, he bent the world on the proper access with a flex of his power as familiar as moving a muscle. It was as easy as stepping through a doorway, so was it like moving between his home and the Pool of the Ancients. Never had he so much cause to visit it so frequently as he had of late.

There was no one there. It was as he left it.

Save for one thing, lying there on the lip of the stone circular platform. A mask sat there, dimly lit in the torches of the glowing crimson lake. The red light painted it in an odd purple hue.

It was in his hand before he realized he had moved. For it was a mask he had once known quite well. It was the face of the man he had murdered so many hundreds of years ago. It had dissolved into dust, like the man himself had done.

Yet here it was.

All the proof that he needed to confirm that it was raining.

Turquoise stones were arranged into a mosaic of a beast. The man who called himself Qta was far happier in his snake-like form than his human one. But when he made the rare concession to take the shape of a man, this was the mask he wore.

"What do you scheme, tyrants of old?" He did not expect a reply from the Ancients he despised so very much. He sent the mask back to his home, slipping it through the fabric of the world and to somewhere safe.

"Hello, Aon."

Turning, he focused on the cold voice that broke him from his thoughts. He was surprised to see the Oracle herself, standing across the platform from him. She was alone. "Where are your fellow traitors, Ziza? Or have you come to die first? You are alone and I am *wrathful*."

"Has the thunderstorm not changed your mind, I wonder?"

"A curious illusion. Maverick's doing, I assume." It was no illusion, he knew. But for now, he wished to play the game. He stalked toward her slowly, but his intimidating presence was ineffective against the Oracle. "Why are you here?"

"A prophecy."

"Yes. I surmised you were given some false vision by the Ancients that led those fools to murder Lydia. You were lied to. She—"

"For once in your life, be silent and listen, warlock!"

He was not accustomed to being interrupted, and it broke off his words into startled silence. Few dared ever speak to him in such a way, let alone the stoic and icy Oracle. "Whatever for?"

Ziza sighed heavily and shook her head, seemingly annoyed at his obstinance. "I have come to deliver a prophecy, Aon. But this one is for you."

THREE

"Where are we?"

Home.

No, home was Boston. Home was her friendship with Nick. God, she hoped Nick was okay. She knew that should probably be the last of her concerns—she'd died, after all. He was a were-whatever. He'd found a place in this fucked-up world. But still, she missed him. She could use a hug right about now.

Lydia took a moment to look around where the strange ghost-snake had taken her. Teleporting from the Pool of Ancients to wherever-the-hell-they-were-now was not nearly so bad as being dragged around by Aon. Or, maybe, something about her had changed and simply could handle it better.

Speaking of the snake, it seemed like he could grow or shrink at will. He had been the size of a cat on her shoulder when he had taken her here and away from the Pool of the Ancients. Now he was at least fifty feet long, curled around the entire circumference of the stone building they were now in, twice. Lydia stood in the colossal stacked-block doorway, watching the pouring rain outside. It was torrential. The water was falling in sheets, and it made it hard to see in the darkness.

Doesn't it never rain in Under? Is this because of me?

Not in fifteen hundred years. And yes.

She tried not to be startled by the snake's answering of her thoughts. Yelling at him clearly wasn't going to do any good. One more thing to get used to.

The building looked like a stone ruin, protruding high over a vast jungle. It was hard to see much in the darkness and deluge of the storm. Everything was enveloped within it. Only in the flashes of lightning could she see the vines that had overgrown the structure and hints of a jungle and other buildings below.

Massive and seemingly entirely impractical stone steps led up to the smaller structure at the top, where they were now. It was a step pyramid. A gigantic, ancient step pyramid. The stones were crumbling and unevenly placed. Carved, but asymmetrical and strange. Depictions of snakes, of jaguars, of screaming and strange monstrous heads dotted the walls.

Under drew inspiration from Earth. And Earth from Under. "Question."

Shoot.

"How do you know it's raining because of me? How did you even know where this place was? If you're inside my head, how do you know things I don't?" She crossed her feet at the ankles and turned to look over at the giant phantasm of a snake. The fact that his wings and feather tufts on his head and tail glowed provided some light in the empty stone chamber, casting the walls in a weird blue-green glow from where it was lying.

When people come out of the Pool of the Ancients, they just Know All The Things. How Under works. Basic facts. You should be like everyone else now, and serve the Ancients, but...

"I was going to go insane. Right. I got that." She shut her

eyes for a moment before looking back to the snake. "So, I made you instead. Can I un-make you?"

Nope! You're stuck with me, Cupcake. And it's not my fault you're stubborn. I don't know what Aon sees in you.

He didn't mean it seriously, judging by his tone and the way he rolled his head to one side. He moved his head like an owl, seemingly entirely detached from the rest of his body.

"Now I'm making fun of myself the other way around." Grumbling, she turned to watch the storm, at the flashing bolts of lightning as they arced through the clouds.

Aon.

Thoughts of the warlock came over her like the black clouds overhead.

Things between them would be different now. She didn't know how. She could barely wrap her head around any of this. Hell, she didn't even know what it was she and Aon had going on *before* Edu had killed her and she was turned into... whatever she was now. She still couldn't process the facts.

Aon had tried to protect her. It hadn't been his fault that he failed. She remembered the image of those arrows piercing through his chest as Kamira, masquerading as Edu, faced off against the warlock.

Kamira had been in on the deed.

That meant... so was Lyon.

Hurt and betrayal stabbed at her like a physical blow, and she felt it twist in her gut. She tried not to cry. Tried. Failed. She wiped at her face to try to keep the tears from traveling too far.

Whassamatter, Cupcake?

"You know what. You're in my head."

Yeah, but I'm trying to get you to talk it out. They say that's good for people.

She rolled her eyes. "They were all in on it. If Kamira was there, then Lyon knew about it. And if Lyon knew, then... everybody knew. Everybody agreed to let Edu kill me."

The thought still brought her visceral pain, and it was surprising. She had thought of Lyon as a friend, as well as Maverick.

They only did what they thought was best. They hate the warlock. Worse, they're absolutely terrified of him. They thought you were some big, bad, world-ending secret.

"I wasn't!"

They didn't know that. They thought Aon was going to do something horrible with whatever secret they thought you had.

"That's stupid. And besides, even if I was, Aon wouldn't..." She trailed off.

Wouldn't he?

Sighing, she stopped, honestly not being able to commit to a claim that Aon wouldn't have manipulated her for his own gain if it suited him. If she were some big, powerful secret... did she honestly think he wouldn't use that to his own ends? He had killed Qta for some unknown reason.

What about now that she was a dreamer?

She trusted Aon when she'd been human. But she wasn't a helpless mortal anymore. The reality of that fact was still settling in and still felt impossible. She was dead. She had died. She should still be dead.

But she wasn't. She was standing here, in a ruined stone nightmare temple, watching a thunderstorm in a world that hadn't known rain for fifteen hundred years. "The Ancients did this to me to save their world?"

Mostly. I'm sure they have other motives. They always have other motives.

"Great." She looked over at the giant Disney cartoon from hell, where he was curled up with his head on a coil, watching her. "What do I do about Aon?"

What do you mean?

"I'm a stupid dreamer now, right?"

The **dreamer. The only one. The Queen of Dreams. So, yes,** he said with a hissing snicker, enjoying how little she was trying to make of it. **You're a stupid dreamer.**

"And Aon killed Qta, the old King of Dreams. Because… reasons, apparently." She threw up her hand in frustration. Aon had given her some crap line about wanting power. She had called him out on that being a lie, and he had confessed that it was. But he still hadn't told her the real reason he had killed Qta. "Do you know why he did it?"

Nope. Sorry, Cupcake. You'll have to ask the man himself now.

Sighing darkly, she put her head in her hands. "I die, and then I get dragged back to life. I wake up with your stupid ass pestering me, and now I have to figure out if the guy I—" She broke off, surprised at the words that were about to come out of her mouth. But she wouldn't admit them. Not silently and certainly not out loud.

The guy you what?

"I don't know."

Liar.

"The guy I care about." She could admit that much.

Yuh-huh. Is that it? The guy you only just care about?

"Don't change the subject."

Don't argue with yourself.

She glared angrily at the glowing creature but couldn't really retort—she really was fighting with herself. In more ways than one. "The guy I 'care' about," she spat the word out pointedly in the snake's direction, "is the same guy who killed the previous dreamer or some bullshit. And I'm wondering if I should be really—*really*—afraid of him now."

No clue. I have no idea how that man's head works. I don't think he knows how his head works, seeing as he's got some seriously stripped gears up there. The creature stretched himself out again to rest his head on his cheek. He let out a contented sigh. **I love the sound of thunder. This world's missed it. I'm tired. Aren't you?**

Holy hell, yes, she was. Everything in Lydia was screaming to shut her eyes and rest. To hope that when she opened her eyes, everything would be right again. That she'd be in her bed at home, on Earth, where she belonged. Not here in Under where things went from bad to worse every goddamn day.

C'mere, stupid.

"Don't call yourself stupid," she quipped at the snake, even as she walked up to him. He moved a coil of his tail for her to sit next to him, and she leaned up against the strange, smoky nature of his body. He was... comfortable. Cozy like a firm sofa. Not at all what she'd expected, seeing as she could see through him half the time. Lydia laid her head down on the ghastly snake and felt exhaustion seep into her like a fog.

Of all the things that were now in question—who she was, what she was, what the hell was going to happen between her and Aon now—she didn't question that this snake was part of her. It felt right. This thing was both part of her, and something more, all at once. And with it, she felt safe. And safe was what she needed right now, more than anything else.

The snake nuzzled his ghostly pale head up against hers, larger than that of a horse. He draped a wing over her, and it was warm. The sound of the rain and thunder lulled her away as her eyes drifted shut.

* * *

Aon heard the crunch of pebbles underneath his shoes as he walked slowly across the stone room. The building was in ruins. The once-vibrant paint had faded and worn away. Of course, it would be like this. The temple of the dreamers had not had an owner in fifteen hundred years. No one had come here to this empty reminder of their doomed existence.

Indeed, for the past six hundred years, it had not existed at all—eaten by the encroaching void that shrank their world with every passing day. This entire jungle had been swallowed up by the creeping oblivion that threatened all their lives.

And yet here it was, rematerialized from nothing. The very ground had risen from the grave.

But this temple in the thick of the jungle was not the only thing returned from the beyond.

He knelt by her sleeping form. Lydia was lying with her head against a stone block, arms folded under her cheek. Her skin was no longer pallid and blue. Her lips were no longer stained with flecks of dried blood. The only proof that she had suffered was that her clothing was tattered and soaked. She was just as Aon had left her, sinking into the lake of blood. Well. Not precisely.

Oh, Lydia…

Reaching out, he touched his ungloved fingers carefully to her cheek, as not to wake her. Her skin was warm. She was alive. He had half expected his hand to pass through her, revealing her to be nothing more than a mirage in his shattered mind.

But this, he could not have fathomed. This, he could not have designed anywhere in the depths of his wildest imaginings. Writing, familiar as it was foreign, decorated her face. Two thin lines arched from the corner of each of her eyes and down her cheeks. One ended in a delicate square spiral close to her ear. On the right side of her face, a fifth line went up from her eyebrow, disappearing up toward her blonde hair.

They were exquisite. They were stunning. They marred not the beauty he had come to admire so keenly. It was not their presence that dismayed him so. If they had been in any other color, he would have rejoiced. Even in red, he would have praised the Ancients for the first time.

But the ink was *turquoise.*

And she bore the marks of a queen.

Ancients of old, what have you done?

He gently stroked a piece of her blonde hair behind her ear. She was shivering. She could not catch a cold and die as she could as a mortal. But she could still be just as miserable, soaked, and freezing. She was now one of them yet foreign all the same.

How had she come to find herself here? How had she known to travel to this temple? Something deep within her must have called her home.

Movement nearby caught his attention. Turning his head, he caught sight of a dragonfly there upon a rock, sheltering from the rain, beautiful with its translucent, gossamer wings in every shade of blue and green and red.

For a moment, it took his breath away. Such things had been dead and gone from this world since the moment Qta's heart ceased to beat in his hand. Yet... like Lydia, like this temple, there it was.

Ziza had told him this temple had risen from the dust of the world. He had not believed her. But the temple, the storm, the dragonfly—and Lydia. Marked in turquoise. The Oracle had told him a great many things of what was to come. Of what he would need to do next and what the Ancients wished of him.

This had been their plan all along, or so they had said.

They had always intended to steal the girl from Earth and raise her as a new dreamer. What they had not predicted—or so they had claimed through their Oracle—was that the girl would fall so willingly into his hands. And he into hers.

But how wonderful that the man who destroyed the dreamers would shepherd in the arrival of the next?

For the Ancients would have never let their world decay and die. No. They just wished to let it come down to the last second.

Or so they had said.

It was all lies and convenient statements, he knew. Yet there was one part that he found charmingly poetic. How laughably ironic—how utterly perfect—for the Ancients to work their will in such a fashion? Edu and the others feared him raising a dreamer so terribly, they murdered the girl to prevent it. In doing so, what transpired was more their doing than his.

Carefully, he lifted Lydia into his arms. She murmured in her sleep and curled her head onto his shoulder. Her hand went to his lapel and grasped it. She recognized him, even in her sleep.

More than that, she trusted him.

For how much longer would that remain the case? There was a deep and terrible task ahead of him, if what the Oracle said was true. He would have to destroy that trust to keep her safe. To prevent the future the Oracle laid out before him. For Lydia's suffering was far from over.

No one else would ever harm her. Never again. If she must endure what was to come, it would be by his hands alone.

He whispered to her, leaning his head down to gently rest his metal-clad cheek against the top of her head. "Oh, my darling little dragonfly..." He took a breath and held it as she shifted in his grasp and nuzzled in closer to him. She was subconsciously responding to the sound of his voice, and the innocent action cinched a vise around his heart. "What am I to do with you now...?"

FOUR

They walked like spiders on two legs and two arms. Long, spindly limbs with flesh that hung from the bone and yet was puffy and swollen, like overcooked boiled chicken. The limbs were far too long to be human. Bulbous heads with too many eyes and distended jaws that drooled and oozed a strange, putrid liquid. They stank of bile and rot.

The monsters were like the bloated corpses that would come out of the Charles River or Boston Harbor. She had one of those on her slab more than once. She remembered the first time she'd gotten a "floater," Nick had insisted on coming to see it. He'd immediately run out of the room to throw up. She'd almost joined him.

Bodies of people who had been soaking in liquid were the only ones that ever lingered in her dreams. Something about the inflated flesh made them seem more grotesque to her than even the worst of car accidents.

Blood was one thing. This was something else.

Lydia wasn't prone to nightmares. Even when her dreams were scary, she tended to just enjoy them like one of her favorite movies. There was something thrilling about being chased by a monster in the safety of her own dreams. Something about it she always found darkly entertaining.

Now that she had been chased by monsters for real, the dreams felt distinctly different. There wasn't a doubt that she wasn't going to find these dreams fun ever again.

The creatures were crawling toward her, tall and gangly, uneven in their gait and yet no less persistent. Terror wrapped itself around her like a claw, clutching at her, twisting viscerally in her soul. Something was suddenly touching her—hands—too many of them. She screamed and thrashed.

Wake up!

The world was a blur now, twisted full of fear and the need to get free. She flailed wildly.

A hand pressed against her chest. The burning points of five fingers, searing into her heart like liquid iron, killing her. Her heart stopped in her chest. Her blood boiled and was thick like syrup in her throat.

Please, no—

Water was in her lungs, taking the place of blood. She didn't know which was worse.

Hey, Cupcake! Wake up!

She was shuddering, lying there in a cold sweat. It took her longer than it should to realize she was awake. Longer than it should to realize she was lying somewhere, her hands dug deep into the fabric beneath her.

The ghostly, nearly disembodied floating skull of the snake-thing was looking down at her with his overly large eyes and empty sockets. He was smaller now, only a foot or two long, and curled up on her chest like a cat.

Y'know, you scream a lot.

He tilted his head to one side then the other, moving too quickly and then stopping too fast, like a crow. The tufts of his feathers at the back of his head draped along his ghastly, smoke-like neck.

Her breaths were coming in short gasps, adrenaline rampaging through her. Taking control back from her panicking mind was easier said than done and slow going. Finally, she managed to smooth her breathing enough that she could think straight. She was shivering from fear, lying on a bed, and wherever she was, it wasn't anywhere she recognized.

The bed she was lying on was small but comfortable. Better than the jail cell she'd woken up in, in Edu's keep. Someone had pulled a blanket over her.

You okay? The eldritch snake tilted his head again to the other side.

"I... think so. I had a nightmare."

No duh. That'll happen a lot now.

"Great."

The snake stretched and moved to slither into her lap, predicting correctly that she wanted to sit up. Looking around, she found herself in a place that could be called a room only in the broadest sense.

It was a huge chamber. The walls domed and transitioned into a ceiling high overhead. Symbols were etched and painted into every surface in a language she was starting to grow familiar with seeing, even if she'd never understand what they said.

A circular platform sat in the middle of the room, some thirty feet in diameter. Around the platform, the stone floor sloped down into the darkness. It was a moat, running around the entirety of the room, some ten or twelve feet wide before it hit the walls that rose up out of the trench. The liquid in it was entirely opaque and looked like black ink. It was perfectly still and gave it the illusion of being a glass surface.

The stone floor of the raised circular platform bore the same style of markings as the walls. Every inch of the space was covered in the esoteric writing of the Ancients. Over the room, at the center of the arch of the dome, hung a chandelier. The electric, antique-style bulbs with their exposed filaments cast the massive chamber in a warm glow.

The bed she was on sat to the edge of the circular platform. There were a few other pieces of furniture. Two chairs, a table on which was a pitcher and a glass. Something else sat there as well, but it was too small for her to tell what it was.

There were no windows. No doors. No way in or out, except for magic. Everything in her life just kept going from bad to worse.

Well, here's an upside for you.

"Oh, do tell."

If it weren't for the wards on the walls and the floor, those bloated people-spiders would be running around in here with us. For better or worse.

"*What?*"

You're a dreamer. You make monsters. You dream them up, they come to life. What do you *think* that meant?

Oh. Shit. "So, this place was designed to contain a dreamer?"

Yup. Keeps all their squiggly-wrigglers from coming to life.

She didn't need to ask the snake who had put her here.

There was only one person she could think of who would have built an entire chamber dedicated to imprisoning a dreamer. She put her head in her hands and felt the dread settle over her like an old friend.

The more things change, the more things stay the same.

She was still the prisoner of the King of Shadows.

Hey, at least he didn't chain you up like he did Qta.

"That doesn't make me feel any better."

She knew next to nothing about the history between Aon and Qta or what really happened during the Great War. She hadn't pushed Aon for explanations before, since she never thought in a million years that it was ever going to be her problem to deal with.

Picking up the snake, she slipped him onto her shoulder as she stood from the cot. She wasn't in the same clothes. Instead of her torn-up outfit, she was in a sleeveless black cotton dress that went down to her knees. It was more like a slip than anything else. She was barefoot, and the stone under her feet was cold.

Normally, she'd bristle about waking up in clothes she didn't put on, but grumbling about the warlock seeing her naked and taking such liberties with her seemed silly at best. She didn't need to look for reasons to be annoyed or afraid, especially since she was his prisoner.

She walked to the table that sat on the other side of the circular platform from her. The third object on it that she couldn't identify before was a small, elegant hand mirror. The details around the edge of the glass were stunning; tangled Art Nouveau vines and asymmetrical details in a polished silver told her without question to whom it belonged.

Why did Aon leave me a mirror, of all things? Why is looking at myself so important that he'd leave me nothing but a—

Ah. Yeah, okay, fine. That'd be why.

She hadn't yet seen what was most certainly etched on her face. Picking up the mirror, she hesitated. Maybe if she didn't look, it wouldn't be real. Maybe her face was still free of the symbols that spelled out her soul. And now, her fate. If only she were that lucky.

"How bad is it?" She glanced over at the snake on her shoulder.

I think you look better with them than without, he teased. **Definitely an improvement, anyway.**

"Why is it that I wound up anthropomorphizing my power into a jackass?"

Says more about you than it does about me, Cupcake.

He wrapped his tail around her neck, casually perching there. He bonked his head into her cheek affectionately.

She laughed once through her nose and reached up to scratch his head. No use delaying the inevitable. She turned the mirror up to her face.

Five lines of thin turquoise writing decorated her face. Four ran in thin arcs away from the bottom of her eyes and down her cheeks, two on each side. Shorter in the middle than at the edges. On the left side, one ran longer and close to her ear, where it ended in a square spiral. On the right side, a fifth line ran up from her eyebrow and into her hair.

The snake on her shoulder was reflected in the glass at her, hovering close to her cheek. He seemed to be looking in the mirror with her, tucking his head close to her. Or maybe like squeezing in for a photo. Something about the little thing made her smile. It was nice to have some company in all this, even if it was, in some weird way, only just herself and the world's strangest imaginary friend.

"What do I call you, anyway? I need a name for you."

It's your job to name things, not mine. You dream things, they become real, you name them. They're your creatures. So'm I.

"It's really annoying that you know things I don't."

Your choice, not mine. You could've just taken in all the power the Ancients were giving you and lost your mind, after all. You chose to keep me separate to keep yourself, well, yourself.

"Maybe it would be easier if I wasn't me anymore."

It'd be easier, that's for sure. But... not nearly as good. Nobody would have been happy with it. Not you, not the Ancients, not Aon.

"Why do the Ancients care if I'm still myself? They did this to me."

No clue. I only have theories.

"Which are?"

One thing at a time. You scream too much as it is already.

She rolled her eyes. "You still need a name."

So, name me already.

After thinking about it for a long moment, she let out a breath. "How about Q? You're not Qta, but you're inspired by him. And it seems fitting. My Trekkie dad would be proud."

Q. I like it. Q. He swished his tail happily. **I am Q! Q, Q, Q, Q...** The snake was trying out the new name, and he fluffed the ghastly feathers of his wings, like a bird showing off.

She smiled at how oddly endearing the little critter was and went back to looking at her reflection and the turquoise marks decorating her face.

The writing made it look like she fell asleep in math class and some aspiring makeup artist with an ultra-fine Sharpie had a little too much fun. Maybe if things had been different, she would have laughed. She would have been somehow excited to feel like she finally had a place in this stupid world she had been dragged into. Maybe she would have felt relief at no longer being an outcast and an anomaly or constantly in danger. Maybe she would have been less afraid of everything all the time.

Maybe.

If it had been any other color on her face. Anything but turquoise.

Nick was going to laugh at her, that was for sure. Not nearly as bad as if she had decided to wear that ugly-ass mask over her face. She smiled despite herself, thinking about how Nick was going to point and snicker at her the next time they saw each other.

Tears threatened to fall and stung her eyes. She missed her friend and hoped he was okay. Wiping her tears away with the back of her hand, she put the mirror back on the table face down. Suddenly, she realized Q was gone. The creature had just blinked out of existence like he had never been there.

A second later, she knew why.

"Hello, my dear."

Ever a knife wrapped in velvet, she knew that voice. It was as familiar to her as it was foreboding. Turning, she saw the man who had appeared standing in the center of the room. Dressed forever in black-on-black-on-black, metal mask glinting in the overhead amber light. Beautiful and terrifying, like a panther.

What could she say to him?

What the hell did she want to say to him?

Half of her felt overcome with relief and wanted to run into his arms. The other half reminded her that everything was different now. His greeting had been unreadable, void of emotion either way. Neither threatening nor soft.

She watched him carefully, and for a long moment, the two just stood there. Finally, she couldn't take it anymore. As she ran through everything that had happened to her, tears threatened to fall once more. She lost the fight.

"Hi." Her voice cracked as she cried. When he stayed silent, she said the first thing that came to mind. "Aon, they killed me. I—I died."

"I know."

The fingers of his bare, ungloved hand twitched as if wanting to grasp for something. She realized his posture was stiff, rigid, and wary. Maybe he didn't know what to expect either. Maybe he didn't know that she was still herself. There was probably a higher chance she had lost her mind than not.

She felt alone. Scared. Terrified. Of him, and yet, of everyone else even more. She took a step toward him, haltingly and unsure. She wanted him to hold her. Wanted to feel his arms around her. But she was a dreamer now. The only one in a world that had been on the brink of oblivion because of what he'd done.

She didn't know if she was still welcome in his arms.

"I'm sorry."

"Whatever for?"

"I tried to run. I tried to hide. They caught up to me. Edu, he—" She broke off, trying to shove the memory deep down inside. Her vision blurred through her tears. "I was dead. And now I'm not. And now this bullshit." She gestured at her face. "And I—" She lost all her words then.

"Oh, my dragonfly..." He lifted his arms out to her. Without even thinking twice, she rushed forward and into his embrace. He caught her, clutching her to him tightly, and a hand cradled her head to his chest. "Only you would apologize to me for what others have done to you, my beautiful, wonderful, silly little creature."

She wrapped her arms around him and held him as tightly as he held her. There was warmth in his voice, a tenderness there that surprised her. Whatever might come—whatever had changed—at least she would have this moment.

"I am the one who failed." He rested his metal cheek against the top of her head. "I could not protect you. I was a fool. I let down my guard, thinking we were safe. I believed the others had come to understand you bore no deep and dangerous secret." His arms tightened briefly at his words. "Please forgive me."

She looked up at him before placing a hand against the side of his neck, wanting to feel his warm skin against her palm. "There's nothing to forgive. Edu's the one who killed me. Lyon was in on this, wasn't he?"

"Yes."

"I'm an idiot. I thought..." Sniffling, she trailed off and sighed wearily.

"Friendship falls quickly in the face of paranoia. Believe me."

She cringed as she felt the twist of betrayal again. "Then they're at fault. Edu killed me. Not you."

"You are a miracle. In more ways than one, it seems." He lifted his bare hand to cup her cheek, running the pad of his thumb slowly along her. She realized he was tracing one of the lines of turquoise writing that she now wore.

The reminder that she now was the thing he coveted so badly during their Great War made fear twist in her stomach. Her hands tightened in his coat, even as he was the source of her fear. She could barely raise her voice higher than a whisper. "Are you going to kill me now?"

"No. Not now, not ever. I will never take your life, Lydia. You are more precious to me than anything else in this world."

"What part? Me or this?" She pointed again at the turquoise ink.

"I would be lying if I did not say both." He let out a weary sigh. "You fear what I will do to you, now that you are that which I sought to resurrect—that which I drove from this world so long ago."

"Kinda, yeah. Do you blame me?"

"Not in the slightest. It means you are wise. Yet you do not recoil from me, hide from me, or shun my touch. Do you still trust me, my dragonfly?"

There he was, calling her *dragonfly* again. He had never called her that before today. He adored calling her an assortment of terms of endearment, but that was a new one. His tone had been hopeful, strained, but seemingly resigned. As if he already knew her answer.

Did she trust him?

She did, once before.

But everything was different now. Wasn't it?

"I don't know. I'm sorry. I'm—I'm scared, and everything's been upended again."

"Do not apologize to me, Lydia. Not now, not ever. You chose not to lie to me, and for that, I am far more grateful." He let out a long breath. "Oh, how I wish I could kiss you, if you would still have it from me."

She smiled faintly up at him and at the affection and desire in his voice that she had come to recognize and yearn for. "Then do it. Use that stupid spell of yours."

"It will no longer work on you, I fear. It was designed for a mortal, not a queen." He tilted his head to the side, just slightly. "But."

"But?"

"Close your eyes, my darling."

"What?" She blinked, surprised. Would he really do that? Would he really take off his mask, on the hope that she wouldn't get curious and open her eyes?

"I trust you."

She felt a lump in her throat. She had just denied trusting him, and yet he was willing to put himself in her hands. Not with his life, but maybe something even more important to him than that.

"Go on, then," he urged her gently.

Shutting her eyes, she vowed to herself that she'd keep them shut. No matter how hard the curiosity burned inside of her to see what he might look like, she wouldn't open her eyes. She couldn't betray him like that.

Fingers tilted her head back, and she felt his breath along her cheek. He kissed her there, once, twice, kissing the lines of ink along her cheek. "You are all that I could have ever wished for," he murmured against her skin, trailing slowly toward her lips. "That you were a mortal was a travesty. That you did not have the power to match the strength in your soul was a crime. Now you are what you should have been from the start—a queen."

He kissed her then, and it stole her breath away. There was so much emotion in that embrace, so much desperation. So much hurt, and agony, and relief, and need. He kissed her as though he thought he never would again, and it had been true.

She kept her eyes shut but let her hands wander to his face, cupping his head in her hands and kissing him back with all she had. All her own trauma, her fear, her terror at what had happened. Poured into him the comfort of being with him, no matter what he might do next.

She realized then, right in that moment, that she loved him.

Even with not knowing what he was going to do to her or understanding how much more complicated her life had just become, it was there. She could feel it burning away in her chest all the same.

But even as he broke the kiss to breathe, to clutch her to his chest like she would be torn away from him a second time, she couldn't say the words. Couldn't tell him what she could finally recognize for what it was.

Her realization was not a happy one.

Aon had killed the last dreamer.

Who knew what he would do now?

"I wept when I found you." He kissed her cheek again, his breath hot against her skin. "I cried for your loss. And when I found you, like this... I dreaded to think what the Ancients had done to your mind. If they had stolen away my Lydia and broken her apart as they have done so many others. Those who go into the pool come out similar but changed... those who come out have within them an innate hatred and distrust of me. I thought perhaps they had given me back a ghost to haunt my nightmares."

"I'm still me. I promise." She wrapped her arms around his neck and hugged him, trying to console them both. *I just have a giant asshole of a snake in my head instead.*

Hey! I'm an awesome, badass, giant asshole of a snake.

Apparently, Q could still talk to her even when he wasn't visible. Aon didn't react to the sound, so it was clear that Q was still speaking inside of her head. Oh, joy. It looked like she was going to have the snake's running commentary all the time now.

You'd better believe it.

Shut up.

Come in here and make me.

"I do not know how or why the Ancients deemed fit to do this in the manner they had, but I could not be more overjoyed." He kissed her once more, slower this time, less desperate, but no less passionate. It was a great distraction from silently arguing with the snake in her head. "No. You are safe. I do not know if I could bear the loss of you a second time."

"I don't want to do this, Aon. I don't want to be like this. I don't want what this means." It was so tempting to open her eyes, but she steadfastly kept them shut.

"I know, my darling."

"Is there a way to give the marks back?"

"No." He traced his hand down her cheek, stroking her skin with his fingertips, once more tracing the ink that he seemingly found fascinating. "To 'give them back' would be to destroy you, and our world, a second time. I fear I do not have the strength to commit either act. And I would destroy anyone who tried."

She let out a small gasp as she felt his hand slip to her chin and tilt it backward, felt his lips kiss the hollow of her ear and start trailing down toward her shoulder. He had switched moods like the flick of a switch.

"I believed I would never taste your skin again," he purred against her as he trailed his lips over her shoulder. "I thought I would never hold you... feel you... or hear your voice cry my name."

Once, she would have recoiled in horror from the darkness in his voice. Her stomach still twisted into a knot, but now it was one of trepidation and excitement. The fear was addicting, and so was he. Letting herself sink into him and tuning out the worry of what was to come sounded amazing right about now. She tilted her head back to give him more room, to let him kiss further down her throat. He dug his claws into her hip slightly, making his intentions quite clear.

She didn't know what was going to happen now that she was a dreamer. But Aon seemed willing to push off the inevitable, if only for a short while. And so was she.

FIVE

Aon did not believe in kindness. It was merely the absence of cruelty. And certainly, he did not think the Ancients ever paid him any such thing that might even resemble such a thing.

But here, now, holding *her*, he was reconsidering his opinion.

Lydia was alive.

When he had found her, asleep in the Temple of Dreams, both the woman and the building resurrected from the void, he had not known what to expect. What could have happened to her in the act of returning from true death?

Certainly, she had lost her mind in the ordeal. There had been no chance that she came out of that pit unscathed. He had only experienced returns from the false deaths of his people, never from what she had suffered.

Or, at the very least, he feared she would despise him and carry with her now the innate and intrinsic disgust toward him that all others bore when they rose from the pool, hand in hand with the ink they now wore.

Instead, he found that neither of these things were true. Unfathomably, she was... unchanged. Terrified, disoriented, distrustful, and wounded, yes. But who would not be so? She had *died.* She had been a corpse, made such by the hands of those she had just begun to trust, in a world she was just coming to accept.

He had believed her gone. She had been gone. It was not a fallacy, a trick, or a lie. She had been dead. Her lips that were like a drug to him had been cold. Now he tasted them again, warm and pleading with him for more. Her breath pooled against his face. It was still so novel, so foreign to him, to feel such a thing.

Now that he had known her lips, he knew that to be devoid of them once more would spell his ruin. He was an addict, and to be robbed a second time would be to kill him.

So, how could he resist tasting her again? But the spell he had so carefully crafted to remove her vision would no longer work on her.

She wore the marks of a queen, and although her body was devoid of the marks she should bear elsewhere, it mattered not. He did not have the time, nor the desire, to build a new spell to hide her vision.

Besides, if she were to peek—if she were to open her eyes and see his face—he would rejoice.

He loved her.

With all his cold, hateful heart, he loved her. And if she stole a glance at him... he would have an excuse to punish her.

Wicked visions came to his mind that ignited in him such a heady, overwhelming fire he nearly threw her to the ground where she stood and took her right then. Images played through his mind of how he wished to strap her to his machines and let them keep her on the knife's edge of release. Leaving her begging and crying for him to let her crest, only to leave her there... and now he could do it to her for *days.*

She bore the marks of a queen.

She was no longer fragile.

How he wished to teach her the extents of her newfound endurance. Oh, how beautiful she would be, bound to his slab, while he took his fill from that fiendishly skillful mouth of hers again, and again. How he wanted to bend her body to his will until she cried and offered up the world and the moons to him, if he would only mount her.

She had not been in his arms for more than five minutes, and already he was devising new ways to torment her! He nearly laughed at himself. He would have, if he were not currently trying to kiss the life back out of her.

All the while, his little dragonfly was holding on to his lapel, clutching to him in trepidation, her eyes shut tight as if she might slip. He tried not to grin. He failed. He broke away from her lips only so that he might trail his kisses down over her shoulder. She shuddered in his arms, and he cinched her tighter to him, and he felt the tension in her body slacken just barely at the gesture.

Lydia was alive. She was still his. She still trembled in his arms. It was impossible... yet if this were his final descent into madness—oh, let it be like this.

She may claim she was uncertain of her trust for him, and it was wise. But her body told a different story, as she let herself lean into him, her soft breasts pressing against his chest. Hunger roared to the surface. They had taken her from him. He would take her back.

If he thought his heart could burst in his chest unprompted, it would have been in this moment. He pressed the tips of his claws into her hip, digging in enough to sting, but not enough to break the skin—there would be time enough for that later. Instead of squirming away, she pressed in tighter to him.

Oh, my dragonfly, you will be the death of me.

How he wanted to chain her, bind her, ravish her. *All of her.* Change his form and take her in every way a man, or beast, could take a woman. Call forth his shadowy powers and claim her as he had always wished to do, but that his burgeoning love for her and her irritating mortality had never allowed.

But now, they had all the time in the world.

These things must be done gradually—each moment savored.

His games were shoved to the back of his mind as the need for her pushed him forward. He did not have the patience to play with her tonight. There had been such an empty cavern of loneliness and pain left behind by her death, and he needed to fill it. He needed it mended. And he needed *her.*

Hooking his hand around her throat, he put the smallest bit of pressure against her. He tilted her back into his arm, sending her just ever-so-slightly off balance, causing her to cling to him now in earnest.

If she did not trust him, she could throw a leg back to straighten herself up.

If she truly did not trust him, she could open her eyes and fight him.

She did neither of those things. Instead, her lips parted as she fought for breath, and she let him arch her backward, jutting those beautiful, delicious breasts up toward him, hardened buds visible through the thin black dress he had given her to wear. Temping him... teasing him.

He was not one to resist temptation.

Lowering his clawed hand, he sliced open the top half of her dress, clear down the center, tearing the fabric easily with the sharp edge. He took his time. He wanted to watch her as he worked. She tucked her chin, her hands grasping tightly onto him. But she did not open her eyes. She didn't straighten her back. She let out the smallest whimper as he—quite purposefully—nicked the skin in the valley between his current obsession.

Leaning down his head, she let out a heated moan and let

her head fall back as he ran his tongue slowly up the cut, tasting her. As a mortal, she had tasted exquisite. As a queen... she was divine.

The noise that escaped her went straight through him like wildfire. Parting her torn dress, he grasped her breast in his hand. He was none-too-gentle about it either. The young woman had a wonderful pain tolerance before, and now he wished to see if it had improved. If so, he would consider himself well and truly blessed by the Ancients.

As he kneaded and squeezed, he let his lips capture the other rose-colored bud, lest it feel abandoned in his attentions. She cried out sharply as he dug his teeth into the tender flesh, before easing her pain with a roll of his tongue.

He felt her hand slip over his shoulder, holding onto him for dear life. When the fingers of her other hand laced into his hair, he expected her to yank his head away. Instead... oh, by the Ancients... she pressed him tighter to her.

"Aon," she moaned breathlessly.

She trusted him.

She wanted him.

She needed this too.

His arousal was painful, the way it throbbed. The way it begged for freedom and for her. His body was flushed and over-heated. His heart was pounding away in his chest like a drum, urging him forward, in time with the surge of his desire. He had never, once in his life, been brought to an inferno quite like that which she could inspire in him.

He ground himself up against her, needing contact to his tortured organ. Still, he did not relent from torturing her soft orbs. She moaned again, whimpering, and when he looked up to her face, she was lost in bliss and need. Her eyes were still shut.

"Please..." she whispered. "Aon."

If he had not loved her before, it would have happened

then. As it was, he nearly wept. Wept for that he had lost her. Wept for that he had found her. Wept for what she was giving him now.

He straightened her up and skimmed his hands over her body. Gooseflesh broke out beneath his touch, and she was shivering. Wordlessly, he slipped her dress from her shoulders, useless and torn as it now was, and let it pool around her feet.

She bore no other marks of a queen, he confirmed once more. A mystery for another day. Now he could not be bothered to spare an ounce of thought over it. Instead, he shucked his own clothing, and nearly breathed a sigh of relief when his straining arousal was finally let free of its confines.

He reached down and took her hand. She jumped at the sudden contact, and he chuckled darkly. How he would always scare her. A demon in the darkness—one that had seduced her—but one that remained dangerous.

Good.

He would have it no other way.

Leading her to the cot he had brought to the chamber for her, he sat down upon the edge. He would worship her this night—his queen—his Lydia. His former mortal and miracle.

The woman he loved.

Is this what it felt like? To love? To feel as though his heart would burst? It was agony, it was suffering... it was ecstasy.

He guided her to straddle him and put her hands upon his shoulders and let her use him for balance. Slipping his hands up her thighs, he wandered his hands to her rump and squeezed her painfully. She squeaked and threw herself forward, reflexively trying to escape his grasp. Which pushed her straight into his chest.

Chuckling again, he set himself to devouring her wonderful breasts, biting at them, making her cry out in agony before kissing away the pain. All while his hands groped and soothed, squeezed, pinched, and petted her.

Not once did she beg for mercy. So, naturally, he pushed her further. He raked his claws down her back, nearly breaking the skin but stopping just short. She arched her back, pressing her chest against him, crying out loudly. But not in pain. At least not entirely. It was the perfect mix of torment and joy. He did it a second time, diagonally intersecting the first set of red welts he knew he was leaving on her pale flesh.

"You are beautiful," he whispered breathlessly to her. "Utterly perfect..."

A third time, and she wrapped her arms around his shoulders, holding onto him for dear life, even as he was the source of her writhing. Clutching him for support and relief.

He nearly spent himself in that moment. It was like lightning, what he felt tearing through him. He needed her. And he needed her *now*.

He spread his legs. She squeaked in surprise as her own legs were forced apart where she straddled him. It forced her onto her knees on the cot to either side of him, her body pressed against his chest, and he looked up at her as she knelt over him.

By all the moons in the sky, she took his breath away.

And *still* she kept her eyes shut. He would see how long that would last. How he would relish spanking her for disobedience if she lost control. This was his favorite scenario—one in which he won no matter the outcome.

Taking her by the thighs, he guided her to kneel over his lap. She hung onto him, both eager and afraid. With one hand, he held his length steady, and with the clawed hand, he pressed it to her hip, urging her lower.

As she obeyed him, the inferno of her body pressed against him. She was like a pool of lava, and he moaned, burying his head into her shoulder, as the first part of him slipped inside of her. Feeling her spread for him, part for him, as he bored into her immense heat, inch by torturously wonderful inch.

He took her hips now with both hands, and he was impatient to fill her, as he always was. He pressed her own against him, nearly with his full strength. Their cries of pleasure mingled, and hers tinged by pain, as he rammed against her end.

He was just—*just*—too much for her. He had to press her down to seat himself entirely within her. But as she quivered against and around him, he knew she relished it just as much as he did.

It was his own manner of torture, not pounding her into oblivion as he wished to do. Instead, he guided her motions, as she lifted and fell atop him. He aided her, lifting her weight and occasionally ramming her back down against him, burying himself to the hilt, making her gasp and wail in pleasure.

But she had an equal hand in this. She was moving against him with just as much fervor, impaling herself on him. His body was throbbing, pulsing, threatening to let loose too soon. Pleasure was arcing through him like a storm with each undulation of her tight body.

He found himself moaning her name without realizing it. Her hands found his face, and shortly after, her lips caught his, kissing him with abandon. His heart hitched, and he was left stunned as her tongue pressed into his mouth. His little hellcat was leaving him breathless and moaning as she took, and he found himself more than happy to give.

At least for a few moments.

He wound his hand through her hair, wrapping it around his palm, once, twice, and grinned mischievously against her. It was her only warning. He yanked her hair roughly, pulling her head back, and arching her back once more. She cried out, her hands clutching at his shoulders to keep from falling backward.

The angle it provided him was superb. The view, even better. He bit down roughly on her already tortured flesh, and she wailed. He kept at it for a few more minutes, pressing himself to the hilt inside her. But soon, his need wore through his patience like an acid.

He kept the grasp on her hair tight, forcing her backward. He pivoted, slung a leg over the other side of the cot, and threw her onto her back, still not releasing her hair or letting them part where they were joined. If he could, he would stay buried in her for eternity.

He pulled on her hair, forcing her to arch further up against him. Her legs were now around his waist, and he laughed as she whimpered and writhed. He leaned his other hand down onto the cot and shifted his weight, slamming back into her violently. There would be no mercy for her now—no quarter. She was a queen.

She was his equal.

He let out a shuddering rush of air as he felt her clench around him, tightening like a vise. "My, my... It seems we've grown to like this manner of affection, have we?" *I love you, Lydia. I love you more than life itself.* He could not say those words, not yet, and so he teased her. Taunted her cruelly.

He was who he was, after all.

She could not speak. She could not find the air. Instead, she cinched her legs around him, pulling him even harder against her. Silently begging him to give them both what they needed. To be as brutal as he wished. To take her how he wanted.

And so, he did. Kissing and biting and licking at whatever he could reach, he took his fill, and gave her all that he was. All that he had. All the pain at her loss, all the agony of her death, all the loneliness, all the joy at her return. All his love, all his wrath, all his cruelty and the kindness he was just beginning to believe existed.

How many times her pleasure crested, he did not know. He had lost count as she writhed and cried beneath him.

And oh... how she cried his name. Each time he sent her over the cliff into ecstasy, she threw back her head and his name left her lips like a song to his ears. Finally, he could not take anymore. It seemed that she, too, was at her limit. Her endurance had grown indeed, but they could only continue for so long.

Pleasure like hot liquid iron built and threatened to overtake him. He let out a snarl, pinning her down to the cot painfully as his motions became uneven and harsh. He felt his body tighten, felt himself crest, and he rammed himself into her, pressing deep to the root, as hard as he could, harder than he had ever done to her before.

She jolted and cried out soundlessly, her head thrown back and mouth wide, as his presence within her tossed her headlong over that edge into wild abandon once more. Her body quivered and clamped down around him as if trying to pull him into her whole, and that was the end for him. He felt himself surge, and he let out a wail of release as he fell against her, his head on her shoulder, still relentlessly pressing his whole weight to where they were joined. He would fill her with his essence, useless as it was, and he would make her his.

Even if she left him, he would be certain she would never forget how he felt.

The pleasure made him see stars, and he blinked them away, his body twitching and shuddering in the throes and aftermath.

She was lying breathlessly beneath him, panting, her head thrown to the side, mouth open for air. Her beautiful blonde hair was strewn about her, and her skin shone with sweat, as did his.

He leaned down and kissed a line of ink that she now bore on her cheek. Turquoise ink... impossible and beautiful. He stroked her hair tenderly. Slowly, carefully, he eased his weight off her and began to kiss her gently. Trying, as hard as he could, to tell her how much he loved her by that method alone.

And yet, even through his kisses, he had to fight a smile.

For she had still not opened her eyes.

SIX

Lydia woke in Aon's arms, lying half on his chest on the ground. He had dragged the bedding off the small cot, as it wouldn't fit both of them, and now she was lying in a nest of pillows, sheets, a comforter, and the warlock.

Last night—or day, she honestly had no way of knowing—they had taken solace in each other. They had pushed away all of what was going to happen and enjoyed the moment and the company. While she'd never consider him gentle by any means, it had felt different than any of their previous forays. There was an adoration, a relief, a desperation, and a deep thankfulness to his actions.

As if he were merely grateful to have her in his arms. It had been to comfort them both, to assure them that the other was still there, and that things would change, but for now, they could just be happy in each other's arms.

She kept her eyes shut as she reached up for his face. She felt metal there and only then let herself open her eyes to look up at him. His dark hair was splayed out around him on the white pillow, and he looked to be sleeping. But without seeing his face, there was no way to know.

He had trusted her to keep her eyes shut throughout their night together. And she had. It had been hard with everything he had done to her.

He was shirtless, and he took her breath away. How gorgeous he was lying there. The ink that ran over his body was a work of art, carefully arranged and covering a third of his body. Someday, she was seriously going to lick every piece of ink he had.

If she lived that long.

If he didn't do something horrible to her.

Unable to help herself, she leaned down and placed a kiss on his chest, on one of the arcs of archaic writing that ran across him. As she did, she heard him hum quietly in his throat, and his clawed hand slid casually to rest on her lower back. "I fear to open my eyes, for that you might be a dream of my shattered mind."

She smiled faintly. How tragic and yet oddly romantic. "I'm here, Aon."

The clawed hand slid up her back, over her shoulder, and cupped her cheek. He lifted his head slightly, and she knew, even without seeing his face, that he was looking at her. "If you are not, I do not think I wish to wake from this vision."

"Man, all a girl has to do is die once, and you get all sappy and romantic." She leaned in to kiss the cheek of his metal mask.

"Do not concern yourself. It will not last."

Lydia chuckled and put her head down against his shoulder. His arms wrapped around her and pulled her flush against him. She took another reprieve from the conversation they were about to have, looming on the edges of the mood like the thunderstorm that had been raging outside.

After a long few minutes of simply lying there in silence, basking in the comfort of the other, he finally began the inevitable. "What do you remember of what happened?"

Wincing, she sat up and rubbed a hand over her chest where Edu had burned holes into her heart. "Edu killed me. Darkness. Then... voices, I guess."

"Voices. Elaborate, kindly."

Standing, she went to grab some clothing that he'd fetched for her. "A bunch at once, but... not. I don't know how to describe it. They were talking in turn, like—"

"Poetry. Seven voices, all at once yet separate. Burning through your mind like hot coals."

"Yeah."

He growled in his throat. "What did *they* tell you?"

"I don't really remember." She blinked at his sudden anger. "Something about choosing. I don't know. I think they let me pick whether I lived or stayed dead. Who were they?"

"The Ancients."

"I—oh." She had never really put much thought into the Ancients and the fact that they were anything more than myths. Gods weren't really things you could just... talk to, like that, where she came from.

"They offer false choices. Only when they feel they know you have no other options do they give you the illusion of walking your own path." He stood from the ground with the grace of a panther. He flicked his hand and was suddenly wearing a full suit.

"Show-off."

"You can do the same."

"I don't know how."

He held his hand out to her, but she hesitated. Even though she had just been in his arms, even though they had just slept together, she couldn't. Now they were discussing what happened and what was to come.

Sighing darkly, he walked up to her instead and wrapped her in his arms before she could tense or withdraw. "I know you cannot. All the power of a queen and yet you are helpless."

No, she's not helpless, you monumental prick. Less yapping, more fapping, motherfucker!

Shut up, Q.

"You have no other marks upon your body. Do you know why this is?"

She looked down at her bare arms. He was a veritable roadmap of black ink, of power and esoteric symbols. She had nothing else on her. Just the ones on her face.

Without a shadow of a doubt, she knew exactly what that was. The irritating snake talking inside her head. Q was her power personified and kept separate from her body. From crashing into her mind and breaking her. So... *he* was her marks.

"No." She lied. She could have told him all about Q. Told him about the snake and why she still felt like a fish out of water, maybe even more so than before she died. But something told her to keep that card close to her chest—to hide the existence of her screwed-up Disney sidekick—until she knew what Aon's game really was.

But that might have been the first time she'd ever lied to him. And it felt disgusting.

A clawed hand lifted to trail through her hair slowly, brushing it back away from her face. It was meant to be comforting, but it sent a chill down her spine as the sharp points grazed her scalp. "I was given a prophecy, my dragonfly."

"Why do you keep calling me that?" It was a piss-poor stall tactic, but it was the only one she had.

"Quite simply, for I adore dragonflies. They have been dead and gone from this world since I killed their creator, Qta. When I found you sleeping in that pyramid, I saw one sitting upon the stones and sheltering from the rain. With you, they have returned." He slipped his gauntleted hand around to tap the sharp end of a claw against her chin. "And you have changed the subject."

There was no arguing that. "I don't want to talk about

what happens next. I don't want any of this. And I don't want to... talk about what you're going to do."

"A desire that I share. If I could spend eternity with you in this room, away from all the others and the world outside, I would. But I feel the need to explain to you what must follow. What I must now do." The way he said it filled her with dread. "The Oracle came and told me of what will come. She told me that the Temple of Dreams had risen from the void and that the new queen lay there sleeping. That I would find our fledgling royal was lost and powerless."

I'll show you powerless! Lemme at him.

No, Q. Quit it. You can't attack him.

Why not?

Just no, Q.

Finally, the snake shut up with a beleaguered sigh inside her head.

"This means you have me locked up why, exactly?" She finally found the nerve to ask the question she had been dreading to ask this whole time.

"To protect you."

Snorting in disbelief, she pushed out of his arms and walked away a few paces. "I know you better than that, Aon. You killed Qta. Now, I wake up here, in a cage. Call me dubious that I'm here for my safety."

"I do not know if your power is out of your control. You would flood this place with monsters and horrors from the darkest depths your mind could reach. I apologize if I did not want my home overrun with such rabble."

She shot him a look. "And?"

"And what? Do you not believe me?" He feigned being insulted, putting a hand to his chest. *There* was the warlock she knew. "Very well. I fear for what Edu and the others may do. He killed you once on the suspicion that you would become some great power at my beck and call. Now he has the proof required to do the deed a second time."

"I am not at your 'beck and call,' Aon. And it's not going to make them any less paranoid if I'm your prisoner!"

"I would rather have you safe! They will make up their minds to kill you, regardless. You know that to be true. And no amount of asserting the contrary will convince them. That you even merely tolerate my existence is proof enough to him that you are compromised by me."

"Compromised?"

"You and I share a bond... do we not?"

Was he just asking her if they were a thing? She put her hand over her eyes and let out a weary laugh, enjoying the sick humor of the whole thing. She was his prisoner, and he was asking her if they were a couple. "Fine. Sure. We 'share a bond,' Aon. And I'm your prisoner. And I'm a dreamer. And you killed the last one. So tell me what game you're playing already."

"What makes you believe that I am playing a game?"

"You always are."

Arms circled around her waist from behind, and she jumped, startled. He could still sneak up on her. Great. His voice was a playful, husky sound into her ear. "I suppose you are correct." Aon cinched his arm around her tighter, pinning her to him. He was still much—*much*—stronger than she was. "You worry that I seek to control you. To bend you to my whim and fulfill some dark aspiration of mine."

"You aren't telling me anything otherwise. You aren't telling me what you really want."

"Very well." His clawed hand snapped around her throat, tilting her head back to rest against his shoulder. Fear, like an old friend, came back to her in a wave. "Then let me tell you more of the prophecy granted to me by the Oracle. It came to me in three parts. The first, where I may find you."

"The second?"

"That one of my fellow kings will come to cause you great suffering and you will be helpless to stop them. That they will rise to destroy you." He dug his claws into her skin just enough to sting. "The third, I will keep my secret for now."

She swallowed thickly. "Aon—"

"Shush." He pressed his metal cheek close to hers, and his voice was a low growl, dangerous and threatening. "I will let no one harm you again. I will not stand idly by while one of those monumental fools takes advantage of your weakness. What do I want? What is my game? I wish for you to stand as a rightful queen."

Somehow, that didn't sound like a good thing. "So, teach me."

"Ah, were it so simple. I would stand a better chance in teaching a fish to fly and a bird to swim than I could teach a dreamer to wield their gifts."

"What are you going to do?"

"I must inspire you to find the need on your own." He dug his sharp talons deeper into her, and she winced at the pain. "When we first met, you feared pain but not death. Is this still true?"

"I—what?"

"I am going to hurt you, Lydia. I am going to take these claws of mine and dig them into your rib cage as I did that night in your dreams. Only this time, it will be real. And when darkness comes to claim you, it will abate once more like the tide. It is only pain. Do you still fear it?"

She struggled. "Aon, don't!"

"Death cannot come for you as it did once before. Not by such mundane means."

"I don't care! I'm not going to let you rip me open!" She tried to kick at him, to strike him, but he had her pinned against him now. The ends of the daggers that were his claws dug into her throat and stung her, and she felt something warm run down her neck.

"Then stop me. Use that which burns away within you and defend yourself."

"I don't know how!"

"I suggest you discover it quickly, or else you will come to learn the true meaning of pain," he said in a low, gleefully sadistic rumble down to her, and she knew in some sick way, he was enjoying this. "And of that, there is no better teacher in this world than me."

* * *

Once more they stood gathered beneath the great, twisting orrery that tracked the movements of their world. Once more, the five of them met to discuss the fate of Under and how best to protect it from the King of Shadows. Once more, Lyon had taken his post of leaning against the wall of the Great Hall, seeking to be unheard and unseen. Only now, a deep sense of foreboding loomed over them, as did the clouds in the skies outside.

It appeared the world, devoid of rain for fifteen hundred years, was making up for lost time. It had not stopped pouring in two days.

The people of Under had found themselves in an uneasy celebration. They rejoiced for the rain and what it meant. Their world was spared, and their eternal lives would continue. News of the edge of the void receding like the tide spread like wildfire amongst them. Kamira herself had taken the shape of the giant tigress she preferred to travel and confirm the reports.

A dreamer had returned. There was no question of it.

But who now wore that mantle? Where were they? The turquoise orb in the orrery glowed brightly on its track, same with the markers for red and black. A new king or queen had awoken.

Yet none could be found.

There were two options, as far as any of them could reason. Either they were smartly in hiding, or the less favorable—and far more likely—option was the reason they were all now gathered here to discuss.

Aon may have them already.

Ziza sat on a bench, her white eyes shut, as she seemed to be waiting for something. She always was. The conversation around them was a tense one.

"I still wonder how much the King of Shadows knew of the girl's fate." Maverick was sitting on a bench, leaning both hands on the end of his silver cane, gazing up at the orrery ponderously. "How much of this he engineered from the start?"

"Ziza did say Aon would be responsible for the rise of the new dreamer," Kamira pointed out.

"Then why not kill her himself?" Maverick asked. "He was not merely passing the blame to maintain the girl's opinion of him. I think she merely implied that it was by his hand she was placed into the Pool of the Ancients once she had died. No, I have come to conclude he knew nothing of her future."

"What makes you say that?" Kamira asked from atop the statue she was using as a perch.

"Aon may be a patient man. But if you were to tell him that if he killed the girl, she would become a dreamer? I think she would be bleeding out before you finished your sentence."

"You assume the girl is the new dreamer," Ylena interjected for Edu, who was leaning against a wall, his large arms crossed over his chest.

Maverick shrugged. "I do not believe in coincidence. And there are far too many here to ignore. Either her death inspired the Ancients to raise Qta, or she is the new Queen of Dreams. I do not see a third option."

"If Qta lived, he would not be hiding." Kamira swished her tail angrily from atop the statue. "He would not have made such an easy prisoner either."

"The Ancients have never once seen fit to raise the dead," Ylena said. "Not once."

"Perhaps they have never found the need," Lyon provided. "But as to why they did not simply bestow upon her the power of the dreamers when she went into the pool the first time... I do not know. It hints to some darker purpose; some deeper reason I cannot ascertain. Do you know, Lady Ziza, why they made her suffer so?"

"I fear I do not."

"So, we're right? Lydia is the new dreamer?" Kamira asked Ziza.

"Yes."

"You could have just said so!" The shifter regent threw her hands up in frustration.

"You did not ask me."

Kamira growled.

The Oracle offered a rare smirk. "Do not begrudge me my very nature, shifter, and I will return the courtesy."

The Elder of Moons let out a frustrated sigh, muttering something under her breath. But, otherwise, she offered no further argument.

Edu shifted from where he was leaning, crossing his arms across his massive chest. His head was lowered, and his long, curly, auburn hair fell around him in waves, curtaining off the skull mask from onlookers. As if he needed to shield his features from view—or as though he may hide his thoughts alone by that action. His mask certainly did the deed well enough. "Then we know where she is, perhaps willingly. We know what has transpired." Ylena's quiet voice carried easily in the acoustics of the Great Hall.

Lyon opened his mouth to respond but did not have the opportunity.

"Oh, pray tell. What would that be, *old friend*?"

A voice, sharp-edged and taunting, cut through the room. It sent Maverick to stand, and even Kamira stiffened where she sat atop the statue.

Aon stepped from the shadows of the room like a nightmare given flesh, materializing from the darkness he so resembled. "How charming to find all the traitors assembled." He gestured his metal prosthetic hand at the lot of them. "It makes this much simpler."

Edu stepped from the wall and toward Aon without hesitation. He held out his hand, and his long, wicked blade appeared from the air in a rush of fire. "Master Edu insists the treason was his work and his alone."

"Truly? I see. Then Kamira's clever masquerade was merely a poorly timed exercise? A diversion for my entertainment? What a dreadful misunderstanding." Aon hissed the last words through his teeth. "I am many things, Edu. But I am not—nor have I ever been—a fool."

"If you have come to kill us all, King Aon, then kindly do so and please spare me your gloating." Maverick leaned both his hands on his cane in front of him.

"On the contrary!" Aon assumed a sarcastically congenial tone as he pressed his gloved hand to his chest. "In light of all that has transpired, I come to tell you that I shall graciously forgive your conspiracies. I pardon you all of your mutinous acts. For we have just regained the balance of our world. Far be it from me to see it thrown off once more in a selfish bid for revenge."

"How is Lydia?" Lyon asked.

"She lives and bears the marks of a queen. She is shaken, confused, frightened, and weak. Oh, and feels quite betrayed by you, Lyon. By all those assembled—but you, most of all. Shame on you, Priest. She trusted you."

Lyon winced. Yes, he supposed Lydia would feel such a thing. They had sentenced her to death, after all. And he, more than most, perhaps, had a hand in her undoing. If only by complacency and his own fear of what the warlock may have plotted.

Aon continued. "I will take a moment to confirm for your paranoid minds that, yes, she is indeed in my care. And there she will remain, lest you all decide to cast her into the arms of death a second time."

Kamira laughed sarcastically, the tone cutting through the silence after his small speech. "Well done, Aon. Well done! A masterful plan, I must say. Having us murder your pet human when you knew it was required all along."

"I knew no such thing. She would have lived out her life in my care, if you all had not interfered. But paint my words as lies if you wish. I do not care. I felt, and continue to feel, nothing but grief at the girl's death and needless suffering. She did not deserve what was paid to her by any of you."

"You must surrender her immediately," Ylena cut in at Edu's obvious request. "You cannot hold her as your prisoner. Where have you taken her?"

Aon put his hand to his chest in mock hurt. "You insult me, Edu."

"Now it is you who assumes I am the fool, Aon!" Ylena shouted angrily. Edu's emotions were leaking into hers. Worse yet, the line between their minds had blurred. It was rare to see her so out of control of her bond with Edu. "Do not think I do not know you hold her imprisoned."

"That is not what I meant, you *remarkable* idiot." Aon laughed cruelly. "You insult me by thinking I would ever tell you where she is."

In a roar of rage, Edu dove at Aon, swinging the massive

sword through the air with the intention of cutting the warlock in half. But the blade passed harmlessly through empty air. The man was gone.

Aon's voice, disembodied and all the more foreboding because of it, rang out through the hall. "The dreamer is in my care. I am the only one of you who sought to protect her. I am the only one of you who sought to save our world. It is therefore only fitting that I protect her from your wrath. Consider it payment in return for sparing your pathetic lives!"

Aon laughed again—a cruel, sick, malicious sound. It faded into silence like the wind and was quickly replaced with Edu's second shout of rage as he planted his fist into the wall. The blue marble cracked and splintered like a spider's web centered about the impact. After a long moment, his head lowered, and the great King of Flames fought to calm his temper.

"Master Edu warns you he will take the dreamer back by force if he must. He will raise his army and take the fight to the warlock. This cannot stand."

"Wait—" Lyon began, but it was no use. A bare moment later and the King of Flames disappeared in a blaze that was his namesake and was gone.

Lyon shut his eyes and bowed his head in a deep sigh. He knew what he must do. He must go to Aon and bid the warlock to release the only prize he had ever desired in all his life. Not a dreamer, as all others might believe. No—a woman he loved.

Perhaps, for old time's sake, the warlock may listen to him once more.

For if Aon did not listen to reason... this would mean war.

SEVEN

Lydia awoke with a jolt. One minute, her world was a dreamless void, and the next, the lights flicked back on. She thrashed as though she were falling in a half-dream state, throwing her arms out to stop herself.

Ah hell, here we go again.

Her hands flew to her stomach, searching for the wound that should be there, for the four, knuckle-deep incisions in her rib cage that Aon had given her. Her heart was racing, pounding in her ears like a drum.

Mornin'.

She was lying on the cot of the chamber, under the covers. Aon had killed her—drove his claws deep into her ribs until the world went dark. And then... what, tucked her into bed?

Fifty percent sadist, fifty percent romantic, one hundred percent misguided fuckwad. Q was curled up on her pillow and lifted his head to look at her. **Welcome back, Cupcake.**

The memory of the pain made her feel ill. She sat up and threw the sheets aside, looking for blood. Looking for any proof of what had happened. There was nothing to be found. In fact, the dress didn't even have holes in it. There was no blood on the floor or anywhere on her.

Different dress, but that's not the point you're making.

"Shut up for one second, will you?" She groaned and put her head in her hands as she desperately tried to process what had happened and why. "He killed me."

Eh, no, not really.

"He stabbed me, and I died."

Don't be melodramatic. He hurt you, but you didn't die. You've died once for realsies. Tell me that didn't feel completely different than before.

Lydia took a breath and let it out slowly and looked up at the domed ceiling and the ornate chandelier. Q, as much as she'd hate to admit it, was right. What Edu had done was real death. This was... like someone turning the lights off. Just one minute awake, the next, not. More like going under anesthesia for surgery. One, two, out.

Death had felt... very much not like that.

Suddenly, she wished Nick was there. Not because he'd know what to do, or what to say—Nick was shit at comforting people or giving advice. No, she just... needed someone there next to her. Somebody who got how much it sucked. "It doesn't mean I have to like it."

Oh, hell no. Of course not. He's being a complete self-serving, sadistic, egotistical, pompous piece of shit. But you didn't really die is all I'm saying.

She snickered. "Tell me how you really feel." Clearly, the snake didn't think highly of the warlock. Aon had said everything that came out of the pond hated him—it seemed Q wasn't immune. She wondered why the Ancients wanted everyone to hate Aon.

Although right now she was starting to see that he didn't do much to help matters.

She felt tired, beleaguered, and overwhelmed. After everything that had happened, now Aon had her prisoner. Again. That wouldn't be out of the ordinary, except that he was trying to inspire her to use her dormant gifts the only way he knew how. "I don't want to do this."

A bony head bonked into hers, and Q nuzzled her like a cat. **I have a solution. Fight back.**

"Fight Aon?" She snorted in laughter. "I can't even beat the man in poker, let alone a fistfight."

Don't punch him, stupid. Use magic. You can do that now, y'know.

"I don't know how. If you told me how I could just... wiggle my fingers and shoot fireballs, then great."

Can't help you there, sweetheart. Either you know how to breathe or you don't. Not even I can teach you how to tap into what you can do.

She flopped onto her back on the cot to look up at the snake, who shifted to perch on her chest and look down at her. "Then how, exactly, am I supposed to fight him?"

Q fluffed his feathers up proudly and flapped his wings.

Me! I can fight him.

"Why didn't you, then? When he stabbed me? Why didn't you show yourself?"

Same reason you didn't tell him about me. You don't want him to know I exist. Q tilted his head at a sharp ninety-degree angle. **I thought to myself, 'Q, you sexy devil, why don't you swoop in there and eat him? That'll give him a run for his money.' But then I felt you say no and tell me not to get involved. You wanted me to stay hidden. So I did.**

She put her head back on the pillow and looked up at the ceiling. Q was right. When Aon had asked her about why she had no marks on her body, despite being a queen, she hadn't said anything about the snake. She was afraid of what Aon might do. "I'm afraid he'll hurt you or use you. Or take you away."

Aww, you'd miss me already? That's sweet. But don't worry, he can't. I'm yours. He can't control me. Not now, not ever. I could take us both away from here, right here, right now. You might not have control over your power, but I do. Do you want to leave?

Shit. *Shit.* No, she didn't.

So... why not?

That was a damn good question. Staring at the ceiling, she didn't know what to do. If Q opened a hole in space right now, she'd hesitate to walk through it. Why?

Then it hit her.

Edu.

Edu and *everyone else.*

That stupid prophecy of Aon's bothered her as much as it bothered him. Another king would rise and try to destroy her. She assumed that meant Edu would probably try to kill her a second time. Lyon and the others had betrayed her. She was—in the most stupid, awful, and nonsensical way possible—safer in this hole and hiding under Aon's wing than she was out there.

"Fuck."

Yeah.

Not to mention, leaving Aon's prison would carve into stone that she was a stupid "queen." That she was a dreamer, and there would be no going back. There wasn't already, but here, she could stall for time. Here, she only had Aon to contend with. "The devil you know, I guess..."

Q snickered at her joke and nuzzled her head again.

Bah, it's not so bad. He's not the devil. He just started some of the myths. Totally different, right?

Smiling slightly at Q's comment, she reached up to pet his head. He let out an odd little hissing purr and leaned into her fingers, happily rubbing up against her fingers. At least, in all this, she had this wiseass of a snake to help her along.

"I'm afraid that things will just keep going from bad to worse if I go out there."

It's possible. But it'll be less... uh... squishy.

Sighing, she shut her eyes. "I was just starting to get used to the way things were. I was just starting to not spend every moment of every day terrified of what was going to happen to me. I was just starting to get used to Aon, and now—"

Q disappeared out from under her hand, vanishing in a blink like he had never been there. A second later, someone was looming over her next to the cot.

"Get used to me, and now, what?" Aon stood over her, sounding amused.

Rocketing up to her feet, she tripped over the blanket that had been put over her, and crashed to the floor in a heap. She would have smashed her head on the floor if it weren't for a pair of arms wrapping around her to catch her. She took him down to the ground in her inertia, and he fell, laughing, tangled up with her.

"You really have moments of astounding grace, you know that?" He continued to laugh. Shifting, he pulled his arm out from under her and looked down at her.

"You need to stop sneaking up on me." She narrowed her eyes at him.

"Never."

"Then you'll keep being treated to such spectacular displays."

Lifting his ungloved hand, he stroked some of her hair away from her face and tucked it behind her ear. "I believe I rather prefer to see you fall about like a baby giraffe. It is terribly fun to watch."

"You gotta get better hobbies."

"That is most undoubtedly true." He tilted his head curiously. "Who were you speaking to a moment ago?"

She cooked up a fast half-truth. "Myself. I don't have anything else to do." It wasn't a full lie. Q was part of her, so she was—literally—talking to herself.

"Perhaps I should get you a pet." He toyed with a piece of her hair. "At the very least I will bring you some books to pass the time."

It was the banter of friends and lovers. Not... whatever they were now. Last she knew, he was tearing his claws through her rib cage. He had hurt her and very much on purpose. Now he was stroking her hair like she meant something to him. She knew the two were not necessarily different things to him. Not in the slightest. "Have you come to torture me again?"

Lowering his head, his shoulders slumped as if he were disappointed she had ruined the moment so quickly. With a resigned sigh, he sat up and shifted to his feet. Reaching his hand down to her, he offered to help her stand.

Refusing the help would just be out of stubborn spite, so she took it and let him heft her up to her own feet.

"No, not tonight. I have not come with such intent." He lifted a finger. "Also, I would rather you think of it as *training*, not torture, if I may draw a line of distinction between the two."

"What's the difference?"

"One is done solely for my pleasure. The other serves a more practical purpose." There was no small amount of fiendish enjoyment in his words. "Although I do admit they are not mutually exclusive."

"You're training me by torturing me. Sorry if I'm not enthusiastic." This wasn't a joke to her, and she didn't appreciate how flippantly he was treating the situation.

It seemed he understood the motive behind her tone, and he shook his head. Moving toward her, he reached out his arms.

When she flinched, he lowered his arms and took a step back. "If you wish the cruelty to go no further, you may end it. You have the power to stop me. You merely need act upon it."

"You know I don't know how."

"And here I am, attempting to show you."

"There's no other way?"

He placed his hand against his chest, fingers dramatically splayed out. "I am but what I am, my darling. Dread warlock, God of Darkness, King of Shadows... This method is the only tool in my possession."

"My dad liked to say that when all you have is a hammer, everything looks like a nail." She rolled her eyes. "I think you haven't tried to think of another plan, because you get off on this one."

He straightened and watched her for a long moment in silence. "Perhaps you may be right. But answer me this. If I were to allow you your freedom, what do you think may happen when Edu finds you?"

She remembered Evie's words. Edu kills... Aon tortures. At the time, the latter seemed like the more undesirable outcome. But even now, she had the will to live. She hadn't wanted to die that night on the streets when Edu burned out her heart. She had made the choice to live when the Ancients gave her the option, and she still didn't want to die now.

Maybe that'd change, once she'd been mutilated in new and fun unique ways. After a few weeks of this, maybe she would have a different opinion.

"Do you think he'd kill me? Just to keep me away from you?"

"Yes."

"But it would doom the world again, right?"

"He does not care. Edu would rather see the void swallow this world in totality than think that I, for once, may have found some measure of solace."

"What the actual fuck does he think you're going to do?"

"Conquer the world, I suppose. Become the King of All he thinks I desire to be."

"But you don't—" She put her hands over her face and growled in frustration. It was so utterly clear to her now that he had no designs on world domination. This whole mess was out of paranoia. Everything just kept coming back to one question —what *did* Aon want? "Why did you really kill Qta?"

When he didn't answer, she lowered her hands to look at him. He was standing stiff, his body language screaming his sudden unease.

"Aon, I deserve to know. I let you off easy before, because it didn't really matter." She pointed at the marks on her face. "It matters now."

"I... cannot tell you. Not yet."

"No, Aon." This time, she was angry. She jabbed a finger into his chest, and was as little pleased when he jumped at the unexpected contact. It had probably been a very long time since anyone scolded him like a child. "You don't get to keep me in a box and torture me and then keep secrets like that! You killed Qta. You killed the last dreamer for a reason. And here I am, a stupid goddamn dreamer now, and you won't tell me why you did it? You tell me it isn't about power. You tell me it isn't what Edu and the others are worried about. But you won't give me any other reason to take its place!"

He caught her hand in his, and for a moment, she worried he was going to hurt her. Instead, he slipped her palm against the side of his neck, warm under her palm. He did this when he wanted to remind her that he was just a man, beneath it all. It broke off her anger like a light switch, and instead tears began to sting her eyes. With her other hand, she wiped them away.

"I have no right to keep this from you. I have no shelter to take, no excuses I may concoct to hide the truth. But I... what you ask of me..." His voice was thick with pain, with regret and sorrow. He was heartbroken. Whatever the truth really was, whatever he wasn't telling her—it cut him to the quick. "Please. Do not demand this of me."

He was begging her, pleading with her not to make him go down that road. Damn her for being such a softie. She stepped into him and hugged him, wrapping her arms around behind his neck. "Do you believe I'll think less of you?"

"I am certain you will. The act itself was selfish and shameful to a level that I think transcends the words themselves. The reason behind it was more so."

"You need to tell me, Aon. You really do. But I'll give you more time. I have plenty. I'm immortal now, right?" She laughed half-heartedly at her own morbid joke.

Chuckling, he hugged her tight to him, squeezing her as if he were afraid she was going to dissolve in his arms. "Forgive me for hurting you."

"The problem is... you stabbed me, and okay, I'm fine. That sucked, that hurt, but I'm fine. I know that's how things work here. But I also know what you did last night isn't even the start of what you can come up with."

"Hardly."

Sighing, she rested her forehead against his chest and shut her eyes. "At what point do you just cut off my limbs, stitch them up so I don't bleed out, and bury me alive to starve to death? Can't we just skip to the end and save me all the bullshit in between?"

He laughed. "My, that was creative. I knew I was fond of you for a reason."

"This isn't funny."

He gently pushed her half a step away and tipped her chin up to look at him. "I hope someday you may truly come to forgive me. Not just for what I have done or for what I will do—but for my very nature. Forgive me, if you can find the strength, for my mannerisms. I am so... very old."

He shook his head. "I have been painted the villain and the worthless, heartless fiend for so long, I find shelter in the cruelty of it. I am too weary to fight what is expected of me. I no longer have the desire. This is not humorous, nor is it a game. The world seems set to put you down this path, and I will be the one to see it through. I will not see you destroyed once more."

He tilted her head away from him with the gentle press of fingers underneath her chin. "So I will hurt you. And yes, I will do so over and over, worse and worse, until you find the means to strike back at me. Until you prove to us both that you can stand in this world on your own." His fingers wandered up over her cheek, tracing the markings on her face with a featherlight touch. "Until you can fight back... I have no choice."

Everything he said left her overwhelmed. She didn't know if she wanted to scream, to cry, to kiss him, or to beg him to just kill her. She never got the chance to decide.

He pulled away from her sharply and suddenly, and the absence of him jarred her out of her thoughts. "But! I digress. You have a visitor."

"I... do?"

"Indeed. The irritating cretin would not stop *howling* at my door until I agreed to let him see you." He gestured, and he procured out of thin air a mask. It was made of turquoise stones in a careful mosaic, creating the visage of a grinning winged snake. It was the mask she hurled into the lake of blood. "You should get dressed." He held it out to her.

"I'm not wearing that fucking thing. Not now, not ever."

"Well, that was a rather passionate answer." He chuckled.

"I'm not doing it. It's dumb, ugly, and it's not me. What the hell's the point in those things, anyway? You can't even read these goddamn things." Lydia gestured again at the writing on her face.

"It is the tradition."

"Your tradition, not mine."

"You are one of us now."

"No, I'm not."

"The marks say otherwise."

"It's still stupid!"

"Most traditions are."

"Nail it to my head if you want. I'm not wearing that thing. Deal with it."

Laughing, he shrugged and walked over to the wooden table by the other edge of the raised platform and placed the mask down on the smooth surface. "I will leave it here and give you something to think on."

"Whatever."

He turned from the table and gestured out in front of him. With fingers stretched, he turned his wrist and pulled his hand into a fist. As he did, a black dot appeared in the world before him and began to grow until it was eight feet or so in diameter. It was the same kind of inky portal Edu had used to bring her from Earth to Under.

Christ, that felt like forever ago. She wondered how much time it had really been. Two months? Three, tops?

Speaking of something that felt like forever ago, the man who stepped through the gate felt like a stranger. So much had happened in so little time, and she hadn't seen him in what felt like ages.

"Nick!" She squeaked as he ran at her and hugged her so hard she thought he might crush her ribs.

Nick was already blathering like a madman, too fast and stepping on his own words. "Lyd! Lyd, shit, oh fuck, Lyd, they killed you! I tried to come. I tried, but they chained me to a goddamn tree, and—"

"Nick—"

She couldn't get a word in edgewise. Nick was on a tear. His wooden mask was digging into her neck. "You died, you really died. I can't believe they killed you, the stupid assholes! They wouldn't listen to me. Nobody ever listens to me."

Laughing, she swatted at his arm until he let up from clutching her like a drowning man would cling to a piece of a shipwreck in the ocean. He held on to her by her upper arms instead. "I tried to come and warn you. To warn either of you. But Kamira wouldn't let me. And then, they tried to—holy shit!" Nick grabbed her face suddenly, clearly just noticing the marks on her face.

She laughed again and shooed his hands off her face. "Yeah. I know."

Nick's expression was one of shock warring with relief. "It's true! Kamira said some bullshit, but I didn't believe it. Shit, Lyd —are you *really* a queen? But... you died. The Ancients brought you back like this?"

"I guess so. I don't get it. I don't know why this happened." She hugged him now that he'd finally calmed down. It was so good to see him, she almost wanted to cry. But she had enough of that for a lifetime already today. She had enough reasons to sob; happiness shouldn't be one of them.

"When Kamira told me Aon had you prisoner, I had to come this time. I had to know you were okay. I don't care what they say. I'm not going to let that asshole—"

"Careful, boy."

Oh, right. Aon was still in the room. She broke her hug on Nick to look over at the warlock with a smirk. He was leaning against the table, arms across his chest, the posture of a man who was utterly bored. "Be nice, Aon."

"He insulted me, might I remind you. I let the flea-infested vermin come see you, didn't I?"

"Is he hurting you?" Nick asked her intently.

"Well..." Man, she didn't know how to answer that.

"He is, isn't he?" Nick growled in his throat, and the sound was entirely inhuman. For a moment, she had forgotten that he was a were-whatever now. A shapeshifter. As she watched, his teeth changed to dangerous points.

"It's complicated," was the best she could do.

"Don't defend him!" Nick snarled, and his eyes glinted dangerously. He turned toward Aon as if readying to fight him.

"And what could you do if I was? Pee on the rug? Hump the furniture, perhaps?" Aon goaded but did not straighten up. Nick was no threat to the warlock, and the king wasn't even going to stand to humor the idea.

She moved to stand in between them. "Aon, stop. Both of you, stop it."

"I, for once, am doing nothing wrong," the man in black insisted.

Nick was still growling like a dog who was upset there was a stranger in the home.

She put her hand over her eyes and for a moment found some strange shelter in the fact that she was surrounded by idiots. Her whole life might be upended, but some things never changed.

"Nick, it's okay. Aon is... it's fine. I promise you. It's complicated. He's trying to help me, I swear." She turned to look up at Nick and did her best to smile. "I'm safer in here than I am out there. At least for the time being. I might have these stupid marks on my face, but I don't know what I'm doing. I can't control my power. If I went out there right now, Edu would just kill me a second time. You know he would."

Her best friend snorted in disbelief but then shook his head and sighed. "Fine. But I don't trust him. He's a selfish, egotistical prick, and I think he's just using you." He threw his hands up in frustration. "But there's nothing I could do to him, anyway."

"Oh, look, the dog has a single braincell, after all."

"Aon!" She glared at him.

He raised his hands as if to say he surrendered and was done with his snide comments.

She didn't believe that for a moment. "Can we have some privacy?"

"Excuse me?" Aon sounded utterly offended.

"I'd like to talk to my friend in private. And besides, this is going to bore you to tears. You know it is." She flashed him a smile, daring him to try to say she was wrong.

Sighing dramatically, the warlock stood. "Very well. Yes. I have far better things to be doing than to listen to you two blather on about how you view my existence as deeply flawed. I will return in an hour's time." And with that, the warlock blinked out of existence like he had never been there at all.

"He's a dick," Nick muttered angrily. "An epic dick."

"He's not so bad when you get to know him. I promise."

"Get to know him, huh?" Nick shoved her arm, and they were back to their old antics. He was teasing her like he would after she had a hot date back in Boston. "So that other rumor Kamira told me was true, huh? You and the douchebag? Really? I thought you didn't like shitheads."

She groaned. "Dude, it just kind of happened." She walked over to the edge of the moat around the platform in the room and sat on it with her feet over the edge. Nick followed suit.

"That kind of thing doesn't just happen."

"I couldn't help it. He isn't what everyone says he is. I don't know how to explain it."

"All right, well, try anyway. Just... please skip some parts." He blanched dramatically, and it was her turn to shove his arm instead. The two began laughing, and the relief she felt at having her friend there with her almost made her lose her fight with tears a second time.

Leaning her head on his arm, she started to fill him in on everything that had happened since she saw him at the gala. Everything she had learned about Aon, about the world, the time spent with him. She included his softer moments—the trip to the museum, dinner. But she did dutifully gloss over the juicy parts. That was the one rule they had when talking about their relationships. Both of them were perfectly happy not knowing the details.

After she finished, it was his turn. She sat there and listened as he told her about the pack he was in, about Kamira, about getting beaten up and learning to defend himself. About the friends he had made already and how much he was enjoying being in Under.

Once again, she was jealous.

"And Kaori, shit." Nick snickered. "I mean, she—"

"No details!"

"But the things she can do with—"

"No. Stop it."

"I mean, her legs can—"

She interrupted him with a disgusted holler and shoved him hard with both hands. The two dissolved into laughter. The lopsided grin he was sporting revealed he was doing it very much on purpose. It was like nothing had changed and nothing had happened. He wasn't a werewolf. She hadn't died and been raised from the grave as whatever she was now.

"Speaking of. You and Aon. Are you two really a thing?" Of course, he glazed over all the important parts, like Edu killing her, the business with Evie, or waking up with marks on her face. Sometimes, he was a miserable gossip.

"I have no idea." She looked down and picked at the hem of the black dress. "I really don't. I don't know what we were before I died, let alone now." She paused. "I care about him, I know that much."

No, she more than cared about him. But that wasn't something she wanted to say when Aon was certainly listening.

Nick sniffed dismissively. "I don't know how you put up with him."

"I have bad taste and a history of putting up with assholes. It's fine."

He snickered at her jab and shoved her. "At least you have one skill in life." He paused for a long time before looking over at her, his tone serious. "Shit, Lyd. You're a queen. Like... a queen-queen."

"I don't feel like one, trust me." She held out her arms. "I feel like a dumpster fire. I'm just as lost, scared, and confused as I was the day I got dragged into this stupid world. And now, Aon can just keep stabbing me, and it's no big deal, so that's the worst kind of party. At least before, he didn't maim me because the damage would be permanent." She was griping. It was pointless, but it felt good to vent, anyway.

"He is hurting you. I knew it." He growled, that same inhuman sound. It was a strange reminder that he wasn't quite the same guy she knew. The wooden mask covering a third of his face didn't help, but the growl was somehow still more jarring. "That sick fuck is doing it to get his rocks off, isn't he?"

"No. Look, it's complicated."

"You keep saying that. Explain it already."

How the hell could she when she barely understood herself? For a moment, she debated telling him about Q. It was Nick. She could trust him with her life. But she wasn't ready to admit to Nick that in some sick way, she was here by choice. Fear and worry over what Edu and the others would do to her, but it was her choice to stay here, nonetheless. Besides, she'd bet everything in the world that the warlock was eavesdropping.

"I don't have any other marks." She lifted her arms, showing him. "None, anywhere. I don't know how to use... whatever power it is I've been given."

You have me.

Shut up, Q.

Can I come say hi? I'll explain it better than you.

Next time.

Who says there's gonna be a next time?

Just no. Not yet.

You're no fun.

Nick must have thought she was pausing because she was upset, having no idea that she was busy arguing with herself. Maybe she had really gone insane. Maybe Q was just a figment of her imagination. Nobody else had seen the snake yet, so it was a possibility. He slung an arm around her shoulder and hugged her into his side. "That doesn't explain why Aon's hurting you."

"Ziza told him a prophecy. That another king is going to come and destroy me. He's... trying to 'inspire me' to figure out how to fight back."

He sighed heavily and shook his head. "That's seriously the best he can do?"

"That's what I said."

"He's a sadistic fuck. That's the short of it. He could do something else, I'm sure. But he enjoys this. You shouldn't be his prisoner. You shouldn't be in this stupid room. He's using you."

"I will not have a rabid mutt judging my methods or my intentions."

Both Nick and Lydia nearly levitated off the ground as Aon spoke suddenly from behind them. The warlock was standing some five feet away, hands clasped behind his back. "Your hour is up."

"I'm not leaving her here. You can't keep her prisoner." Nick clambered to his feet. His voice was half that animal snarl again, triggered by his anger.

"You are, and I can. And she may leave on her own, as soon as she discovers how." Aon shrugged dismissively. "You may come see her again in a day or two, if I allow it."

"If you allow it?" Nick stepped toward Aon, his fists clenched. "Listen, you insane, piece of shit cocksucker—"

Oh, Nick. Guaranteed to make a bad situation worse.

"Devolving into obscene name-calling again? You modern children and your lack of imagination." Sighing as though he were dealing with a toddler, he waved his hand dismissively. "Very well."

A black hole in space appeared in the floor beneath her friend, and Nick plummeted downward with a startled scream. And just as fast, the portal closed.

"Aon—"

"Before you lecture me or worry, he is quite fine. I merely dropped him in a lake in the woods outside my estate. The worst he will contract will be the smell of wet dog."

She pinched the bridge of her nose and tried to hold back the long, angry lecture she wanted to unleash on the warlock about how he was not doing himself any favors. No wonder people didn't like him. "You didn't have to do that."

"No. I did not. But it was immensely enjoyable."

Yup. No wonder people didn't like him. Shooting him a weary smile, she decided to change the subject. "It was nice of you to let me see Nick."

"I had little choice. He was going to scratch my door to oblivion if I let him sit upon my porch and maim the wood-work as though he were the family dog left out in a storm."

Walking up to him, she wrapped her arms around him and pulled him into a hug. He was trying to downplay what he had done—to brush off his bringing her friend to see her as only serving his own agenda. She could see through it now for what it was, a bad attempt at dodging what he had really done. Which was, for once, to do something *nice.*

Or to make up for what he was going to do to her.

Either way.

He folded his arms around her and drew her against him. His façade didn't last. "Did it give you some peace of mind?"

"It was nice to talk things through with him. He's been my

best friend for five years." She hadn't realized how much she had missed Nick until she had seen him.

"And what insight did the idiot pup have to provide?"

"He said he doesn't know what I see in you."

"Hm. A valid observation. I truly am a valueless, worthless cretin. To see any redeeming value in an abhorrent gargoyle such as myself would be to question one's sanity." He tightened his grasp on her. "I do wonder if you came out of that pond with your mental faculties intact—either the first time or the second time. Have you considered you might now be insane?"

"Takes one to know one." She grinned up at him.

He laughed and rested his head on top of hers. "Touché."

There was a long pause as she felt the mood deflate. She knew what was going to happen next. She tried not to hold it against him, but it was hard. "How bad is it going to be this time?"

"You can stop it. You can fight back."

Fear knotted in her stomach. "You know I can't..."

He sighed and lifted his bare hand to stroke her cheek. "Then let us begin."

Something snaked around her throat and suddenly yanked her backward. Lydia screamed and tried to pull whatever it was off her, but it was no use. It dragged her off her feet and to the ground.

She kicked and fought, trying to get free of the thing around her neck that was keeping her pinned to the ground. "Let me up!"

"No."

Stepping over her, he knelt and pinned her legs to the ground as he sat atop her. When he ran his hands to the collar of her dress, she grabbed at him.

"Don't you dare!"

"What, rape you? Please. Do not think so little of me. I

would hardly be so puerile. I merely need your skin exposed for what I will do."

She couldn't stop him as he used his metal claws to slice the dress open down the center. She punched at him, trying to shove him off her.

"You know you cannot stop me in such a fashion." He grabbed her wrists and yanked them up over her head. Something slipped around her wrists—something like rope. But rope that could move. When he released her hands, she couldn't pull her arms down from where she had put them. Looking up, there were tendrils of black... nothingness coming up out of the floor and weaving around her wrists and beginning to squirm in between her fingers. Her heart was pounding in her chest with the adrenaline brought on by fear.

"When the worlds of Earth and Under align, we go and gather what books and media we can, to bring back with us. Music, films, books, and so on. Maverick is the keeper of such things. He is particularly interested in the medical profession, as he was part of it back in his mortal days. Recently, I had a chance to peruse the additions to his collection." He watched her, his tone dry and oddly detached.

Why the hell was he telling her this?

The tips of his metal talons touched the bare skin of her chest, and she jolted at the sudden sharp sensation.

"One book I found amongst the volumes reminded me of you. A book on the forensic sciences. Particularly one regarding corpses."

Oh no.

"I wonder, my dear Lydia, when you took a scalpel to flesh..." His voice was a deep and sensual rumble in his chest, even as he pressed the metal point of his finger into the skin just below her right collarbone.

She tried not to scream—tried her best not to beg him to

stop. She knew he wouldn't. She knew he would only tell her to fight back.

He was digging the claw through her skin now, slicing into her. Dragging a painful diagonal line toward the center of her torso. Hot blood welled from the wound, pooling on her skin. She felt it run up over her shoulder and onto the floor.

She knew what he was doing.

She'd done it a thousand times.

There would be two more lines to follow before the pain even really started.

He was performing an autopsy.

"Tell me," he said, breathless in his enjoyment of her suffering, "did you ever wonder how it might feel?"

EIGHT

"No! Edu, you can't be serious!"

Evie could become quite shrill when she was angry, Edu decided. He had returned to his keep to ready his armies for war. He would march on the warlock to free the Queen of Dreams or whatever he may find within Aon's prison.

Noting his mood, Evie had pestered him until he revealed to her that not only was there a dreamer alive, but that it was her former cellmate and fast friend. Evie had still not fully forgiven him for taking Lydia's life. How she had wept when he had Ylena deliver the news. She had punched at him until her anger broke, and he held her until she calmed.

Now it seemed her anger had found purchase once more. Ylena stood nearby, as even Evie's clever reading of his body language would not be enough to convey the intricacies of what was at work.

"Let me get this perfectly straight, cowboy. You wanna march your army to Aon's home and storm the joint to, what? *Rescue* Lydia?"

He shrugged. Rescue or kill again, he wasn't yet sure.

"First of all, she ain't gonna be happy to see you." She

planted her hands on her hips, and he wanted to pin her to the wall and take her right then and there. He found her anger kindled his desire in a way that little else in this world had ever done.

Misjudging his silence as evasiveness, and not as he was busy listing all the things he was going to do to her if she stopped hollering at him, she continued. "Don't tell me you ain't thinkin' to pick a fight with the bearcat all over again. You can't! She's my friend. She don't deserve this."

He shook his head. Ylena spoke for him, as always. "Master Edu knows your friend does not deserve the fate she suffers. But if she is a danger to this world, it must be dealt with. Edu does not know what he shall do. Regardless, she cannot stay as Aon's prisoner. Would you have him leave her there? After what Aon did to you?"

Evie blanched at the memory and looked off with a wavering breath. "You're goin' to go there to save her, right? Nothin' else?"

That was a promise he could not make. Ylena remained silent for a long moment before his empath came up with a better response than he could muster. "Master Edu insists that his choice is not yet made. First, he shall free the girl from Aon's prison before he judges what must be done for the sake of Under." Ah, Ylena, always finding words when he could not do so. Literally and figuratively.

Evie let out a long sigh. "All right. All right, you big lug. I'm trustin' you. Don't hurt her. Not again, please. I don't think my heart could take it a second time. Please."

He only held out his arms to her, inviting the girl into his embrace. She walked up to him, and he scooped her up into a hug, lifting her clear off the ground. Evie squeaked and laughed, throwing her arms around his neck, quickly forgetting her anger at his plan for war.

He would do a great many things to give Evie anything her

heart may desire. There was little she could ask for that he would not grant to see a glimpse of a smile. But... Lydia's safety, he could not promise.

For if Aon was using her to become the King of All, he could not let it come to pass.

Whatever the cost may be.

* * *

Lyon stood in the library of Aon's home and looked up at the soaring bookcases with idle interest. He had been waiting here for some time. Navaa, Aon's second in command and regent of the House while the warlock slept, was pacing back and forth in front of the fireplace. It burned low, the wood and embers nearly spent. Its master had not been here in many hours. He needn't wonder where Aon might be. It was what actions Aon may be taking in his absence that left Lyon troubled.

Navaa and Lyon knew each other well. They were not friends but peaceful colleagues. Time was once that their rank was the same. Navaa was far faster in his judgments than him and far more prone to bursts of violence. But such was the way of those Aon cultivated, he supposed.

"Do you know precisely where he is?" Lyon asked the agitated man.

"Of course not. He would not tell me, even if I asked. This matter is far too serious to have any trust in anyone but himself."

"Do you know much of the young woman? How she fares?" Perhaps he might glean some information from Aon's House, if not from the man himself. "I worry over what Aon may do."

"No. No one here has seen her since she was raised. I did not believe it myself, until you came."

Ah. Well, there went that hopeful idea. Lyon would have to find another means.

Navaa continued speaking. "As for what he's doing? Who knows. He guarded her fiercely when she was mortal. He said that all those of us with masks may never speak to her—that we were not even to *approach* her. I have not even met her. Only the servants were allowed to interact with his new ward. What manner of foolishness is that?"

"Perhaps he wished to keep her free of political entanglements." Lyon looked up at the bookcases once more. So much knowledge was kept within these walls, and yet all of it fell flat and useless in the face of what was transpiring around them.

Lydia was prisoner to Aon still, but now her situation had become far more dire. Lyon had been pleased, when she was mortal, to see Aon caring for her as he might a guest and not a fugitive, as had opted Edu.

It was plain to see that the warlock delighted in her naivety and her clear mind. She was a rare creature in a world like theirs, and to see the King of Shadows pursue her as a lover did not trouble or concern Lyon overmuch. Indeed, he lauded the man's restraint in dealing with the mortal woman. Better he seek to possess her than mutilate her, as some suspected he might.

But now, everything had changed. She was no longer a bird in a gilded cage, protected in her confinement from the raging storm that was their world. She would not have survived a day in the wilds of Under without some manner of protector when she was mortal. All of them had conspired to cast her to her death, and now she was a dreamer. *The* dreamer. The only hope to breathe new life into a dead and withering place.

Lyon had his hand to blame in all this as well. He, too, had wished desperately to believe Ziza's words, that Lydia must die to save the world. They had believed it would save them from the wrath of the King of Shadows, not that she must need die for their world to continue to exist at all.

Aon had not raised the Queen of Monsters.

They had.

His heart bled for her, for all she had suffered. For the fear she must feel now, her future uncertain and in the hands of a man who may or may not be benign in his intentions. Lyon knew quite well that even when Aon was being benevolent, he found the cruelest way possible to enact the deed.

Now they stood on the brink of war once more. It was for that reason Lyon had come. Edu had, in his rashness and foolhardy righteousness, demanded she be surrendered to him immediately. Even Lyon, in his desire to think the most of all parties, could not fathom a world where a recently maligned victim might be returned to her attacker and not desperately desire otherwise.

That was before one took into consideration Aon's feelings for her. The warlock was a covetous creature on the best of days —but to hand over the woman he loved, so recently returned from death...? Impossible.

If Edu knew the truth for what Lyon suspected the warlock may feel for Lydia, he did not doubt the warrior would kill her for that reason alone. Edu was many things—but his hatred of Aon ran deep.

When Aon refused to surrender Lydia to the group of them, he triggered a series of events that Lyon knew were now in play. Edu would amass his army and lay siege upon the warlock. He would attempt to destroy all in his path to wrench her from his grasp by any means necessary.

As was often the case with such heated rivalry, both Edu and Aon were wrong in their actions. Both men were misguided in their singular desires. The truth lay somewhere betwixt them as it most often did when the Kings of Flames and Shadows found themselves embroiled in a debate.

The victim in all this—save for Lydia, of course—would be the world of Under and its people. It was for them that Lyon stood here, wishing to plead to the warlock for a generosity of spirit. It was for this world that Lyon put his own life in the balance. Kamira had begged him not to come, for it may mean his doom. Aon had "forgiven" them their trespasses, but he needed no reason to take a prisoner. Especially not now when he had his greatest desire to protect.

"Does he know I am here?" Lyon needed to distract himself from the turmoil and dismay in his own mind.

"I did what I could, Priest," Navaa snapped. "He does not answer to me."

"I am quite aware. Forgive me, I am attempting to make conversation. I have been told I should not endeavor into such territory that to me remains so unnatural." Lyon smiled, if faintly, at his own dry moment of self-deprecating humor.

Navaa huffed a single laugh, and Lyon was at least proud that he managed to defuse the man's mood, if mildly. "Where has that fat weasel been in all this?"

"Otoi is claiming 'general malaise' and that he cannot leave his bedchambers. He fears what may come of all this. No one minds his absence." He hated to speak so poorly of someone who was, in technicality, his regent.

"I certainly do not. Nor, for the record, do I understand this asinine 'law' that forced you to relinquish your mask in the first place." Navaa huffed angrily, and picking up an iron poker, jabbed it into the dying fire. Embers kicked up, carrying in the invisible rise of hot air up the black stone chimney. "We're a horrible, violent, doomed lot. Politics be damned, let us have our love where we find it, I say."

Lyon turned to look at the man fully and was surprised at his words. Navaa rarely said a kind word to anyone for any reason, and to hear him speak so now touched him to a surprising degree. "Thank you, Navaa. I wish it were not so. But

I find I do not miss the piece of porcelain I wore for so long." Lyon touched the spot on his face that bore his soulmarks. Sometimes, he still expected to find the smooth piece of pure white clay that had been such a part of him for so long. "Too much do we distance ourselves from those without. We are not so superior to them."

Navaa made a dismissive grunt. "For that, I do not care. Such was the decree of the Ancients, not us. The law that keeps you from lordship is our invention, not theirs."

"That is a degree of piety from you I would not expect. Yet I appreciate the sentiment all the same."

"Don't expect more." Navaa sneered. "I have a quota."

Lyon laughed and found the gruff, dark-skinned man was grinning in his enjoyment at the joke. When he grinned, his metal mask shifted on his bald head, creasing into the skin. "Well said. Well said, indeed."

The feeling in the room shifted as a dark presence filled it. Power blew into the room like a dread wind. Without a doubt, it could only be one person. Turning, Lyon saw Aon standing at the end of the table, wiping his metal hand with a black handkerchief. He was bending each joint one at a time, cleaning something out from the hinges in his prosthetic. The rag was wet, and Lyon could see the barest glint of crimson in the light of the room. Dread welled again in his heart at what that may portend.

"My king." Navaa bowed to Aon sharply. "I kept him here as you requested."

"Thank you," the warlock responded. "You are dismissed."

Navaa vanished in a swirl of black smoke. That left the two of them.

"To what do I owe the pleasure of this visit, Priest?" Aon continued to idly clean off his hand from the blood that stained it.

"Is that hers?" He honestly dreaded the answer. He feared he already knew it.

"And if it were, dearest friend of mine?" The seemingly friendly words were a spoken threat as Aon walked around the table to stand a dozen feet from Lyon, moving like a shark might circle its prey. "What then? What would it matter?"

"I would ask why you harm her when you grieved so terribly for her loss."

"I grieved for her loss, and I rejoice in her return."

"Then why?"

"She is as though nothing has changed. Her mind remains her own and free of the influence of our vile Ancients. She is powerless, yet she bears the marks of a queen. Ironically, I believe her gifts may yet lay sleeping and dormant. The desperate protections of an injured mind against the ravages of such enormity as she has absorbed. I seek to ensure she has command of herself before releasing her." The warlock shrugged. "I am merely giving her a reason to find the skill to resist me."

"By such means?" Lyon sighed and shook his head. "Only you, my king, would seek to mend injury with further injury."

"I must teach her all this world may have in store for her." Aon tossed the bloody handkerchief into the fire. "I was too compassionate when she lived as a mortal. She trusted too much. I cared for her happiness, and see what it wrought? Now she cannot die so easily. Now I can teach her in full to prepare what will wait for her. I would have her rise from these ashes as a force with which no one would dare trifle. Not a pawn in our tired games."

"And if you fail?" Lyon stepped closer to the man carefully. "What if she is not so strong? What if her powers never wake to stop you?"

"Then she will break and be mine in mind, in body, and in soul." Aon laughed. "Either way... I suppose I win."

Lyon felt the cold creep of horror well over him at the man's words. Such was a tactic that only the warlock might devise. It was perfect in its broken brilliance and matching madness. "You would torture her mercilessly for fear of what others may do." Lyon hung his head and shut his eyes. Perhaps he was too late. "This ploy is horrific."

"I am quite proud of it, thank you."

"If I cannot beg you to think of her welfare in all this, I must beg you to think of your own. I saw how you held her in your arms." He hesitated. This was a risk. "Do not think me so naive not to know love where it is written so boldly."

Aon's words came in an angry hiss, though the warlock did not turn to face him. "What I feel is my own business, *Priest*, not yours."

Lyon looked up at the silvered mirror that hung over the fireplace, shadowy in its reflection of the dark room. He was growing exasperated with the warlock's stubborn adherence to his line of thinking. He should not be so bewildered, as the King of Shadows had always been this way. "You at the very least care for the girl. These actions of yours are irreparable. How do you think she might feel for you when all is said and done?"

"It does not matter. My goal is simple—her salvation. At the end of this bloody road, either she will despise me and look upon me as the worthless, fetid, and foul thing as you all have come to do—even my oldest 'friend,'" Aon shot at him spitefully, mocking their once-close nature. "Or she will shatter and be my devoted servant."

"Aon... please, this is madness, even for you."

"Have we met?" The warlock laughed, perhaps at himself. "It is what must transpire. If I do not show her the cruelties of this world and allow her to walk freely, I would do her a disservice that will end her life a second time."

"Then stand at her side and protect her! Guard her from

these evils you think may find her. Take her under your wing, and—"

"As I did once before?" Aon said through a furious shout and punched his metal hand into the back of the chair at the table, splintering the wood. "I kept her here as my guest! Every need of hers was met! I treated her as a princess—as *my* princess —she wanted for nothing! All my secrets were laid bare to her, if she would have them. I would have tended to her until she died of old age, and I would have done so with joy. And *you* took that away!"

Lyon flinched and found himself looking down at the wood floor. Guilt stabbed at him, harder than the warlock's words.

Aon was not finished shouting. "You showed me, all of you, precisely how naïve I had been to think I could save her from the wanton, bloodthirsty nature of this doomed place. And do not think for one second that I do not hold you responsible most of all, dear Priest! If you said one word against them, not even *Edu* would have dared to act as he did. You fell prey to the delusions just the same as the others. You are responsible for her suffering, same as that idiotic oaf. Same as I am now!"

The silence hung painfully in the air. Finally, Lyon broke it. "You are correct." When Aon did not respond, Lyon continued. "I suspected the double-natured meanings hidden in Ziza's words. But when she talked to us of saving this world, Aon... I had to let it come to pass. You know I do not delight in the pain of others. I would not have sent Lydia to her doom without the hope of what it may bring. I do not wish to see this world burn. Nor do I wish to see it dissolve into the silence of the void. If the girl had to die for this to come to pass, then... so be it."

Lyon lifted his head finally to look at the other man. He was standing facing the fire, his back to the priest, hands clasped behind his back. "For that, yes, I am guilty of dooming her to this suffering the same as Edu. But I beg you, Aon, spare the girl the pain you wish to bring her. Spare her this suffering. If you feel for her as I suspect, surely you cannot bring yourself to do what you say."

"Oh, my dear old friend. That is the worst of it all. You see before you a monster willing to commit such acts of horror against her tender flesh. But what you even now refuse to admit?" He lifted his metal hand in front of his face, examining it as if fondly recalling what it was that had just brought the girl harm. "Is that before you stands a monster who can do such acts and find great joy within the deed."

Lyon felt revulsion rise in his stomach, and he held it down. But he did not truly believe the warlock's assertion. He could not, for then there would be nothing left to redeem in the man who stood before him.

Either way, his heart wept for Lydia and where she must now find herself. Confused and lost with her lover and only protector now turned tormentor. Aon was right in one thing—such acts would either break her mind or free her of her chains of fear. "You were not always like this."

"And Edu was not always such a belligerent, righteous fool." Aon waved his gauntlet dismissively. "Time changes us all. Even creatures such as we who shall never die."

"Edu will come with an army to free her. Dubious in light of recent acts, I know—" Lyon headed off Aon's argument at the man's sudden exclamation of laughter at the idea. "But in his mind, he sees only the protection of Under as valuable."

"*Protection?* Of a world that would be shrinking and dying now, if not for all your accidental blunders. He cared not for saving this world when it lay on its deathbed! Now he wishes to rise as the 'kind' King Edu? *Please!* He would rather burn this world than see it continue with me in it. Do you think he would not kill her again if given the chance?"

Lyon could not disagree. "I do not know. He has not said anything to such an effect. Only that he does not wish to leave her in your ownership."

Aon paused for a long time and looked down into the fire. "Believe me or not as you will, I do not intend to keep her, Lyon. Not if she is capable of what I believe her to be. If I have my way, none shall hold her chains, myself chief among them. Not again, not ever. If I must buy for time to prevent him from interfering and harming her, so be it. Let there be a war."

The warlock placed his hand upon the mantel of his fireplace and leaned on it heavily. He lowered his head, his dark-clothed shoulders drooping. "I did not wish for this. I did not want it this way." He paused for a moment as if debating if he would continue speaking. "I received my own prophecy from Ziza, after Lydia had risen from the pool. I will protect her at any cost. Even if it means she learns to revile me. I do what I must, my old friend."

For the first time, Lyon heard the term of endearment not pitched as an invective in his direction. There was sincerity within it. Taking a chance, he walked up beside Aon and placed a hand gently on his shoulder. It was the first time in many centuries that he had seen him in a moment of reflection or of doubt and dismay.

"I have missed you, Priest. Even if your consult is more irritating than useful."

"And I you, my lord." Lyon squeezed the man's shoulder. "If I cannot convince you to spare the girl such torture, I must beg you not to let this world fall into war once more."

"I will do what I must to prevent Ziza's vision from coming to pass."

"What did she tell you?"

"That is my secret to hold." Aon straightened, and Lyon let his hand fall back to his side. "I will not let this world fall to ruin, Priest. For that, I promise you."

"May I see Lydia? May I speak to her?"

Aon tilted his head thoughtfully and considered his request at length. "Yes. You may. But she is... resting currently." The way he said the words were with such pleasure that it almost made Lyon's skin crawl. "Return tomorrow morning, and I will take you to see her."

Lyon bowed his head, thankful, at least, for that. "Thank you, Master Aon."

"But I would ask for something in return. I would have you bring the others—without Edu—here to my home. I will then tell you all precisely what I will see done in exchange for peace."

It should have brought him great hope to hear Aon speak of a possible truce with Edu. But instead, it only carried more dread. "I will do what you ask." Lyon bowed his head.

"Do you truly think the worst of me, Lyon? Do you think I mean the end of this world or merely warp it to serve my own ego?"

"No, my lord. I do not think you wish to destroy us all. I believe you when you say that you wish to see us continue. As for serving your ego?" Lyon paused, thinking it over. "That, I cannot say I do not suspect. You do much in your own honor."

Aon chuckled and nodded. "Touché." The warlock waved his hand at him, dismissing him from his presence. Lyon bowed and turned to leave. He was halfway out of the room when the warlock stopped him by speaking. "There is a path in which I do not survive what lies ahead, my friend. Either in body or soul."

Lyon winced and turned to look back at the silhouette standing in front of the fire. He was surprised to find that he did not desire such a thing. A world without the dread king would be just as barren as one where he reigned alone. Yet to say such a thing would feel too much like a platitude. Finding himself without words, he turned and left without saying anything at all.

NINE

There was nothing grander than watching an army prepare for war.

Edu stood on the parapet of his keep, looking down at his troops gathered around their bonfires that blazed strong, even in the raging storm. The torrential pouring had tapered off to a steady rain, turning the ground thick with mud. The sound of metal on metal echoed against the trees as they trained and readied for what must come. Battle was glorious on its own, but this war was a righteous one. Theirs was a just fight.

Aon *must* be stopped.

The lunatic held the new dreamer in his prison. Likely in the same chamber that he kept and tortured Qta until he killed the former king. Fifteen hundred years ago, the madman had tried to bend the King of Dreams to his will. Now he had a chance to do the same. With the woman he had seemed so oddly obsessed with before her death, no less.

Edu did not believe in coincidence. With the warlock, it was never the case.

"Assuming we can take Aon and his bastards down." Oanr, his elder and second in command, rubbed the back of his hand across his nose. "The new snake queen ain't going to be happy to see you." He was sitting on a bench, running a stone over the edge of his favored axe, sharpening it. "You two ain't friends."

Oanr had fought—and continued to do so regularly—to carry the rank of regent. Many fell by the blade of that same weapon. He was born into Under a servant with no mask to hide the single, large red mark that blazed over his face. No, the Ancients had not made him the Elder of Flames. Oanr had earned his position.

Edu believed that one should only ever have exactly what they deserved. He huffed a laugh. "Master Edu knows she will not care to see him. She may well try to kill him. But she cannot remain as she is, prisoner to a tyrant." Ylena was standing beneath an overhang, sheltering from the rain.

"Who says she doesn't want to be there?" Oanr shot him a look through his blond dreadlocks. The man had been a Viking in his time, and he still wore the style. "I've heard the rumors. So've you."

Yes. The whispers were flying. Aon had doted on the displaced mortal; that much was clear. The warlock had kept her in his home like a treasured guest. And she, in turn, had been seen pulling him by the hand through the streets of M'url, peppering the cretin with questions and laughing at his stories and dark humor.

It was sickening.

Lydia did not understand—could not understand—what the warlock was capable of. Of the damage, the heartache, the pain he had caused all who lived in this world. Of the depths of treachery and evil he could descend to when the mood struck him. The warlock was a madman and had destroyed millions of lives on a whim.

She would learn, if she was not careful.

Edu's leather gauntlet creaked as he gripped the edge of the stone crenellation. The rain did not trouble him, nor Oanr. It was rather nice to stand, preparing for war, in anything other than the utter lack of weather that Under had known for centuries upon centuries prior.

Evie would undoubtedly complain that he smelled like a wet dog when he went back inside. He could hear it in his mind as though she were already there. He imagined her shrieking in laughter and swatting at him as he scooped her up to share his soggy condition against her will.

Edu smiled at the thought of his impetuous little redhead. She was a natural spitfire, and all those in his home—even Oanr —had learned to fear her temper. After making a grab for her rear during a dinner, he discovered precisely how good the woman was when wielding a cast-iron pan.

She was now one of his House of Flames, if only as an honorary title. She still bore the purple mark on her cheek that he viewed as a sin against her nature. She deserved to wear red, more than most.

"Edu." Oanr was attempting to get his attention. "Edu, are you listening to me?"

No, he hadn't been. Edu shook his head.

Oanr laughed, clearly appreciating Edu's honesty. He and Oanr were old friends, and Edu's mannerisms would never offend his second in command. "What'll you do with Lydia when you free her?"

Yes. A good question. One he didn't yet have an answer for.

To kill Lydia would be to doom the world to the void once more. He would happily greet oblivion if it meant he would deny Aon a chance to sit as the King of All. But he was not certain without a doubt that she was his pawn. Lydia may still be of her own mind. Or of no mind at all, if Aon had seen fit to torture her until she was as mad as him.

It would not be the first time the warlock reduced an enemy to an empty shell. There were fates far worse than the death Aon was forbidden from performing.

He had not wanted to kill the woman the first time. He hardly wished to do it again, when the cost was so very much more. Edu saw three outcomes from what lay ahead. Lydia may be the unwilling prisoner of the warlock, or she may already be a broken thing. And finally, worse still, she could be there of her own accord.

If Lydia was the plaything of the warlock against her will, he would put an end to it. If Aon had shattered her mind with his ways, Edu would imprison her until he could have others mend the damage or leave her there to live out her days.

If Lydia doted on the warlock by choice—if she felt a perverse and sick attachment to that fetid, rotting corpse of a man—it may be too late. The corruption may be too deep.

She would have to die by his hand once more.

* * *

Being stuck in a room with nothing to do was starting to become maddeningly boring. Lydia had walked the circumference of the platform around the edge of the moat at least a few dozen times by now, just that day alone.

Worse than the boredom was what was left in its wake.

She had time to *think*.

Thinking meant she had to debate in her head the situation she was stuck in, and that was a miserable endeavor. She shivered at the memory of what Aon had done to her the night prior.

He had performed an autopsy on her while she was *still alive*. While she was *still awake*. The feeling of his claw cutting into her skin had been one thing... feeling him peel it away and dig for her organs was another.

Normally, shock would have taken over and sent her into the safety of death or unconsciousness. But it hadn't come for her. Apparently, she was a bit more resilient now that she was a queen of Under. *Lucky fuckin' me.* She could go longer before dying, and she learned how quickly she could heal.

All it did was keep her awake for longer before passing out from blood loss.

Queen of the House of Dreams, Aon had called her as he taunted her and watched her writhe in pain. What a fucking laugh. A "queen" who was no more than a game of *Operation* for a madman.

The whole time, Q had begged her to let him out to stop Aon.

The whole time, she hadn't let him.

If she stopped Aon, if she escaped this stupid room, that would be it. She'd have to face down Edu and all the others. She'd have to spend the rest of her life—no, correction, *eternity* —desperately trying to defend herself from people who had already proven how badly they wanted her dead.

Her mind circled around the "people" in question. She had trusted the Priest. She had even counted him as a friend. But he betrayed her, doomed her to death like all the others. Maverick as well, she thought she had been on good terms with. Even Kamira, she would have figured would have taken her side.

But it'd all been a fart in the wind when it came to stopping Aon from some... imagined misdeeds.

She didn't want to go out into that world. In some back-assward way, she really did feel safer with Aon. Even if he was torturing her. She was glad at least that she had a high pain tolerance. It was news to her, but it was something to be proud of, she supposed.

Or maybe she simply wasn't afraid of it anymore.

The pain wasn't such a big deal when the fear of death was gone. When the fear of mutilation wasn't there. When she knew no matter how bad it got, she'd just pop back to normal in a few hours, and it would all be an ugly memory. Pain was only that... pain. She didn't like it. But she could compartmentalize it off somewhere until it didn't matter anymore. Apparently, she was good at that.

Case in point!

Q was flying around her head like a bird, circling her and swooping. He was also bored to tears but was amusing himself by doing aerial acrobatics around her as she paced the edge of the circle.

"I don't like being a queen. Not in the slightest."

You'll get used to it. It has its serious upsides. You just are too afraid to find them.

"I'm not afraid."

Oh, yeah, you are. If Edu came in here right now, you'd shit a brick.

"No, I wouldn't."

You're lying to yourself. Literally.

Yeah, fine. The pain was less terrifying than what Edu would do to her. She could put up with the pain. But she had absolutely no desire to die a second time. "Could you protect me from Edu?"

Edu by himself? Maybe. Edu and his army? Nope. You're a one-gal band right now, and he's not. That's the problem.

"Aon would help me."

Of course, he would. But Aon can't always be there. You learned that the hard way. No. You gotta stop hiding.

"I like hiding right now."

That's fine, but it won't last. You know it won't. You can't stay in here forever.

"I know."

'Cuz I'll go wacky being stuck in here. Then you'll have to contend with two nut jobs.

"I just need time. This is all a lot to adjust to in short order, y'know."

"There is no doubt about that."

She turned sharply upon hearing Aon's voice.

Q, predictably, must have vanished the moment before the warlock arrived.

The man in black was standing in the center of the platform, watching her. The memory of what he had done to her the night prior twisted in her stomach. He held his arms out to her, but she didn't move.

He sighed as if resigned to his fate. "Again, I find you speaking with yourself. Perhaps I should at least bring you a houseplant, hm?"

"Or a television set. Do you guys even have those here?"

"Yes, some cities do. I find that manner of diversion atrocious."

"You prefer torturing people, I know."

The way his shoulders slumped made her feel awful for her snide remark. Suddenly, she regretted her words, but it was too late to take them back.

"I have come with another visitor for you."

Her mood ticked up. "Nick?"

"No. The Priest."

Cringing, she looked away. *Great.* She was still very upset with the vampire, and all hopes of a conversation that might cheer her up were dashed. "What the *fuck* does he care?" Oh yeah, she was still bitter.

"He comes to see if I have hooked you into one of my machines. I can send him away if you prefer."

"No... it's fine." Throwing up her hands, she sighed. "This has to happen sooner or later."

He gestured, and another portal opened in space next to him. Stepping out of the black gap was a figure in white. Tall, thin, and ghostly pale. As soon as Lyon passed through the gateway, it closed behind him. The Priest looked to her and cast her a thin, forlorn smile. His eyes screamed of sorrow, even more so than they usually did.

"My lady." He moved to cross the platform, but hesitated and looked back to Aon.

The warlock had become seemingly distracted with his cufflinks, and Lydia suspected it was a cheap ploy to look disinterested in what was happening. He was leaning against the table, his ankles crossed. When Lyon's gaze flicked to the turquoise mask upon the table, Aon huffed a laugh. "Whatever you do, do not ask her about the mask. *Apparently,*" Aon teased her, "she has strong feelings on the subject."

"I... see." The Priest turned his attention back to her. He approached her tentatively as if worried about what she might do.

Maybe he doesn't know you can't do anything fancy. Or he thinks you've completely lost your fucking mind. You could be stark-raving mad and licking the walls, for all he knows.

There was a much higher chance you'd go nuts than not, honestly.

Q's voice rang in her head, and she managed to keep any annoyance or expression off her face at the intrusion. The live-action version of *Pop Up Video* in her head was irritating, more so when the snake wasn't around.

I'm always around. They just can't see me.

She almost slipped and yelled at Q to shut up, and that would have been incredibly awkward. But she swallowed her words just in time and masked her annoyance by running her hands through her hair. She took a moment to gather herself. "Hi, Lyon."

"I am glad to see you are... I would say well, but I do not know if that is the case. How do you fare?"

"Why the *actual* fuck do you care, Lyon?" There wasn't a point in hiding her anger. "You're part of the reason this bullshit is happening to me!"

You'd think she slapped him by the expression on his face. "It is for that reason I have come." He closed the distance between them down to a few feet and, with that, sunk down to a knee before her. He was so tall and yet moved gracefully for someone his size.

She pulled back in surprise. Even Aon stopped fiddling with his cufflinks to watch what was unfolding.

Lyon bowed his head. "I was complicit in your death. I knew what was transpiring and I did nothing to stop it. Indeed, I, too, felt that the act was necessary. I fell prey to the same fears and paranoia as all the others. When I saw the great orrery with its turquoise orb restored, I was terrified for what it may mean."

The what?

I'll explain later.

The Priest continued, blissfully unaware of the conversation in her head. "I am as guilty as Edu for your death. It was by my actions that Edu was seemingly adhered in his theories, even before the Oracle told us you must die to save this world. She merely confirmed actions that were already in motion. I fear instead my words may now have still doomed us all."

"What did you do, Lyon?" Aon snarled. He went to storm toward Lyon.

She raised her hand to stop him and was shocked when it worked. She begged him silently to let the Priest talk. Aon didn't retreat but stood where he was, fists clenched at his sides.

Lyon kept his head bowed low in shame. "Lydia, the night you told me of the nature of his research, I fled to Edu in fear. I told the King of Flames of what Aon intended—to raise the House of Dreams from the grave. We all feared what he may do if he held in his hand the powers of the Ancients. I myself have seen proof of it in days gone by."

"What do you mean?" She furrowed her brow.

"Go no further, Priest. That story is mine to tell, not yours." Aon's warning was no bluff, she was sure of it.

What the hell was this story that Aon wouldn't tell her? She knew Aon could be an asshole—really, she was starting to know that literally firsthand—but was it so bad, compared to oblivion?

Lyon looked up at her. "Please understand. I lived through the bloody war that decimated our world. It cost us millions of lives and left a deep gash upon us all. All of it was done at his behest. When Ziza told us you had to die to save this world, I was eager to pretend it meant your death could prevent his rise to total power."

"You're all so afraid of him that you voted to let Edu kill me?" She was getting seriously sick of this entire ordeal.

"There was not a vote." The regret in Lyon's voice was palpable.

"Whatever." What was a little more insult to injury? "You all decided to kill me to keep him"—she pointed at Aon— "from having control over another dreamer? You *knew* I had nothing to do with any of his stupid mark-stitching science experiments from hell. You *knew* that!"

"I did. I wished to believe you were some unknown secret key to his plans. That is my folly."

"You all had me killed to prevent exactly what ended up happening." She laughed at the sad irony in the situation. "Tah-dah! Well, *fuck you*."

Lyon was silent where he knelt before her. Even kneeling, he was still incredibly tall. *Stupid assholes, the lot of them.* But her anger simmered and couldn't hold as she thought it through.

Aon was a madman. A power-hungry, egotistical, unstoppable force of nature. He always believed his methods were correct. She knew how violent he was, and she stood on the precipice of learning exactly how sick and twisted a man with his reputation could be.

But she also knew he was much more than that. Her opinions of the warlock were a convoluted, tangled mess, especially now. She loved him. She wanted to feel his arms around her, to hear him laugh, and to banter with him. She wanted to hear his stories, even with everything he had done and was going to do.

She missed Aon while he was gone and dreaded him while he was here.

But he wasn't evil.

She was starting to think there was no such thing as evil people. Just evil deeds. But that was an internal debate for another time. She watched the Priest thoughtfully.

How bad could that war have been for Lyon—who by all accounts was a sympathetic creature—to lose sight of the facets in Aon's personality? She had to ask. "Do you really all hate him that much?"

Aon snorted in laughter.

After a long moment to find his words, Lyon answered. "I have grown to deeply fear him. It consumed me. Now, in the pale light of what I have wrought, I see my actions plainly for what they were, born not of concern for the safety of our world, but of cowardice."

She could understand that. She didn't want to, but she could. He was only doing what he thought was right. Even Edu, when he killed her. All of them—they were only doing what they thought they had to do.

They were all as afraid as she was.

They were all terrified of what might come or what this might mean for their lives. Killing the little mortal to save the world was regrettable but not a hard choice. It was a small price to pay for saving them from the horrors the "Great Evil Aon" might bring them.

Stepping forward, she put her hand on Lyon's shoulder. The white suit he wore was soft under her touch, even if he had no body warmth to go along with it. Right. Vampire. "I forgive you."

Lyon looked up at her, uncertain and surprised.

"If there's one thing I can sympathize with, it's fear. You

were all doing what you thought was right. None of it was personal. So… I guess I forgive you for what you did."

The Priest lifted a cold hand and placed it over hers, clasping it, thanking her silently.

"But," she added, "I have a favor to ask you."

"Anything, my lady."

"I want you to go tell everybody this. If I can't hate Aon, even now, then you pansies can seriously *shut the fuck up about it.*"

Lyon blinked and rose. Her hand slipped from his shoulder as he did. The vampire pondered her statement, opened his mouth to speak, stopped, shut his mouth, repeated the action dumbly, and then bowed his head in acceptance. "Yes, my lady."

"And I want you to repeat that to them word for word," Aon said with an air of great enjoyment. He flicked his wrist, and the black, swirling gateway opened again. "You are dismissed, Priest."

Lyon cast a look back at her before disappearing through the void. The circle shrank and blinked out of existence a second later.

Walking to the edge of the cot, she sat. She needed a second, after that. Elbows on her knees, she put her head in her hands. "Let me get this straight. The Ancients told Ziza to tell them all to kill me?"

The sound of wingtip shoes on the floor heralded Aon's approach. "Yes."

"I don't think I like the Ancients very much."

"In that, we agree."

She felt Aon crouch in front of her, her legs between his. His metal hand fell lightly on her thigh as he stroked the other through her hair. "Do you mean what you say?"

"What part? Telling them all to go fuck off?"

"That, I know you mean without question." He chuckled. "No, that you do not hate me."

Lowering her hands, she studied him. His metal visage tilted slightly in curiosity. The man she loved. The man she would always be afraid of, no matter how long they spent together. He was a rabid panther, tamed only to a point, able to snap at any time. But she couldn't help it. "Of course, I don't hate you." She reached out to put her hand against his metal cheek, and he leaned into her touch, even if he couldn't feel it.

"Even with what I have done to you? That I have hurt you?"

"If you were doing it just for fun, I'd be far more upset."

"Well, then. I suppose I now know not to ask. You have saved me an embarrassing evening, thank you."

She laughed at his dark humor. "But, like them, yeah, you scare me. I'm afraid of what you're capable of. And I don't mean the torture. I've seen *Saw*. I'm afraid of the pain, sure. But whatever. I can't die now, so what's a little maiming between friends?"

He continued to stroke his hand through her hair, and his touch made her slip her eyes shut. "Then what about me frightens you?"

"Because I'm not stupid. I know you won't stop there. You'll find some other way to hurt me. I'm afraid of your motives, Aon. I don't know what you're after. You wanted this world not to die. You wanted to bring back the dreamers to save it. Check. Done. But *now* what? What do you *want*? Why did you kill Qta in the first place?"

He touched his fingers to her cheek, tender and warm. "Keep your eyes closed, Lydia."

His hand tilted her head closer to him, and she felt his warm breath against her lips. He had taken off his mask. A second later, he claimed her lips with his own. It wasn't violent or rough, but it gave her no room to argue. Not that she wanted to. She sank into his embrace and let her hands curl into the fabric of his lapel.

He pulled her up to standing and cradled the back of her head in his hand as he deepened the kiss. Finally, he broke away, allowing them both some air. "Forgive me. I felt the overwhelming need to do that."

She chuckled. "I won't complain."

"You may reopen your eyes now."

When she did, she shrieked. Quickly, she ducked her head and covered her eyes.

He hadn't been wearing his mask!

It had taken her a split second to notice that his face was not covered in black metal.

"Aon, I—I'm sorry!"

He was laughing. "Oh, come, now."

"Your mask!"

"As if I did not notice? It did not *fall* off."

"But—"

"I know."

"But I—"

"Are you so afraid you will find me repulsive? A worthy concern, I suppose, to have your fantasies so ruthlessly shattered." He pulled her hands away from her face, and she squeezed her eyes shut tightly. He kissed her again, and she let out a small sound as he did. He held it for a long time, slowly becoming more passionate, before he clearly forced himself to stop. Still, he hovered near her, and she felt him place a kiss by her ear.

"But you've never shown your face to anyone." She clung to him, keeping her eyes squeezed shut.

"Correct. Not once since I cast the Ancients into the lake in which they are still prisoners has any living soul seen me for what I am. Not since I designed my mask has anyone seen me without it."

"Then I..."

"I appreciate your reservations." His hand stroked through

her hair slowly. "It means the world to me that you are worried over what this may mean. But I am certain in this, my dragonfly. Open your eyes."

Still, she kept her eyes shut like a kid being led down to see a Christmas gift. "No. This is a trick."

"Oh, you are impossible!" He laughed at her fear. "Suddenly so shy? I did not realize our 'stupid traditions' carried such value to you." He reached behind her and roughly pinched her ass, and that brought her eyes shooting open as she yelped and jumped from the pain. He was grinning at her.

Grinning.

She could see his face.

His expression faded to a smile, and he studiously smoothed his expression. He straightened his shoulders as if for examination by an army superior—doing his best to look regal and presentable.

Oh good God.

Or Gods, she supposed.

She had seven of them, now.

Her heart skipped a beat as she took him in.

Framed in jet black hair, with just the rare strand of gray, his face was just as pale as the rest of him. Four dark lines of cryptic symbols ran down one side of his face from hairline to jaw and three on the other. Seven in total, archaic and razor thin in black ink.

They didn't do anything to stop how... goddamn handsome he was. Holy hell. No, he wasn't just handsome, he was *gorgeous.* Sharp cheekbones and a matching jaw. His lips looked slightly chapped and uncared for. His eyes were such a deep, dark color that they looked black. Of course, they were. Of course, they wouldn't be anything else.

"Well... hi." She reached up to touch his face, and she watched as his spilled-ink eyes slipped closed. He leaned into her palm and let out a wavering breath—she realized he had been holding it—and pulled in another deep one to fill his lungs.

"Oh, my dragonfly." It was so strange to see his mouth move in time with the voice she had come to know.

She had become used to his metal mask, even with how foreign and unnatural it was. She had started to accept that, to her, he didn't really have a face. "Why did you... why are you letting me see you?" She was awed, wary, and confused all at once as she let her hand run along his face, exploring it for real for the first time.

He was obviously lost in the bliss of it and was unable to form words for a moment. When he did, his voice was low. "In exchange for what I have done. For what I will continue to do. At the very least, I could give you this part of myself in exchange."

She could watch him talk for days.

"I thought..." she started and hesitated. He stepped into her and wrapped his arms around her, pulling her into his chest. He was warm, and the smell of old books and leather washed over her. He was fascinating. She couldn't stop touching his face, tracing the lines of writing that ran down him in almost straight lines.

"You thought what?" He opened his dark eyes. When they found hers, he captured her in his gaze. He smiled. His expressions came quickly. He had spent so many lifetimes behind a mask, she supposed he wouldn't try too hard to hide emotions from his face.

"I thought you people didn't show each other your faces unless—" She broke off, afraid to put the thoughts together. She shouldn't assume. She shouldn't let her mind wander that way.

Without warning, he leaned down and caught her lips with his, kissing her passionately again. He pressed her tight against his chest and let out a sigh of contentment against her. When he broke away, she was breathless. "Unless what? You are so painfully shy sometimes. It is quite adorable. Have you not suspected, my darling? Is this not enough proof for you?"

"Proof of what?"

His metal thumb was against her cheek, tilting her head back, as he kissed her jawline up toward her ear. A small moan left her throat unbidden as he kissed the hollow just below the lobe. "You would have me say the words, then? You would have me admit it out loud, to embarrass myself. What a cruel mistress you turn out to be."

"I don't know what you're talking about." She found herself clinging to the fabric of his vest and coat, fingers tangled up in the lapels.

Aon leaned his head to whisper to her. "I would have you rise as my equal in this world. I would have you tear down all who stand in your way. I would have you build this forsaken world to be your throne. For I love you, and I think I always have..."

TEN

Lydia stood there in Aon's arms, stunned. She was locked solid, wide eyed, watching his expression as he confessed that he... loved her.

He loved her.

Her first reaction was to call bullshit. That he was playing games to manipulate her. And maybe if she couldn't have seen his face, she would've been able to convince herself of that. But the look on his features—and more importantly, in those abyss-black eyes of his—showed her just how much he meant those words.

His expression was drawn into a look of tired and beleaguered acceptance and heartbreak. Like whatever she was about to do would be one that he deserved. He was a man at the executioner's block, resigned to his death. Still, a smirk curled the edge of his lips as if to say he knew this would happen. He was somehow superior, even in his pain.

A smirk suited him, she decided.

Watching him, she knew she loved him back. She'd known it for a while, but she just... didn't know how to tell him that in the moment. Everything was too complicated. What were his motives? What did he want from her? He loved her—but what was he going to *do* with those emotions?

What came next?

She couldn't say the words.

But she couldn't give him nothing.

A smirk suited him. And she decided she wanted to taste it. Placing her palms to his cheeks, she watched as his expression smoothed as she ran her fingers along his skin. As she pulled him gently closer to her, his eyes slipped shut in bliss.

She remembered how little he had ever been touched in all his centuries of life.

Meeting her lips with his, she kissed him with all the emotion she couldn't put into words. Everything warring within her. All her hopes, her fears, her uncertainty—but most of all, her love.

His arms wrapped around her, clutching her close. First, hesitant in his own right as if he didn't quite believe what was happening, before a tidal wave unleashed itself on her. He must have been so certain—so absolutely *sure* that she was going to reject him—that he hadn't considered the chance that she would have done anything other than laugh in his face.

Curling her hands into his suit coat, she urged him toward the cot. It seemed he was of the same mind. There was too much rushing through her, too many thoughts and emotions tangling together.

He loved her.

And she could *see him*. Something so mundane for everyone else was, for him, such a revelation. Every time she touched him, every kiss, every gesture, washed over his face like a firework. She backed him into the edge of the cot, and he sat, allowing her to straddle his thighs and sit on his lap.

How she wished she could tell him that she loved him.

It wouldn't be a lie.

And she knew he wanted to hear the words more than

anything. But she knew it was crossing a point of no return. He'd killed Qta and still wouldn't tell her *why*. And until she knew the true story—until she knew why this horrible torture chamber had been built, she just couldn't trust him with her whole heart like that.

Not like he hadn't already literally ripped her heart out once.

Great. Now she was starting to think like Q.

Aon distracted her quickly as he dug his claws into her thigh, slipping her dress up to her waist as he quickly turned their embrace more passionate. It was easy to lose herself in him, in each flash of pleasure that washed over his handsome features, of each flicker of emotion in those void-like eyes as he watched her.

She gasped as he filled her effortlessly, as they moved together in a dance that felt somehow different than before, somehow *changed*. He loved her. She wasn't just a toy. This wasn't just a game. This was love.

This was *real*.

Despite it all.

This was *real*.

Their passion ended in a tangled mess of limbs, him on top of her, panting into her shoulder, as she clung to him in her own release. She let out a wavering breath.

With a low groan, he kissed her cheek before climbing to his feet. Without a word, he got dressed before heading to the table on the other side of the platform. Casually, he poured himself a glass of water, drank it all in one go, then poured himself another. Turning, he leaned his weight on the edge of the table and looked down at the glass.

He shut one eye as he peered into it, a curious expression on his face. "I think I must spend all my days painfully thirsty. I wonder if that is why I am always so irritable. Fascinating. To think, how many deaths could have been spared if I had only been able to drink a glass of water?" He took another sip and could not help but look at her with that same playful and knowing smirk. She wasn't the only one who found shelter in cynicism.

Putting a hand over her eyes, she laughed. Just laughed. It was weak, weary, and a reflection of how ridiculous this all was. She wasn't laughing at him—no, she was laughing at herself. At the situation. At everything. Putting her dress back on, she climbed off the cot and walked up to him.

As she approached, he reached out to put his prosthetic hand against her hip and drew her in to stand between his legs. She felt his metal, clawed fingers twist nervously in the thin fabric of the dress she wore.

He must have been worried sick she was going to tell him she was only in this for the sex. Probably still was. She had avoided saying anything about his confession and decided to screw him instead, after all. She watched his features, still fascinated by them. "Do you mean it?"

"Unfortunately, I say little I do not mean." His voice was unreadable, but his face was not. It betrayed his exposure and his wariness of her and what she might say or do considering his confession.

She wondered how much she had missed—how many things he had said to her whose meanings she lost—because she couldn't see the real emotion behind it.

"Everything is a mess right now, Aon. I don't know what I am, let alone—" She choked off. Why was she suddenly about to cry? Damn it all, she was never a crier; why did she have to start now? "It's all too much."

Shushing her, he wrapped an arm around her tenderly and kissed the top of her head as she tucked it up against his chest. "That you do not refuse me is more than I could have ever asked. For that you feel anything but disdain for me, I am content. I did not show you my heart, or my face, in hopes of garnering anything in return. To expect such from someone in your predicament—toward her jailer and tormentor, no less—is asinine. I am selfish, but there are lines to be drawn in all things."

"Thanks." Shutting her eyes, she just tried to enjoy being there with him. He loved her. Her heart should be doing backflips. She finally understood what she meant to him, and it was far more than she could have imagined. Instead, she just had the same heavy cloud of dread over her. "I care about you. I just—I just..." She stopped. She couldn't.

"Do not thank me. Never again should you thank me for anything. For I have shown you this part of myself in hopes that you may understand why I do what I must." He laughed derisively at himself. "I hope against all reason that someday you may even come to forgive me for my actions."

When she looked at him, there was a pained but determined expression on his face that quickly turned to grief. Emotions registered on his face like it would on a child—unweathered by time and a thousand ugly social interactions. It seemed he knew this, and he turned his face away from her, hiding behind a curtain of black hair.

"What do you mean?" She put her hand against his cheek and turned his face back to look at her. She left it here, running the pad of the thumb back in forth. He couldn't help but sigh and lean into her touch, his eyes drifting closed in the bliss of it.

He bowed his head to rest it against her shoulder, and she felt the tightness in his shoulders loosen. Both arms wrapped around her back, and he held her tightly as though he might lose her again.

Or as if this were the last time she would let him hold her.

Something was wrong. Very wrong. And for once, he didn't seem to want to answer her. For once, he wasn't talking. That was worse than his evil gloating as he had cut her open and made her exceedingly nervous.

"Aon, you're moping. Want to stab me a few more times to cheer yourself up?" She smirked and nudged him.

Her sarcastic comment made him raise his head and bloomed his expression out of pain and into a fiendish grin, his obsidian eyes finding hers and flickering in mischief. That had been her goal, to see what he looked like when he was himself, and it certainly didn't disappoint. He was somehow more intimidating without the mask than with it, now that she could see the detail in the darkness that burned in his eyes. There was a surge of that familiar fear and delight that mixed together whenever he was around. He was a monster. But he was *her* monster.

"Oh, do not tempt me with such a charming offer." His expression darkened, and she realized it must be more common to him than not. "But I fear I am already late for a meeting with the others. Edu has taken offense at my holding you prisoner. I must deal with his threats of war."

"*He's* offended? Edu can go fuck himself! He's the reason I'm like this."

"Oh, I share your sentiment. But he believes you must be freed from my evil clutches." Aon smirked and accentuated his comment by digging the claws of his hand into her.

"Why, so he can kill me a second time?" She sighed. "Yeah, sure, that makes sense."

"To him, it does."

"I'm starting to think you're right. I don't think he's terribly bright. He really thinks I would rather let him kill me than stay here?"

"He believes I am the doom of this world. He thinks whatever I may do with you will spell the ruin of all."

"Well, you did kind of do that once, to be fair..."

He chuckled and shook his head. "You are even bolder now, I believe. I see your fear of me has faded."

Smiling, she leaned in to kiss the corner of his mouth. He

grinned and chased her lips with his own, seeming to bask in the simple expression of affection. She was reminded how he was so unaccustomed to anyone touching him, let alone his face. He was fascinating to watch, and she could spend all day like this, doing just that.

When he broke away, he studied her for a moment. "Are you afraid of what Edu may do?"

No point in lying. "Yeah. I am. I'm more afraid of what he'll do to me than what you'll do to me."

His expression darkened. "While that is a deep compliment, it is misplaced."

"What do you mean?"

"Edu will not touch you. No one will harm you again. No one but I."

The foreboding statement was meant to be comforting. It was meant to show his dedication to her. It was meant to declare his love in the most selfish, possessive, and self-aggrandizing way possible. But it, like the dark and dangerous look on his face, suited him perfectly.

"You're doing this to protect me."

"Of course."

"Then... I trust you." It was undoubtedly stupid, but it was true.

"Oh, dragonfly," he said through an exhale and buried his head into her shoulder. He nuzzled into her, and she realized how strange and foreign any touch on his face must feel. "Not once, in all my years, has anyone said those words to me in truth."

"Then I'm an idiot, huh?" She let out a small laugh.

"Most assuredly." He lifted his head to look down at her, and there was a tiredness in his dark eyes. A man with a million miles yet left to walk. "I fear I must go. I have lingered too long."

"Screw them. Stay here with me."

He smirked—he did that a lot. It really did suit him perfectly. She couldn't help but let her fingers run along his face again, and his features smoothed once more. She had that power over him, and it was addicting.

He lifted his hands to grasp a chain around his neck and pulled something out from under his shirt. It was the little glass chrysalis, with the blinking false insect inside. It was still flashing its strange black light. "I believe you should have this back." He pulled it from around his neck and slipped it instead around hers. He gently pulled her hair out from under the chain and settled it down around her.

"You kept it?" She was amazed. He had expressed nothing but annoyance over the little ball of magic. "I thought you hated it."

"I despise it. But it was all I had left of you."

It hadn't really dawned on her what had really happened. It hadn't clicked together. Not until right then. He said he had loved her and always had.

Edu hadn't just killed her; Edu had killed the woman Aon loved.

Her heart cracked in half at the realization of the grief he must have felt, finding her there like that. Thinking he had failed her. Knowing he had lost her.

All she could do was take his face gently in her hands and kiss him, embrace him as though that alone could mend what he had felt. She kissed him to remind them both that somehow, miraculously, she was still here. She felt the warmth beneath her hands and held the moment for as long as she could.

He let out a sigh as she finally broke the kiss. One of a man in paradise and one of a man knowing he was about to descend into hell. It was clearly time for him to go. He straightened from where he was leaning on the table and summoned his mask from thin air in a rush of black smoke.

"Do I ever get to do cool stuff?" *All I get is an annoying ghost snake.*

I'm not annoying, I'm awesome.

With a laugh, he slipped the mask back over his face, and once more he was the Aon she recognized. "Time will tell. Do not forget I have several thousands of years of practice that you do not." Straightening his coat and tie, he looked like he did in the nightmare when she first met him. So much had changed in the short time she'd been in Under. And yet, so much stayed the same.

He moved away from her several paces. "I will return in a few hours' time. Do not be pleased when I do, my love." He bowed his head and disappeared in a blink.

Q appeared and drifted down to curl on her shoulder.

He does not know to make an exit.

"Shut up, Q."

ELEVEN

"To what do I owe the pleasure, Master Edu?"

Edu walked down the center of the Great Hall to find Ziza waiting for him. She stood beneath the silently twisting orrery with its three glowing glass orbs. Red, black, and now turquoise. The other four sat dormant and unlit, unmoving on their tracks.

Ylena hovered to the side and responded for him. Time was once that Edu would have talked with Ziza in private, but such days were long dead and gone. "He has come for guidance, Oracle."

"I fear I have none to give," came her cold response. "If I had a vision to relay to you, I would have sought you out. You know this."

Edu's hand fisted at his side, and he forced himself to relax. He could not very well hurt Ziza, for more than one reason. That she was the lady of a House and the Oracle of the Ancients was not enough. It was their history alone he could not bring himself to raise a fist to her.

He let his eyes slide shut as he let out a long, weary sigh.

His world stood on the brink of destruction, even as it

appeared it may be saved from the void. "What would you have him do, Ziza?"

"As the Oracle, I cannot take sides."

"He is not asking the Oracle."

When Edu looked back up at her, her beautiful features were creased in uncertainty. If but briefly, perhaps, before they smoothed back to their placid calmness. She put even the Priest to shame in her unemotional quality.

It had not always been so.

Once, so very long ago, before Aon and his dread war... Edu and Ziza had been in love. In those days, she did not bear the burden of the Oracle. It had been before her heart and soul were torn from her like fruit from a tree, leaving her barren and empty.

He remembered those days with increasing sadness and bitterness. He had never once looked upon them fondly. Not with her always standing there, like a ghost of her former self, haunting his heart. But like a specter who walked the cold hallways of his home, she was no more herself now than smoke from a candle may be the flame.

In his pain and his jealousy, he had even subconsciously chosen and modeled Ylena to be so like the Elder of Fate who stood before him. His empath resembled the pale figure in blue. His selfish need to feel something like her in the dark reached through the veil of his mind and had guided his hand unseen to that end.

He could keenly remember the nights Ziza and he spent together, the days exploring their world, talking of the future, of the past... of nothing at all. They had been happy. It was a great boon for him to fall so deeply in love with the member of another House. Queen Ini, Ziza's mistress, encouraged them and found great happiness like a mother in Ziza's joy. Soon, she became his consort and stood at his side. All was well.

Until Aon saw fit to change that.

Edu had dared to stand against the warlock in his selfish, endless desire for power. To control the Dreamers was madness. To seek to rule the world above all was intolerable. And so, they all rose to fight him in his desires to enslave Qta and his ilk.

In the dark, Aon came to hurt him. But he had not come alone. For merely burning Ziza's soulmarks from her face and taking her life would not be enough to sate the warlock's thirst for revenge.

Edu would never forget the night that Aon had burst through the doors of his keep, dragging the Oracle of the House of Fate behind him, hand caught in the woman's dark hair. If he admitted it to himself, he could not even remember the name of the former Oracle. Her face was bleeding, her mask removed. Aon had already sliced it from her face, leaving her vulnerable and mortal.

Edu remembered the flash of the warlock's dagger in the firelight. In those days, he had no clawed hand. The words he spewed like venom into the air. "We shall both be denied!"

The words made no more sense to him now than they had the day the warlock had issued them. More insanity from the mad King of Shadows.

He remembered the touch of Ziza's hands on his arm as he pressed the girl behind him, to protect her. But the warlock had more insidious plans than simply attacking his lady.

It was not enough to kill Ziza.

Aon would have her haunt his soul for the rest of time.

He remembered the gurgled cry of pain that the previous Oracle made as he slit her throat wide and dropped her dying, twitching body onto the stone floor of his home.

The Oracle was dead.

There must *always* be an Oracle.

A power, ghastly and pale, came from the woman's mouth like a spirit. It would find a home, the closest it could, now that its host was dead. It had taken to Ziza instantly, and as it entered, her own heart and soul fled. She had collapsed, her eyes going white and sightless, her heart emptying of all things other than the entirety of the burden she now carried.

Aon did not stay, as Edu held Ziza in his arms. Edu had wept, knowing what the warlock had done. He had torn out her heart but left her alive. Left her in such a state so that he would always be faced with the reminder of what he had lost.

Edu would never forgive that act.

Edu would never forgive Aon.

Not until one of them lay dead as dust.

"Those days are gone," Ziza reminded him coldly. "They have been for fifteen hundred years, Master Edu."

"He knows," Ylena said from beside him. Her own voice was haunted by the pain of what Edu felt, the memories that dredged to the surface each time he saw Ziza. "He has still come for advice, nonetheless."

Ziza sighed, and her pure white eyes drifted shut. She shook her head and turned to walk away from him. "I have none to give you. Do not force this upon me."

Edu stepped forward quickly and caught her wrist in his hand. He needed to stoop to do so. But it was a familiar movement for him, even with it having been fifteen hundred years since last he caught the hand of his lover in his.

Ziza stopped and turned to face him. Edu lifted her hand to his chest and gently placed her palm against him. Her hand looked so comically small against the expanse of his own body.

He clasped his hand over the back of hers, over his heart. "A dreamer has risen. The girl he put to death with his own hands is now Queen of Nightmares. At your instruction, he has done this."

"The vision told me the girl must die to save Under. You interpret my words whatever way you desire. You always have. And you wished the girl dead to spite Aon long before you knew it might have any salient bearing on this world." She spoke no lie.

Edu wished the girl dead for many reasons. Fear for what Aon may do with a secret such as she may hold, yes. But Edu had seen how the girl acted in the streets of the marketplace at the side of the dread warlock. Like a woman who was there with him of her own accord. She was no weeping, terrified prisoner. Aon doted on the girl. Entertained her strangeness. Took her through the streets of the cities of their world as though she were his *princess*. The mortal girl was a bauble of amusement to the warlock. A shining toy. A distraction.

But the way she had smiled at Aon?

Edu had killed her to save this world.

But he had also killed her to *spite him.*

"Master Edu will not apologize for his actions," Ylena replied.

"I ask you, would you repeat them?" Ziza pondered.

"Speak plainly."

"I merely wonder, would you kill her again and doom the world to hurt the warlock?"

Edu dropped her hand from his chest and sighed darkly. What a wonderful question. Would he? If Lydia's death simply brought the warlock pain, he would do so once more in a heartbeat. But to do so now would doom them back into the void. It made the matter more complicated.

"He is undecided."

Ziza shrugged dismissively. "Such is your decision to make. If you are to kill Lydia twice, know you will doom this world in finality. The Ancients will not intercede a second time."

"So be it," Ylena replied.

Edu turned to leave, but this time it was Ziza's small hand on his arm that stopped him. "Wait."

That was not the cold voice of the Oracle. That was a voice overtaken with strain. He turned to look at the girl, and he took hold of her. Her eyes were not white. They were the emeralds he remembered. But she looked weak and overwrought.

"I cannot—" She gasped for air. "I cannot hold this for long. Edu, I—" Her knees gave out, and he caught her easily in his arms. He knelt, cradling the girl he had once loved so very much against him.

Ylena was stunned to silence and could not speak for him as he wished to profess to Ziza how much he had missed her. How much his heart burned a hole in his chest with every day that passed without her. He could only clutch onto her, his head lowered, feeling tears sting his eyes behind his mask.

"Do not—do not destroy her, I beg you. Please. Have compassion. She has suffered—will suffer so much. I can see what waits for her, and it is beyond tragedy. Do not add to her pain. You must find forgiveness. Not for her, but for him. You are so strong, my love. Be strong," she begged him, even as her voice was fading to weakness. Her emerald eyes rolled into her head as she began to lose consciousness.

Silently, he begged her not to go. Not to leave him once more.

It was too late. Ziza was unconscious. It had taken a great show of power to push through the force of the Oracle that possessed her. Such things could not be sustained for long without destroying what was left of her.

How he would have wished to speak to her but once more. How many hundreds of years did he spend, desiring one last chance to see the woman he loved restored?

Now that he had it... he was not glad for it. He wished he had never come.

A fresh wound bled in him as if cut by a sword.

Edu held her to his chest and wept.

Compassion. Forgiveness. Those things in him were long dead. They lay in the hollow shell of the woman he loved.

He would bury them all with the warlock.

* * *

"Must he always find the need to keep us waiting?" Maverick commented idly from where he sat at the great table in Aon's library.

Lyon found that rather ironic, as the doctor was generally the one who was always late.

No one answered his complaint, save for Kamira, who huffed a single sarcastic laugh from where she stood by the wall. Her tail twitched in nervous anticipation around her legs.

Ziza was said to have been unwell, and instead she had sent the next ranking member of the House of Fate. The man looked to be in his early forties, hailing perhaps from somewhere in China. A blue, Venetian-style mask that was their House's style covered a third of his face. He, like all those in his House, sat quietly and observed. If he was not mistaken, his name was Yuandi.

Lyon was horrible with names, all things considered.

Neither Edu, nor anyone from the House of Flames, had been invited to this parley.

This was a meeting of the regents of the Houses whose kings and queens still slept. Even Otoi had seen fit to be present. He was sitting in a chair, running grubby fingers along the stem of a glass wine goblet from which he was drinking. Lyon was asked to attend by Aon, a fact that continued to annoy the "real" Regent of Blood to no end. "He wants his errand boy present," Otoi had grumbled as they had arrived.

Lyon did not trouble overmuch for Otoi's words and constant belittling. He pitied the little man for taking in name only the rule that he had once shouldered. No one respected Otoi. Including, he suspected, the man himself.

"We all know where he is. Who he's with. He's distracted." Otoi cracked a disgusting grin across the table at Maverick. "I would be, with a girl like that. Mmh. Especially now that she's worth the effort!" He looked around the room to see if anyone would enjoy his crude comment.

Kamira made an exaggerated blanch. Her antics made Lyon smile from where he stood across the room from her, even as he shook his head. His wife was never subtle in her feelings.

"Speak of her that way again, Otoi, and I will make you regret it such as you have never done anything else in your wretched life." Aon's voice came from nowhere, carrying through the room, foreboding and detached. Maverick visibly shuddered, a rare break in the man's reserved exterior. Even Yuandi seemed unsettled.

"I—I meant no offense—" Otoi stammered to the invisible presence. A moment later, the warlock materialized, seeming to emerge from the shadows, seated at the head of the table, a dark shadow against crimson upholstery. "Forgive me, Master Aon!" Otoi knew the man would be wrathful, given everything that was unfolding.

Ignoring the apology, Aon addressed the room. "I will make this brief and not waste any of our time with trivialities. I have much to do this evening. My spies tell me that Edu is preparing to go to war to see the dreamer freed of my care. He would see her 'rescued,' with no sense of irony in the matter. Worse still, we all suspect that he would kill her a second time, should he find the opportunity."

"Surely, he would not be so foolhardy," Yuandi said. "To do so would destroy Under a second time. We have just seen the void retreat. Would he really bring it upon us again?"

"I don't think you really grasp the depth to which these two men hate each other." Kamira snickered.

Maverick nodded and leaned back in his chair thoughtfully. "If Lord Edu suspected even in the slightest that the death of the new dreamer would bring Aon duress, he may see it done regardless of the consequence."

"I, for one, do not wish to die," Otoi interjected.

"None of us do, you idiot." Kamira was agitated, her tail swishing like the angry cat she often resembled.

"Regardless." Aon resumed control of the conversation. "As Lyon has most certainly reported, Ms. Lydia does not yet have command of her power. I have seen nothing from her, save the marks she bears on her face, to show she is capable of defending herself. I keep her here for her own sake, not mine."

"Truthfully, Aon?" Maverick found the nerve to ask that which they all suspected. "You do not keep her here for your own ends?"

The warlock was silent and seemed to debate how to respond. Anger would have been expected. But the King of Shadows seemed to find the desire to be unpredictable as of late. "I would keep her as mine if she were content with such an arrangement. It is for her opinion of such matters that I would find her imprisonment untenable, not yours."

A stern rebuke, but a peaceful one. It could have ended with Maverick's visible yellow eye removed from his skull and plopped on the table, after all. The doctor winced all the same and bowed his head to the man in silent apology.

Aon continued to speak. "I have the means to ensure she is free come the morning. I know what I must do to see that she is released of me before Edu's armies begin to march. I would see it done." He let that hang in the air. Lyon stood from where he was leaning against the wall. Kamira made a similar movement in mirror of his own—a response of surprise.

He could not be serious. There were no circumstances he could fathom where the warlock would simply *let her go.* It meant an inevitable chaos would ensue when Edu found her. And when Lyon had seen Lydia, she had been as Aon said. Unchanged, save for the marks on her face. She had no means to defend herself.

Lyon knew the others had different concerns. They did not believe Aon would merely give away that which he had sought for two thousand years. They were all missing one key piece of information, even Kamira. He had not confided in his wife what he had seen in Aon the day Lydia died. He had not told her of the love the warlock felt for the young woman who had lain dead in his arms.

They did not realize that in Lydia, Aon had found hope of having what he had desired more than anything else in his five thousand years—the love of another. Even still, the warlock was a possessive, protective creature. It would be easier to seduce her into loving him if she was his prisoner, would it not? Not to mention, to set her loose would be to place her in grave danger.

Yet with Aon, nothing was ever straightforward. What could he be planning?

"I assume you will not do this out of the kindness of your heart." Maverick finally broke the silence.

"Of course not. There is always a price." Aon leaned back in the chair and steepled his fingers in front of his masked face. "To see her freed immediately, I will need a promise from all of you to be paid unto me, at a time and of a nature of my choosing. A favor, if you will."

* * *

Aon had warned her not to be happy to see him when he returned. Between that, and how dodgy he was being on a few seriously key subjects, it had Lydia on edge.

She should be ecstatic that he had confessed his love for her. That her feelings were mutual, even if he wasn't as conflicted over them as she was. Instead, she dreas moping. Moody, afraid, depressed, and nervous.

She was sitting in the chair at the table, as sitting on the bed got boring. She was looking down at Q, who was currently the size of a ferret and curled around her fingers and wrist. For once, she didn't even have any questions to pester the snake with. They were waiting. Both of them.

She had spent the past few hours sitting here with him in silence. There was comfort in having someone there with her, and Q seemed to deeply enjoy it when she scratched the feathers at the back of his head. And so, they sat. Saying nothing. Doing nothing.

Nothing, except thinking.

Her life had been a train wreck since this whole mess started. Just a steam car racing off the rails, ever since that tattoo appeared on her arm. She wasn't ever in control of what was happening to her. Everything was just thrust at her at a rate that kept her reeling and trying to catch her breath.

The fact that she was a dreamer was still sinking in. She was the only hope for a world she didn't even know. One she didn't even really understand. Yet she had to admit the few days she had spent with Aon as he took her around to show her the sights had been wonderful. Some of the most fun she'd had in, well... a very long time.

If she was being honest with herself, exploring this weird and twisted world with him at her side made her happier than she'd been in years. Long before coming here. Her life had never been interesting. *She* had never been interesting. If Aon came in right now and opened a gate for her to go home and told her she could go back to Earth and her old life—she knew deep down, she couldn't do it.

It would doom a world she had been just starting to enjoy, in its weird, fantastical, and twisted way. Without her, they'd all die. That included Evie. Aon. Gary and Kaori. Nick. That old man who had made the lanterns. Who knew how many countless others she'd enjoy meeting?

If she lived that long.

But most importantly, it would mean she would never see

him again. And God damn her to hell, that thought hurt her worst of all.

She'd also been fidgeting with her necklace the whole time, thinking about the warlock. What a convoluted, complicated man. Torturing her, tearing out her heart, confessing his love to her and promising to do more, all in the same breath. And he meant every word. All of it was true, all at once.

You really do love him, don'tcha?

Q broke the silence for the first time since Aon had left. Rare for the chatty thing, but she needed some quiet time to think, and he had simply known to stay silent.

"I don't know."

Q looked up at her and tilted his head to one side, clearly not buying it. A ghastly, turquoise, smoke-like tongue flicked out from under his jaw.

You're lying to yourself again.

"Fine. Yeah, I love him. But how am I supposed to handle that right now?"

Never said you had to tell him. I don't think you should yet. I was just curious if I could get you to say it out loud.

"God damn it all, I need a vacation. I need everybody to let up for a hot second." Lydia slouched low in the chair. She looked down at the little blinking insect in the glass cage. "What do you think has him so upset? What do you think he's going to do when he gets back?"

I have an idea, but I really hope I'm wrong, so I'm not even gonna say it.

No need to add to her paranoia. She had plenty of her own theories, so she didn't press for Q to voice his.

Either way, say the word, and I get us both out of here.

He nuzzled its bony head into her fingers, and she couldn't

help but smile and pet him. Man, she was happy to have Q here with her, even if he was annoying half the time.

No. Aon, and whatever he was planning, was better than facing down Edu and the rest of the world. Well. At least she hoped so.

Without warning, Q disappeared. She knew what that meant. Someone was coming, and there was only one option.

The temperature in the room shifted suddenly. There was a hum and a strange whooshing sound. She stood and turned in time to see one of those black gateways in space open in front of her.

A figure emerged, shadowy and familiar. Aon had come back. He wasn't alone. Her dread vanished at seeing who followed behind him. Nick! Her friend quickly hurried around Aon to hug her, and she returned the gesture. So much for not being happy to see Aon when he came back.

This must be Aon's method of apologizing for what he had done to her last night when he autopsied her.

"You doing okay, Lyd?" Nick asked, smiling down at her.

"Yeah. Nothing I can't handle."

"We shall see about that."

Lydia really should have trusted what Aon had said.

She really shouldn't ignore his threats.

She really shouldn't have been happy to see either of them.

Chaos happened quickly. It never came with warning. Something snaked around her throat and yanked her downward at the same moment Nick was dragged backward, pulling him off his feet and hard to the ground.

"*No!*" She didn't know what was going to happen—but she could guess. "Aon, no. *Please!*" The tendril of darkness that had snapped around her throat pulled her to her knees without any care for the stabs of pain that shot up her legs as it dragged her down.

Nick was snarling and howling, tearing at the force that was pulling him across the floor back to Aon. But he was helpless against the strength of the warlock. Nick tried to change forms, his bones snapping and skin growing fur as he tried to transform into the werewolf he had become.

"Ah-ah," Aon scolded like a schoolteacher. With a flick of his wrist, Nick screamed. She watched as a ceremonial magic circle was emblazoned on his chest, burning through his shirt. The wound began to bleed instantly, and Nick collapsed. Whatever the spell had done, it seemed Nick couldn't change shape. "Down, boy. Good boy. Stay," Aon taunted gleefully.

"Fuck you—" Nick tried to fight.

Aon dug his talons into Nick's scalp as he dragged him up to his knees. He stood behind the shapeshifter, keeping him easily under control. Her friend was now bleeding from his hair, crimson running down over his face. Quickly, it began to cover what was not hidden by wood in a mask of red instead.

"Aon, no—please!" Panic was building in her, quick and harsh.

"There is a third part to the prophecy given to me by Ziza, my dragonfly." Aon ripped the wooden mask from Nick's face and tossed it across the floor. It skittered to a stop in front of her. "Allow me to finally tell you her words to me in full. 'Travel to the Temple of Dreams and find the queen where she sleeps. She will be lost and powerless. If you do not take great care, another king will rise to destroy her. Be wary, for her friendship with another will be her undoing.'"

"Aon, *no!*" She yanked desperately at the black tendril that had snapped around her neck like a chain, keeping her planted on her knees.

His voice was dark, hollow, emotionless. "Tonight, you will learn to hate me like all the rest. Now your friend will die."

TWELVE

Aon couldn't be serious.

He had to be bluffing.

There was no way he could go through with this!

Lydia watched on in horror as Nick's arms were lashed behind his back, keeping him unable from even reaching up to wipe at the blood that poured from the cut on his forehead and into his eyes. Aon held the wounded man's head cranked backward, normal hand twisted in his hair. Nick was unable to do much to fight back.

"Don't do this, please, Aon!" She yanked on the tendril of black power around her neck. "Anything but this, please!"

Aon shook his head, *tsk*ing at her. "You prove my point. Do you think there is another way? Do you not know in your heart that he is a liability to you? Say I let him walk this world. Do you believe Edu or Dtu would be so reluctant to do the same as I do now?"

"Please!"

"Fuck off, asshole!" Nick snarled up at him and received a fist to his head for his trouble.

"Edu already once sought to wield Nicholas against you. He

sought to use your weakness to lure you away from me, the night you died. Kamira took his place to protect her worthless new mongrel."

Tears stung her eyes as she shook her head, not wanting to believe it. But why would he bother lying?

"Do you think he would not try again to use him against you? Or any other, for that matter? If that worm Otoi asked for your 'service' for this man's life, would you give it?" Aon's voice was cruel and distant.

"People aren't liabilities, Aon!"

"Ah, but I beg to differ. That is all we are to each other in the end."

"Then what am I to you? Am I not your liability, then?" She struggled as hard as she could, but it was useless. The fucking tendril wouldn't budge from where it was pulled tight into the black hole it came from out of the ground at her feet.

"I am well aware, my love." Aon's voice was cold as ice. "Such is a risk I am willing to take unto myself."

"And I'm willing to take it with him!"

"You are too young. Too new and weak in your gifts. I have the power to defend myself against such a burden as what you may bring. You do not." Aon shook his head.

She lost her fight to keep the tears from flowing down her cheeks. "Just please, please don't hurt him—have pity!"

"I allowed you to see him before so you may have one last memory with him. That is the extent of my mercy. I will not allow you to be destroyed by another. I will not allow this prophecy to come to pass."

"I'll do anything. I swear. I'll be your slave or whatever, anything!"

"You continue to prove my point."

"It's okay, Lyd." Nick tried his best to grin. "It's okay. Fuck this guy." Nick broke off in a grunt as Aon's metal fist impacted the side of his head. It would have sent him falling to the ground if it weren't for Aon's other hand twisting into Nick's collar and yanking him upright.

"Wait, please!" She was frantically ripping at the thing around her neck and could feel her nails sting and tear her skin as she did. She didn't care. Even now, she begged in her head that he *couldn't be serious.* He couldn't mean it. He couldn't possibly go through with it! It was a bluff. It had to be. She loved him. He loved her. He couldn't do this to her.

"No."

Aon's metal hand burst into black flame, and Lydia couldn't react fast enough. Before she could even send Q in to stop him, the warlock grabbed the side of Nick's face, placing his metal burning palm against where the soulmarks were inked onto her friend's skin.

While both would haunt her for the rest of her days, she was certain, she wasn't sure which was worse.

The sound of Nick's scream echoing throughout the domed stone chamber...

Or the smell of burning flesh that filled the room.

It was acrid and pungent and turned her stomach over. She couldn't even hear her cries for Aon to stop, pleading and begging with him, over Nick's painful howls. He thrashed and struggled, but Aon was inescapable. The grasp of the metal prosthetic on his face could not be avoided.

The smell of burnt hair joined the rest, and something else she only knew because of her line of work. Because of that car accident where the man had burned alive. Then came the smell of charred bone.

When, exactly, she started to weep, she didn't know. She didn't care. Nick had stopped screaming, and the silence was more awful than the sound had been.

Aon dropped Nick to the floor at his feet, and the poor man was twitching, curling reflexively into a ball and covering the seared half of his face with his hands. Smoke was rising in wisps from his skin. What she could see of his face was charred black and in the distinct mark of a hand. He had lost his eye. And likely far more than that.

"Damn you," she swore at Aon, yanking on the thing around her neck harder. "Damn you to hell!"

"Where do you believe we are?" Aon let out a sharp, vicious, and mocking laugh, holding his arms out at his sides. "Where do you think inspired all those great myths of the underworld? And who do you believe inspired the worst of such tales but I?" He stood over Nick's body like some great nightmare. "Here I stand before you, Lord of Darkness, Black Angel of Agony. I am he who brings this upon you!"

"Fuck you," she snarled at him. "You egotistical sack of shit!"

Nick was trembling and likely going into shock. There was an ooze seeping from his face. He wasn't even making a noise. He was in too much agony. He was going to die.

"Stop this. Save him!" She was desperate.

"Ah, still you have hope. Such an insidious poison. No. Now, he dies."

Send me in, Coach.

"He can't be serious," she whispered. "He won't let this happen."

"Hm? I did not hear you."

Aon rolled Nick onto his back with a shove of his wingtip shoe. Nick's hands turned weakly and uselessly away from his face. He was unconscious. "Do not fret. He does not have long. Nor does he suffer... well, he does not suffer *much*."

He was, in this moment, the King of Shadows. Not her lover, and not her friend. He was the dreaded King of Shadows. The one every single person here had seen fit to warn her about. The monster she hadn't believed existed.

Let me finish this. Let me give him some payback.

Burying her head in her hands, she let out a sob, feeling

everything in her just wanting to crumble up and fall away into the ocean. "This isn't fair."

"What is the saying, my pet? Life is not fair?" The smugness in his voice made her want to hurt him.

"I wasn't talking to you, asshole!" And that was it. She could almost hear it in her as she just gave up trying, like the tone of a bell ringing through the mayhem. There was an immense clarity and a strange kind of peace, knowing this was the end of the line for how much she could take. Something in her broke. Somewhere, she couldn't take it anymore.

Nick was dying.

Her best friend for the past five years. Her cohort and drinking buddy. Her coworker, her ally in all things. The one who sat there patiently and sighed his way through every video game with her. The one who she rolled her eyes at every time he wanted to watch some new anime with her because he insisted, *"You'll like this one, I swear."*

She was going to have to watch her best friend die right in front of her, at the hands of the man who said he loved her. At the hands of a man she—maybe at least until right now—loved in return.

All she had done since she had come here was take it from people. All she had done since the day she woke up with that fucking mark on her arm was to eat the misery other people shoveled onto her. Wading through hell night and day, trying her goddamn best.

Every time she adapted, every time she thought she was going to be okay, more and more of this bullshit was piled on top of her. Magic appearing tattoo? Fine. Chased by a man-eating corpse? Fine. Abducted? Fine. Nearly drowned? Fine. Rejected? Fine. Threatened? Fine. Murdered? Fine! Raised from the dead as a dreamer? Fine! Mutilated and tortured? Fine!

But Nick? Killing her friend?

Going after someone else to hurt her? No more.

That was too far.

That was one step too goddamn far.

If her friend was going to die, she was going to make Aon pay.

Anger boiled in her the likes of which she had never felt before. She had never really known what it meant to be *furious*.

She wanted to stand. No, she was *going to* stand. Wrapping her hand around the thing on her neck, she silently demanded it was gone. She simply told it to fuck off. If there was power in her—if she was indeed a dreamer—if she was some worthless fucking queen of Under, this was all going to stop. This all stopped right here, right now.

The tendril came apart in her hands like dust, and she looked down as it dissolved into strange turquoise sand that fell to the floor around her knees. Climbing to her feet, she watched with idle fascination as she saw twisting, glowing, turquoise symbols that were winding their way around her arms as though they were liquid. They were fading in and out of existence, as though they were sinking up and down through waves. As if they only existed when she demanded it.

She wasn't in the habit of demanding much in her life. She supposed that was going to change now.

When she finally looked up to Aon, he was silent, standing there still as a statue over the body of her dying friend. Whatever he was thinking, whatever expression was on his face, she'd never know. Honestly, she didn't give a rat's ass right now.

"Q?"

Yeah, Cupcake?

"Kill him."

"Oh, I thought you'd never ask!"

Aon went rigid, his head tilting back slightly. He clearly heard the voice she had only known in her head until now.

The feeling of the room shifted. There was the sound of

liquid moving as something around the edges of the room stirred. In the moat that ran the circumference of the room, filled with that black and inky opaque liquid, something was moving. Until this point, it had been smooth as glass, but something had come to life beneath its mirrored surface.

The warlock whirled as a shape pressed up from the liquid. Coils of a giant snake whose body was as black as the liquid from which it emerged. Rising from the water was Q, and he was huge. He coiled around the room several times over, and the black liquid ran in rivers from his empty eye sockets and ghoulish skull. His body was just as ghostly and smoke-like, fading in and out at the edges.

Q snapped his blue-green wings open wide, spanning the curved walls in a *crack* that echoed like lightning. The sound made even Aon take a step back away from the great beast. The glow of Q's wings dwarfed the chandelier overhead, casting the whole of the room in an eerie turquoise light.

Aon's hand exploded into flame again as he quickly moved to defend himself. But he was caught off guard and unprepared. Q attacked, almost faster than could be seen like the strike of a cobra. Aon's shout of pain choked off as the giant snake wrapped the coils of his tail around the warlock's rib cage and arms and hefted him easily off the floor. Aon fought, but every time he squirmed, Q squeezed.

"Feel that? Feel that hopelessness? Feel that pain? Each time you breathe in, you have to blow out. And every time you blow out, I'm waiting... right there." Q squeezed tighter, and she heard a crack of Aon's bones. **"Just like that, every time. Yes! Yes, do it again! Feel that? Isn't it divine?"** Q was mocking Aon's ecstasy and words from last night when Aon held her own beating heart in his palm. **"You know what? You're right. This *is* fun."**

Aon twitched, gagging, choking for air. He coughed, and it was a wet, sloppy sound. There was blood in his lungs. She watched, morbidly fascinated, as Q slowly constricted himself tighter and tighter around the man. It might have dragged on for minutes. She wasn't sure. This was taking longer than she would have expected, but then again... it was Aon. Five thousand years of living and dying was a long time to learn how to suffer.

"Aaaaaand..." There was a sickening, horrible *crunch*. **"Pop goes the weasel!"**

Aon twitched once and then went limp, his head rolling forward.

Q dropped him to the floor unceremoniously, not caring in the slightest how undignified the King of Shadows now was, a crumpled and broken heap on the ground.

Now that Aon was dealt with—at least for now, he'd be back—she ran to Nick. He was lying lifeless on the ground, arms splayed out to his sides, uncaring for the burn that consumed most of his face.

Oh God... Now that she could see it, she realized the burn hadn't just taken his skin. It had taken most of his skull with it. He hadn't just lost his eye. She could see the matter underneath, charred and blackened.

There was nothing she could do to save him. It had been hopeless the moment Aon put his hand on his face and set him ablaze.

Sobbing, she knelt at his side, doubling over and pressing her head against his chest. It was still rising and falling, but shallow and weak. She just stayed there, holding on to him, weeping. There was nothing else to do. Nothing else to do but stay by her friend's side and wait for him to die. The only thing she could do was make sure he didn't go alone. With the damage he'd suffered, it wouldn't take long for his body to give up.

Her only solace was the fact that he felt no pain. He would have no idea what was happening. "It's not so bad," she mumbled to him, knowing he couldn't hear her. It didn't matter. She was going to see him off, anyway. She took his hands in hers and held them tightly.

"Dying isn't so bad. I promise you'll be okay. The worst of it's over. After this, it just doesn't feel like anything at all. It's just quiet. It's peaceful. Oh God, Nick." She sobbed again, feeling her ribs hurt from how hard it wracked her body. She doubled over, pressing her forehead against his chest again.

She'd been right. It didn't take long.

He spasmed where he lay, his body convulsing as it came to terms with the lack of an owner. It could no longer keep up the work without artificial help. She could only hold on to him, tears blurring her vision, as he wheezed and then lay still.

He was gone.

She wailed, a sound of pure and utter pain and loss. She prayed to any Ancients or Gods or God or anybody who might hear her. She prayed to anyone who might listen to her for someone to take care of her friend.

How long she stayed there, she couldn't say.

A gentle weight settled around her. Q was trying to comfort her. The coils of his tail gently picked her up, scooped her away from Nick. **There's nothing more you can do.** Wrapped in the very tip of his tail was something, and he handed it to her gently. A wooden mask etched with dark green symbols. Nick's. **Except remember him.**

She leaned back against Q, whose main trunk of his body was as thick as a tree, and clutched the mask to her chest. "Let's go home."

There wasn't a single thing in this world anyone could give her—except the life of her friend—that would make her stay in this place for another second. And something told her that the Ancients weren't going to pull that trick a second time.

With a swirl of a turquoise wing, they were gone.

THIRTEEN

This time, it had been Aon who had summoned Lyon to his library and not the other way around.

It was not uncommon in days gone by that Lyon would find himself standing here in Aon's home, debating the warlock in matters of politics or science. Despite his belonging to the House of Blood, and in the service of King Rxa, he had shared a keen friendship with the King of Shadows.

After the Great War, which took such a massive and aching price from them all, Aon had ceased calling him to his home for such discussions.

The warlock was sitting in a tall, wingback chair in front of his hearth. The amber firelight cast flickering reflections off the man's black metal mask and matching prosthetic gauntlet. He was leaning back, his chin resting on the back of his hand, one ankle on top of a knee. Aon very well might have been here for hours, by the look of things.

Lyon approached, bowed, and waited to be spoken to by the dread king. There was a chance Aon may not know he was yet here. The warlock was prone to becoming lost in the corridors of his mind.

"It is done." The statement from the king carried immense weight.

Lyon had trouble believing it. "You have released Lydia?"

"She released herself." Aon's tone was unreadable. Lyon had once been proud of his ability to discern the moods of his former friend. Regrettably, those days, like all the others, were dead and gone.

There was a matter he hated to ask over but knew he must. One that his wife had brought to his attention earlier that day. "Do you know where Nicholas may be? Kamira reported he came here once more to visit his friend."

"He is dead."

Lyon could not hide the shock from his face. "My lord, please tell me you jest."

"He is dead. Furthermore, I killed him."

Lyon let out a long, heavy sigh. It was not just for the boy's death that Lyon was concerned. Aon had committed a grave sin in killing another in cold blood. Kings were allowed to commit the act if there was suitable need. But Aon, as part of the treaty signed ages ago after the Great War, was banned from such a thing.

Once more, they found themselves balanced on the brink of war, this time not in a bid for Lydia's freedom but revenge for Aon's act of murder. Edu would not require much to challenge the warlock, and this was undoubtedly worthy enough a cause.

That Aon seemed utterly indifferent to the act to which he was confessing was also cause for concern. The warlock was a sadist and took great glee in his schemes and games, but he was a staunch opposer to any death sentence since repenting from his acts during the war. To see him so apathetic... worried Lyon. Now less so for the world, but perhaps for the man who had once been his friend.

"Why?"

"I needed to break her of her fear. I had to free her of her dependency upon me." It was only then that the warlock shifted to look down at his clawed hand. "The methods I find more personally enjoyable were not proving to be efficacious or lasting in their impact. Lydia is stronger than perhaps even I gave her credit."

"I would question the truthfulness of your desire to remove from her any need of you." Lyon kept his tone gentle as to avoid angering him. "But I know how you feel for her."

The warlock let out an exaggerated, irritated sigh. "Yes, Priest, very well. Will it please you to hear me say the words?" Aon snarled. "I love her! There. Are you quite happy?" The warlock leaned farther back into his chair. "It is meaningless now, regardless. And your overwhelming desire to witness romance unfold around you is sickening and childish. I do not understand how Kamira puts up with you."

Lyon bowed his head with a faint smile. "Neither do I, my king." Aon's jabs at his expense were not unfamiliar to him. The warlock had often spent as much time tormenting and teasing Lyon as he did confessing to him his most profound thoughts. The man was now, and would always remain, a double-edged sword.

The moment of strange humor was gone. Aon's tone darkened once more. "She did not desire to use her gifts and instead would have remained happily within my care. All this has been thrust upon her. I knew there was little I could do to push her far enough for her to leap from that cliffside. Understand that I wished deeply to keep her by my side in such a fashion. My proclivities are no mystery." He paused. "But to keep her my prisoner would trivialize what she could become. To do so would be a crime against our nature not even I could commit."

Lyon pieced together the depth of the situation and sighed heavily. It weighed on his shoulders like a palpable force. He moved to stand closer to the fireplace and leaned his hand upon the elaborate, ornate mantel.

Aon had sacrificed the boy to force the girl to spread her proverbial and perhaps literal wings. The warlock had done so out of love for her. To keep Lydia in chains, cast in gold as they may be, was to do her a deep injustice. Now she was freed of him, and if the death of her friend did as much damage as he suspected it might, she might have shirked her bonds to the warlock in full.

"Ziza came to me with a prophecy when I went to the Pool of the Ancients during the rainstorm. She told me where to find Lydia. Told me she would be lost and helpless. She warned me that another king would rise to destroy her. Most troubling, that... a friend would prove to be her undoing. I could not let it come to pass, Lyon. I could not. I love her."

"Does she feel the same in return?"

"Does she, or did she?" Aon huffed a sarcastic laugh at himself. "As of this morning, I believe she was on the cusp. If her situation had not turned so dire, I believe I could have earned her heart. Now I have committed against her a sin that I do not know if she can forgive."

Lyon shut his eyes and bowed his head. This had all become a cruel joke played by the Ancients that even Aon could not find the strength to speak out loud. Lyon understood, all the same. Aon needn't draw the conclusions for him.

Lyon knew the truth of the Great War, after all.

So very long ago, Aon found his world lacking in only one way; he was alone. No one had ever come to love the warlock king in all his thousands of years of life. All those who stood at his side in such a fashion were only liars and seekers of influence. Rxa, Dtu, Ini, Vjo, and Edu all found companionship when they desired it, and love bloomed for them like flowers in their seasons. But they no more mourned the fading of their affairs than one might mourn a rose. It would come again in time.

But no such thing grew for the warlock, not once. And Aon was ever desirous of that which he could not have.

In thousands of years, never Fell to Under a soul that had become enamored of the King of Shadows.

He sought to find a bride in the only way the twisted man could devise—he would make his own.

For centuries, he had fashioned puppets and automatons to sculpt a creation. But to create a soul was beyond even the warlock's dark powers. All his manifestations were empty of such things.

There was only one creature who could mold from the ether creatures that seemed to live under their own will. King Qta. The father of all the monsters that had not been born of the Ancients. Even those who dwelled within the House of Dreams could not sculpt a soul from cloth such as did their king.

Lyon did not know what transpired between Aon and Qta the day the House of Dreams fell to dust. All he could get from the warlock was that he claimed he had been given hope, only to have it dashed away from him. That the Ancients saw fit to mock him once more in his agony.

And now it seemed they had decided to do so once again.

For only when Aon had surrendered all hope—only when it seemed that their very existence would cease to be—would they give him someone with the capacity to care for him. A fragile glass rose. A mortal in a world of cruel and bloodthirsty monsters.

Only now would they summon for him what he had always desired. Someone who might love him for who he was. And to let their sadism unveil in such a fashion was all by design.

The Ancients must have planned this from the start. They had twisted them all to their designs so that Aon would have to suffer the reality he now endured.

There was another who could have loved him in return.

And for her sake, he had no choice but to destroy that love or render it false in his selfish desire.

To make her a dreamer was a far crueler twist of the blade to the warlock's ribs. To taunt him with the very thing he had nearly destroyed this world in his quest to own was too much. It brought Lyon a heartache that was visceral. "Oh, Aon..."

That was why the warlock had called him here. Lyon was the only soul alive on this forsaken plane who knew the truth of the story, save the dread king himself. The only one who might see the magnitude of the suffering he now shouldered.

"I need you to go to her, for I cannot." Aon kept his voice quiet and measured, but Lyon suspected the wound in his soul must be bleeding. "She will be in need of a friend."

Lyon bowed his head, this time in acquiescence. "Of course." He would do so gladly. "If the others ask for what has become of the boy, what shall I say?"

"Tell them the truth. However much of it you see fit."

Lyon blinked in surprise. He did not merely mean about the death of the shifter. His tone, empty and devoid of life, revealed Aon meant about all of it. "No, my lord. That story is for you alone to tell." He tilted his head thoughtfully. "And I will not mention to anyone your feelings toward Lydia. Should Edu find wind of it, it may put her in harm's way once more."

"Edu will not stop. He will seek her life on the gamble that it might irritate me. He needs no confirmation or denial to do the deed."

"I will do all I can to stop this."

"I think she may be able to handle herself." There was a hint of pride in Aon's voice. "I only hope I am there to witness it."

Lyon smiled faintly. Yes. That was distinct pride in what the girl had become. He was eager to see it for himself. Aon waved a hand to dismiss him, and Lyon bowed at the waist and turned to exit the room.

"Oh, and Lyon?"

The Priest paused.

"Be wary of her new companion. It is... oh, never mind. You will discover it on your own. I am sure you will be fine. You are the *amenable* one of us, after all."

That brought Lyon no comfort.

* * *

Everything was a mess.

The ruins, her thoughts, her life, all of it. The stone city was much larger than just the enormous step pyramid that dwarfed all the other buildings near it.

The pyramid sat at the end of a reflecting pool. It was hundreds of feet long and at least a hundred wide, rectangular, and designed to show off the buildings that surrounded it. The liquid looked clear, but she suspected it was much deeper than the one outside the library near the Opera House in Boston. She wasn't about to go jumping in to find out.

On the other end of the reflecting pool was a much smaller step pyramid, one with a much larger building atop it—shorter and squatter. Q had taken her there last night and said it was once Qta's home. Awkward, but she didn't much care right now.

She found the room that Qta must have used as a bedroom, and the wooden furniture was wrecked and destroyed, rotted and overgrown with vines and trees, reclaimed by the wildlife. There was a large, smooth stone platform that had tattered pieces of cloth on it. It was a bed, whose cushions and sheets had long since rotted away. She cleared it off until it was as clean as she could get it and curled up on the stone surface, using Q's tail as a pillow.

She felt as desolate as the bed did.

Waking up had been another story.

At first, she thought Q must have been to blame. Or Aon. Or somebody. Somebody had to have brought the cushions of all sizes and shapes, a giant collection of multi-colored pillows embroidered in wild patterns. It wasn't exactly traditional, but man, it was comfortable.

Q had been buried in them, using them as a pet snake might use substrate in a tank to hide. The sight of his nose poking out with his flicking turquoise tongue had made her laugh. She had needed to laugh. He said she was the one who had done it. That her being home was repairing the city.

And sure enough, the ruins of the room looked much less, well, "ruin-y." The place she'd fallen asleep in looked straight out of Indiana Jones. The room she woke up in had furniture that was intact and whole. Moonlight streamed uninterrupted through holes in the thick stone walls that served as windows. Rolled dried sticks tied together with strings like porch shades draped in front of them, swinging gently in the breeze.

Healing the world, healing the home. Kumbaya or some bullshit.

She'd also needed a change of clothes. She didn't want to wear the simple black cotton dress from Aon's home any longer. Standing in front of a pane of what looked like antique silvered glass, she looked at herself.

Turquoise lines on her face, in writing she couldn't understand. She looked down at her arms and saw no marks floating beneath the surface like she had last night. Her hair was disheveled, and she was just... a mess.

At least she could look dignified. She demanded to be different. Just willed it. Just as she had when she dissolved Aon's weird dark tendril around her neck, she reached out with herself and reshaped the world to better suit her.

Everybody in this world tried to look as badass as possible, as much as possible. Lydia didn't know if she was going to be capable of that. Start small, she figured. A turquoise tank top and dark gray linen cargo pants. Strappy sandals. Casual but comfortable if she was going to be bombing around a humid jungle.

She wondered if it was a real jungle. It was hot enough to be one. *What constitutes a real jungle, idiot? Of course, it's a real jungle.*

How queenly, Q remarked on her clothing choice.

"Shove it," she shot back but smirked. Q flitted across the room and changed his scale to curl around her neck, and she kissed the side of his head affectionately. He nuzzled her cheek in response. "I'll dress fancy when I have to. I don't even know what that'll mean, but I'll figure it out when I get there."

Mmhm. Sure. You could always just go naked like Kamira.

"Yeah, no. Thanks. I bet that chafes."

One last thing she had to do before going out and about. There was a stone shelf on the wall. Really, it was a rock that just jutted out more into the room than any of the others near it, but it would do. She picked up the wooden mask from the bed where she had left it and ran her thumb over the dark green carving on its cheek.

Wiping her tears, she sighed. Q nuzzled her cheek again as she walked over to the stone on the wall and gently placed the mask on it, standing up on its edge.

"He died because of me." The heartbreak threatened to boil over into sobs again. "You can try to say he didn't, but if I were still dead, he'd be alive. If I'd never come here. If I had just—" She broke off and pulled in a deep breath and let it out in a wavering sigh. There weren't any more what-ifs for Nick. There was no point in wondering what could have happened if she had done anything differently.

He was going to kill Nick, anyway. Even if you escaped earlier. You heard him.

"It doesn't make it any better."

I know. I'm sorry, Cupcake…

Shaking her head, she walked out of the room to go explore her new home. She'd have a long time to mourn Nick. She wasn't going to age and die now. Death by other means was still in question. She had plenty of time to deal with her grief unless Edu put a stop to it.

She tried to break herself out of her sulking. Grief was never something she coped with normally, to be honest. Every time she lost a pet or a family member, she would try to make herself as busy as possible to focus on anything other than the pain. And she had ruins to clean. A home to rebuild. Focusing on something practical would help.

The sky was dark and dotted with clouds. It had still been pouring when she arrived last night, and it seemed the rain was just starting to let up. Several moons were glowing overhead, casting the clearing of the city in beautiful mixed light. And around them were… stars.

There were *stars*.

Under hadn't had any stars in fifteen hundred years. Not since Qta died.

She had brought them back. Just by her being alive like this, the stars had come back.

Beautiful in their thousands, glowing brightly in their numbers with no light pollution to hide them. Lydia made her way down the massive steps of her new home to the reflecting pond that stretched out in front of her. The lake cast back at her the image of the night sky.

It was stunning.

She lay on her back on one of the colossal stone blocks that ringed the pond and looked up at the sky. None of the patterns of stars were recognizable. Although she didn't expect them to be. This wasn't Earth.

Q was flying overhead, circling the pond as he glowed eerie and turquoise against the night sky. Well, it was always night.

She also had no idea what the hell time of day it was. It didn't matter.

She couldn't stop staring at the stars.

Everything in her life was messed up.

And that—that view right there—was why the Ancients had done it. "Hey, Q?"

Yeah?

"Tell me this place has wine."

FOURTEEN

Well, it hadn't been wine, per se.

It was more like hard alcohol. It tasted like honey whiskey—thank God it wasn't tequila—and she couldn't complain about the flavor. What it was, though, was intense as hell. She had to pace herself to keep from getting trashed.

I wonder what my alcohol tolerance is now.

Well, let's find out.

She was still lying on that stone, looking up at the stars, the bottle next to her on the block. Q had decided to go for a dip and was in the reflecting pool somewhere. The snake loved to bury himself in things or be in the water, and she could tell he was super thrilled to be home.

It'd probably been hours since she started looking up at the stars and thinking. Coming to terms with what she was certainly came easier with a bottle of alcohol in her hand and proof of why she had to suffer.

Seeing the weight of what she represented, she couldn't very well jump into a fire and kill herself. This world needed her to live.

At least until Edu killed her.

This world needed her to live, fine. But Edu didn't seem to care. He would come for her, and he'd try again. She wasn't sure what his excuse would be this time, but he didn't really need one.

There was the movement of wings nearby, and something flitted in the corner of her eye. She lifted her head and saw Lyon materialize a dozen feet away from a swarm of bats. He was wearing all white like he always was, looking like a pale drop of paint on a dark rug.

"Oh, hey, bud!" Lifting a hand, she greeted him.

"Are you drunk?" Lyon eyed the bottle.

"Goddamn working on it." Sitting up with a huff, she swung her legs over the edge of the block. She held the bottle out to the priest, offering him some. It was a dark green onion bottle, clearly hand-blown and ancient.

Lyon considered it for a moment, shrugged once, and walked toward her to take the bottle. He sniffed it, took a sip, and handed it back. She patted the stone next to her, inviting him silently to join her. He was obviously here to talk, and honestly, she was a little surprised nobody had come sooner. It'd been a solid day. She expected to have been mobbed the moment she had shown up.

"Dare I ask you how you are?" Lyon furrowed his brow.

She took a swig from the bottle and handed it back to him. "On the verge of a mental breakdown. Angry—no, *fucking furious*—at Aon."

He took another drink before setting it down between them. "I can imagine." Lyon's stoic features creased briefly in sympathy before smoothing back to their perfect alabaster finish. There was always a deep sadness in his eyes, mournful like the carved statues in a church. "Just at Aon? What of the rest of us? I have come to see if you are well. If you are... what is the word..."

"Coping?"

He nodded.

She pointed upward.

Lyon looked up and immediately pulled in a startled breath. Apparently, he'd been so focused on her until that point that he hadn't noticed the clouds had cleared. After a long stretch of silence, he reached down, grabbed the bottle of alcohol, and took a hard swig.

Laughing, she leaned back on her elbow. "You're all right, Lyon."

"Thank you?" He was clearly dubious that her modern words were a compliment. Lyon shook his head and looked back up the stars. "It is still raining everywhere, but here. I... this is... a miracle."

"I've been laying here for hours, just... staring. Thinking. Trying to understand what it was like to live in a dying world for *centuries*. And I guess... I have to not be so mad that they turned me into a dreamer." She lay back on the stone and folded an arm under her head. The rough block was prickly otherwise. "It's hard to be pissed at a world for making you when you see why."

"That is very wise and compassionate of you, Ms. Lydia."

"Just call me Lydia. Or, hey, call me Lyd, that's what Nick called me." She paused and then snorted in laughter. "And all your idiot kings have three letter names, anyway. That's really funny."

He was smiling down at her. "Yes, it is quite fitting. It gives me great hope to see that you are not beside yourself. I did not know what to expect when I found you."

"I'm trying to deal with one thing at a time. I can't come to terms with anything else if I don't start at the top. So step one is being okay with what I am now and understanding why it had to happen. Step two is to try to sort out all the rest of this bullshit."

"Which is what, specifically?"

"Aon. Edu. Aon killing Nick. What I'm going to actually do now." Ugh. She was feeling anxious. Getting back up, she paced away from Lyon, needing to stretch her legs. "He killed my best friend, Lyon. In front of me. Right *fucking* in front of me." Tears stung her eyes, and she pressed the heels of her hands into the ridges of her cheekbones, trying to get them to stop.

"I know, and my heart weeps for your loss. I cannot express the extent to which I wish it were not so."

She stopped her pacing. "Thanks. I just—" She didn't know what she even wanted to say. The subject of Aon was such a giant, ugly disaster, she didn't even want to open that box. "Sorry. I don't know what to think."

"It is quite all right. Please do not apologize. You have nothing for which to do so. You are handling this with more grace than many." He stood from the block in order to bow to her like the over-the-top gentleman he was. "I am here if you are ever in need. For counsel or simply for someone to listen."

He was offering himself as a friend. If it were anyone else, she wouldn't trust him. She'd suspect it was a political ploy. But all she'd ever seen from Lyon was that he was a stand-up guy. She honestly did forgive him for his betrayal. He was weird. Definitely weird. And with the emotional range of a ceramic bowl. But he was honest, and she believed he meant well. "I'd like that, Lyon. Thanks. God only knows I could use more than one person to talk to."

"Hm?" Lyon blinked curiously. "Who is the other?"

As if on cue, sensing his chance to make an entrance, her ghostly snake companion loomed up out of the reflecting pool behind Lyon. He was now fifty feet long or more, and his clawed wings grasped the ring of stones as he lifted himself up to tower over the man.

Lyon was still unsuspecting as Q bent his long neck over the vampire to look at him upside-down some five feet in front of the poor man.

"Sup."

Well, there was a new emotion to add to the logbook for Lyon. *Startled-as-shit terror.* The man in white let out an undignified noise and threw himself backward from Q, staggered, tripped over himself, and landed heavily against the stone block. He had tried to get away from the floating head but instead had fallen toward where the giant winged snake was perched.

Lyon looked up at the massive creature over him, and he froze, unsure of what to do or how to run from something like that.

Q snickered loudly and fluffed the glowing feathers of his wings. **"Ooh, that's fun. I like scaring people."**

"Stop it, Q. He was being nice." She put her hands on her hips. When Q darted at Lyon, causing the Priest to jolt in fear, she rolled her eyes. "Quit it already."

"Fiiiine." Q let out an exaggerated sigh. **"Spoilsport."** He changed to the size of a horse and coiled himself at Lyon's feet, reared up like a cobra. **"You can get up now, y'know."**

Lyon obeyed, unsure and stuttering in his movements, and used a palm against the stone to push himself up to standing. "I... suppose you are the one about whom I was warned."

"By who? Aon? Yeah. I squeezed him to death. Squished his internal organs and broke every bone in his torso. Asshole had it coming."

"Well..." Lyon stopped, still stunned, and began again. "Lydia, is he your creation?"

"No. Well, not exactly. As far as I can tell, Q *is* me." She stepped over Q's tail and reached up to ruffle the feathers on the back of his head. Q shrank again and curled up on her shoulder, wrapping his long, smoky tail around her neck. "He's all the knowledge and power that I should have received from the pool, all bottled up. It was either that or I stop being me. I guess

I somehow knew to make the world's most annoying sidekick instead. Or at least that's what he says."

"I am not the sidekick! When you use magic, you're plugging in to me. That makes you the sidekick."

Lyon blinked. "I... see." It was clear he didn't.

Laughing, she shook her head. The vampire was adorable, in an awkward way.

They fell into silence as Lyon stared at Q, wide eyed and confounded. Q probably went against everything he understood as the laws of his world. A person went into the pool, a person came out with power and knowledge of their world. The end. Twice now she'd come out of that lake of blood not the right way.

"This is all very unusual." Lyon walked over to the stone block and sat once more. Lydia followed and sat next to him. Q, over his fun of scaring Lyon, was now crawling around the man's shoulders and down his arm. Lyon looked as though he had a rabid raccoon on him—doing his best to hold still yet incredibly nervous at the same time.

"Everything's unusual to me, so I guess it doesn't count." She shrugged.

Lyon lifted a hand to tentatively invite Q to climb onto his palm. The little snake did so, looking up at Lyon with a flick of a forked, turquoise tongue. Lyon flinched as it did.

"Oh, simmer. You're fine. I'm not going to eat you. I actually *like* you."

"Thank you." Lyon sounded dubious at best but took it for what it was worth. "I think."

"What do I do now, Lyon?"

The blunt question pulled Lyon out of his fascination with the snake, and he looked over at her. "That is challenging. I suppose we should take it one topic at a time. Aon... it is clear he cares for you."

"He said he loves me."

Lyon smiled faintly, but it didn't reach the sorrow in his eyes. "I am glad he told you."

"You knew?"

"Aon and I were once close friends. The Great War saw the end of those days. But when he came to bury you in the Pool of the Ancients, I saw his grief for what it was."

Lydia shook her head and picked up the bottle of alcohol to take a swig out of it. "He killed Nick. He did it to prevent some stupid prophecy from coming true."

"It does not soften the blow, nor does it make his actions righteous or forgivable. You have every right to be upset with him. How do you feel about him?"

"Right now? I want to shove his head so far up his ass he has to cut holes in his nipples to see."

"And I'll help!"

"You and my wife will become friends. I fear for all of Under the day this comes to pass." Lyon chuckled quietly and sighed. "You have every right to be angry at him. But..."

"You're asking me if I love him back?"

"Yes, I suppose I am."

"I don't know, Lyon. I really don't. Right now, I really might hate him." Staring down at the bottle of alcohol, her shoulders slumped. "And don't tell him I said that."

"We speak in confidence."

"Mmhm, just like last time." Fine, she was still a little bitter that the Priest had run to tell Edu all the details she had learned about Aon's experiments.

His features creased. "This world has done poorly by you, Lydia."

"Cheers to that." That deserved another swig from the onion bottle. "So Aon's a hot mess that will take a while to solve. What about Edu?"

"Do you feel ready to face him, not knowing his intentions?"

"Fuck, no."

"I might be able to take Edu if he comes alone. Might. Don't know. If he doesn't? That's the problem."

"I am not certain he will come with the intent to take your life. But I will admit it is more likely than not."

"Can't someone just tell him he's already used his Lydia-killing quota already?"

The vampire laughed. "You are a little drunk, aren't you?"

"No. Maybe. I'm just done putting up with people's shit, I guess."

"Then here is my suggestion to you, my friend. Go out and see this world. Edu will come here looking for you in short order, and he will find you wherever you may be. So, instead, go learn of this world. Explore it. It is yours now, same as it is all theirs. Make it your home. It will be easier to understand where you belong within it if you can see the whole of its parts."

It seemed risky. She wasn't so sure about that.

Lyon placed his hand on her shoulder. "You do not seem someone shy to follow her heart. Many will come to see you out of curiosity, to know where you stand and what you may mean to their lives. Be patient, for what has happened to our world in your wake is," Lyon paused as he looked up at the stars, "quite remarkable."

"Yeah." She understood. She was going to have a lot of curious people around her. All she wanted was to curl up somewhere and spend some time thinking it all through, but they weren't going to give her that kind of patience.

"Perhaps go see them instead. On your terms."

With a blink, she realized something. For the first time since coming here, she wasn't afraid of what might live out in that world. Every dark shadow might have held a monster waiting to eat her, but now she had Q backing her up. She was finally free of that constant threat. She had plenty of others, but that one was now gone.

"What is it?" The Priest squeezed her shoulder lightly.

She smiled at him and felt a weight had been lifted off her. "I think I'm going to take your advice."

FIFTEEN

At first, Lydia stuck to the woods, to the edges of the wilderness around the cities, as she wandered. Q made for a fantastic tour guide, it turned out. He had the answers to most of her questions, even if he was kind of a wiseass about it most of the time.

She was walking along a beach, watching the blackened waves of the ocean wash up over the shore. The moons overhead cast the waves and the rocks in a beautiful array of blues, whites, and ambers. It was plenty bright enough to see. Q was swooping in the air around her, adding streaks of glowing turquoise as he went.

The beaches are back? This is awesome!

"They were gone?"

Most of the world was gone. It's all back now. But everybody scrunched into the cities around the Pool of the Ancients when it was clear the void was going to eat everything. The rest of the world is abandoned. But people are like a gas. They'll expand to fill their container in time.

When she went to argue with his crass metaphor, she realized she couldn't. She shrugged. "Why were they centered around the Ancients?"

They aren't omnipotent. Not really. They're centered there, where they're kept as prisoners. They're super powerful, but they aren't gods in the same way you think of them. Everything is relative. You think about bugs a certain way, and they think about you exactly the same.

"That isn't comforting."

Nothin' really is. So, anyway—Ooo! Hold that thought!

And with that, Q dove into the ocean. In mid-dive he grew, nearly tripling in size, before disappearing beneath the waves. Shapes surged and thrashed, splashing and sending crests of water hurling in different directions some thirty feet off the shore. It was clear Q was wrestling with... something. His turquoise wings were flashing beneath the surface, reflecting up like a glowstick dropped on the bottom of a pool. It was like watching a radioactive shark wrestle with a killer whale. Whatever Q was battling was *big*.

Finally, he crested through the surface, and in his jaws was a creature that resembled a huge swordfish. Its scales were thick and heavily stacked like plate armor. Q flew to the shore and dropped it onto the sand with a *whump*. It was already very dead. Her snake friend had nearly bitten its head clean off.

Look, Ma! I caught a fishie!

He was so proud of himself, she laughed. "Yeah, you did. Good job. What're you going to do with it?"

Eat it, silly. Want some?

"No... I'm good, thanks."

You should eat. You haven't since you came back from the dead.

"I—" Blinking, she realized he was right. It had been... at least a week. Maybe longer. And she wasn't even hungry. Until he said it, she hadn't even thought about it. Huh. "Sushi really isn't my thing. Could never get used to it."

Suit yourself. More for me!

Q started mowing into the thing, ripping it apart with sickening crunches of bone and wet flesh. It wasn't until the fish's head finished coming off its body and wound up near her foot that she noticed something.

All the creatures she had seen—even the monsters that came out of the pool—had marks on their faces. The bughorses, the Hellhounds, the giant monster that those idiots had fought in the market square. They all had soulmarks. This fish... didn't. She flipped it over onto the other side with the end of her boot to be sure.

It wasn't a person. Not ever. Q was gulping down the last of it, using the talons on the tips of his wings to pull open the rest of the carcass. **So don't feel bad, unless you're suddenly vegetarian.**

"I thought everything in Under was a person."

Yeah, except for the monsters that the House of Dreams creates. This one is one of yours. So technically, I guess I'm still committing cannibalism. *Tasty, tasty cannibalism.*

Tilting her head to the side slightly, she studied the fish. She didn't remember dreaming up a super-armored swordfish.

This world taps into you the same way you tap into it. Remember what Aon told you about the Ancients? You're the branch on the tree of their power, but they created this place. Subconsciously, you're balancing out this world because they want you to.

"That's... unsettling."

Q shrunk in size and swooped up into the air again before landing on her shoulder, well-fed and purring contentedly. Her snake, it seemed, could purr. Why not?

Welcome to Under, Cupcake. Where everything is

creepy and the murder party's the best party because the murder party never stops.

Tiredly laughing, she once more found herself smiling at Q's snide comments. He was like her inner monologue, just with the sass level turned way up. He might only be the world's most elaborate imaginary friend, but she was glad he was here.

Shucks.

"So, wait. Now that there are normal creatures in Under, nobody else has to eat person-beasts anymore?"

Nope! They can go back to hunting all the beasties you dream up. I mean, they still will eat each other. It's more fun. But they won't have to all the time. It goes back to a sport or a game and less of a necessity.

That was some small solace, anyway. At least her existence spared people like Evie the task of being dog chow day in and day out. "You said the Ancients are using me to balance out the world. They're controlling my mind?"

Eh... not in the way you're thinking of it. They're driving you to create beasts in your subconscious. You're doing it without realizing.

"I don't like the Ancients, and I don't want them mucking around in my head."

No dice, too late. You're wearing the marks. You heard their voice. If you want out, the only way is by dying for keeps a second time.

Okay, she was starting to get why Aon didn't like them very much. "What do they want from me?"

I dunno. Nobody does. Maybe Ziza, sometimes. As Oracle, she gets visions direct from the Ancients. She might know. Why not go see her? Besides, it'll be good to socialize. You've been playing Rapunzel since you showed up here.

"That's not my fault. First Edu locked my ass up, and then

Aon. This is my first time being able to walk somewhere on my own without getting chased around like a goddamn rabbit."

And so here we are, exploring, so go explore what matters. I love the scenery and all, but let's go see Ziza. See if she has answers for you.

Maybe she could confirm this prophecy she gave Aon and see if the warlock had been lying when he said he had killed Nick to spare her some upcoming tragedy. "Sure, I—"

The ground under her feet suddenly moved. The sand in front of her began to bubble up, and she fell back onto her ass. The rocks stung her hands, but it was the least of her concerns.

Rising from the sand was a giant, bus-sized insect. It looked like a rhinoceros beetle if you crossed it with the first half of its namesake. Like everything in Under, it was twisted and warped. The horn that came off its head had strange, angular curls in it. Its carapace split and opened, and Lydia winced as it buzzed its enormous wings.

It stepped toward her, the feet on the ends of its long, spindly legs flexing out to keep it from sinking into the sand. It bent down, and Lydia pulled in a nervous breath and held it as it... nudged her foot with the end of its horn.

What?

Aw, how cute. It's saying hello. Q flapped his wings. **"Hey, buggo!"**

"It's saying hello?"

"It's another one of yours, silly. No marks. To it, you're Momma. It just came over to say hi. Didn't you, you adorable, truck-sized freak?" Q flew up to the creature and curled around the end of its horn. The bug seemed quite content with that and... sat on its hind legs with a *whumf*, kicking up sand with its weight. Q was talking to it in the tone that somebody talks to a family pet, childish and silly.

"Who's a cute li'l freaky buggo? You are! Yes, you are!"

Getting up, she brushed sand off her legs. She was its *what?*

This was going to take a long time to get used to. She walked up to it slowly and reached up her hand to touch it. "H-hey there, buddy."

The beetle leaned down and rubbed its head up against her torso and nearly knocked her over in its exuberance.

Squeaking, she laughed and patted its head, smiling. All right, fine. It was cute.

"If Edu tries to kill you, this is how you should defend yourself. You summon monsters. That's your gig. If he shows up with an army? You create your own."

Yeah, right. Her? With a monster army? Fat chance. She was in mid-pat on the giant beetle when the creature suddenly decided to move on. Q took the hint and flew back to her shoulder as the creature got to its feet.

The giant insect scrambled up the rocks and into the forest at the top of the embankment.

This was her world now. A world of monsters and creatures that were both friend and foe. But at least not everything that went bump in the night was trying to eat her now. And those ones were her freaky pseudo-*attack-pets*. "All right. Let's go see Ziza."

* * *

Q's teleportation stunts were not nearly as jarring as Aon's. Or maybe, now that she was a queen, it just sucked less. The jury was still out. He brought her to the city of Yej. The Great Hall that the House of Fate called home was off the main courtyard of the city.

The main courtyard where the marketplace set up once a week.

The courtyard where Lydia had run for her life... and then promptly died.

She stood there in the shadows of a building, hiding in an alley, away from the main thoroughfare. She had created a black coat with a hood and pulled it up over her face to help hide who she was. Nobody might know her face, but the marks were a dead giveaway.

The memory of the fear and the pain of Edu burning out her heart came back to her like a freight train. It hit her so hard that she had to lean against the wall to try to calm her breathing. She scratched her chest with her nails.

It's okay, Cupcake. Deep breath.

"Shut up, Q. You're not helping."

The snake settled down on her shoulder and wormed his way inside her hood. He nuzzled into her cheek. That actually did help. She reached up to pet him and tried to chase away the memory of Edu's hand burning into her like molten metal. She shuddered despite herself.

"Do come inside, Mistress Lydia. It is a much better place to talk than here in an alley."

Jolting, she looked up. There, standing across from her, was Ziza. She was dressed in a long, sapphire blue gown, and her white hair was pulled up in an ornate bun at the back of her head. Her pure white eyes were looking in her direction, although Lydia suspected she was blind. She also suspected it didn't really matter.

"How did you know I was—" She stopped herself. "Stupid question."

Ziza's expression cracked in a brief and faint smile. "You will adjust in time. Come."

Lydia kept her head down and her hood pulled tight as she followed behind the woman in blue. She shoved her hands in her pockets, desperately wishing she could crawl in there and hide.

Luckily, it wasn't long before they were inside. As she stepped into the grand, marble building, she looked up and couldn't help but let out a quiet "whoa." Q had called it the Great Hall. It was literal.

The building arched up around her in blue and white marble. It looked like a building from Venice or one of the grand palaces in Italy. She had never seen anything like it in person. Candles burned in sconces and added warmer tones to the cool blues of the rest of the building. The windows that stretched up higher than a story cast in light from the city and the moons outside.

But that wasn't the most impressive part of the building. Ziza led her through the room to stand closer to the huge, twisting metal structure that hung overhead. She had never seen anything like it. It was suspended in midair, floating what must be eighty feet over her head, and held up by... literally nothing.

Magic. Right. Eventually, she'd get used to that.

Circles of copper and brass some twenty feet in diameter twisted around each other. It was moving in slow motion, tracking in all different directions. There were orbs and symbols that made no sense to her. It took her a long time to realize there were seven glass shapes on the tracks, one per circle of copper. One in each color for the Houses of Under. Three were lit—red, black, and turquoise. Edu, Aon... and her.

That's the orrery, Q said silently as he had disappeared the moment they came inside.

"Wow," was all she could muster.

"Think of it as not just a celestial map, but a guide to our world. Every force that pulls upon us is represented here. You can think of it as a form of astrology in your world, if such sciences truly ever held weight."

It seemed Ziza wasn't immune to Under's sense of superiority of Earth. Lydia smiled faintly. "If you could read this, it would tell you what'll happen in Under?"

"No. Not precisely. This merely helps us understand what is, and by that, may we see what will surely come." The woman stood beside her and folded her hands neatly in front of her. "Such as a torch in the darkness. That which is closest to you is the easiest to discern. All after that fades and grows more obscure with distance."

"Huh. Gotcha." At least she thought she did. Suddenly, Lydia remembered her manners. "Oh. I'm sorry to bust in on you—"

"She knew you were coming. She always does."

Lydia blinked and turned, not realizing there were other people in the room. She had been too engrossed with the giant magically floating copper whatever-it-was to see two figures sitting by one wall. Both of whom now stood to approach her.

Well, this was fitting. They were there when she first woke up in Under. It should only serve she see them again now. One of them was regent of a House, after all.

"Hey, Maverick. Hi, Aria." Why was she suddenly nervous?

The doctor and his wife stopped a few feet away, and Maverick bowed to her. Aria even curtsied.

The action brought a burst of laughter out of Lydia that echoed in the giant chamber. "No, no, no! Stop that. No bowing. No scraping. I'm just me. I'm barely me. Don't be all 'Mistress Lydia' or any of that crap. I'm Lydia. You fixed the hole in my arm and lectured me about my horrible surgery skills."

"You are now a queen, though," Aria pointed out, as if she'd really have forgotten.

"I guess. But I don't feel like one, and I certainly don't want you—or anybody—treating me like one. It's awkward and I don't know what to do with it."

"Well, I for one am glad I do not need to lick the floor before another egomaniacal despot." Maverick smirked at her. "Lydia, it is good to see you. I am... we are... very sorry for what happened, and I must apologize for my hand in it."

Lydia looked at Ziza. "You told him I was coming?"

"I told the Houses of Words and Moons that you would be attending me here, in case they wished for a chance to speak with you. Kamira said, I believe, 'I'll find her on my own terms.'"

Oh, good. Now she had *that* to look forward to.

Turning her attention back to Maverick, she sighed. He was still hanging on his apology. She couldn't be angry. She really couldn't. She understood. She was going to carry that trauma with her for the rest of eternity, but she couldn't blame them for making what they thought was the right choice. "Call us even, Maverick. For both the times you patched me up." She held her hand out to him.

Maverick smiled and shook her hand. "Gladly."

She tucked her hands back into her pockets as she looked up at the thing over her head. "Ziza?"

"Yes?"

"Did the Ancients tell you I had to die?"

"I am afraid so. I was given a vision that foretold your death. I knew that you must die to save the world and that it was connected to the rise of a new dreamer. I did not know, although I suspected, that you would become she." Ziza's voice was quiet, but it carried easily in the echo chamber that was the giant marble hall. Lydia thought she could hear classical music playing from somewhere. It fit.

"Can I ask you some questions?"

"Of course. I will give you the answers, if I know them."

"Why me? Why did the Ancients pick me?"

"They saw in you the potential to survive what would have destroyed many. Your resilience is your true strength."

She rubbed the back of her neck. "Well, isn't that the worst superpower ever? 'Hey, you're good at handling massive amounts of the bullshit we throw at you. Here's some more.'"

Aria chuckled, and Maverick smiled. Ziza looked like

emotions might shatter her face, so Lydia didn't take it personally when she didn't do anything.

Second question. "Okay, fine. But why did they reject me
the first time? Why let me nearly drown? Why not just raise me
as a dreamer then, if they could do it all along?"

"I believe the reasons are twofold." Ziza moved a short
distance to light some candles that sat on a table nearby. "One, I
suspect a living body could not contend with that amount of
strength. I believe it had to replace all that kept you whole, for
you to be the vessel for what the Ancients needed. The other six
kings and queens were made in a very different fashion to all
those who followed them here."

Lydia bristled at being called a vessel, but she didn't
interrupt.

"The second..." Ziza paused and tilted her head to the side
slightly and cast her a glance with a rare smile upon it. "I think
you would not have made the friendships you have were you
one of us from the start."

The look on her face screamed what she was implying. She
wasn't talking about Evie or Lyon, that was damn sure. The
Ancients kept her mortal so she could form a bond with Aon?
"But why? Why are those friendships important?"

"That, I do not know. The Ancients enjoy their games.
Even though they cannot influence directly as they once did
when they were free, they find their strings to pull, even still."

"I don't like being a puppet."

"Welcome to Under, I am afraid," Maverick interjected.

"One last question. Aon told me you gave him a prophecy,
just after the thunderstorm began. What was it?"

"My words were for him and him alone."

"Right, but if he told me what you said, can you tell me if
it's true?"

"What are you asking me, Queen of Dreams?"

Lydia winced at the use of her title. She looked back up at

the hypnotic movements of the copper structure overhead. "I want to know if he was telling me the truth. If what he told me was real or if he made up a prophecy to try to manipulate me."

"What did he tell you I said?" Ziza's voice was as emotionless as it always was.

"He said you delivered him a vision in three parts. The first was where to find me and that I would be weak and lost when he did. The second part was that a king would rise to destroy me. The third was that a friend would serve to be my undoing."

"That is not precisely what I said, word for word, but it captures the meaning well enough. Yes, that is the intention of what I said to him on behalf of the Ancients."

Wincing, she shut her eyes tightly. She felt tears sting her eyes once more. Aon hadn't been lying. Some part of her almost wished he had been. It would have made everything so much easier if he had just been using her, manipulating her feelings to his own ends.

It meant he would have been easier to hate.

But Aon killed Nick to *honestly* try to prevent some terrible future. He had torn out her heart to save her life. It didn't make it right. It didn't mean she forgave him. But it didn't help her turmoil. It would have been so simple if he had just been lying.

She blinked as someone took her hand. Aria. She was holding her hand between both of hers, looking at her intensely. The woman was kind and gentle. She was looking forward to getting to know her more. "When Maverick told me what had become of you, I wept. You seemed like such a clever, bright thing. I so hoped you would Fall to the House of Words and give my husband an assistant with which to match wits. But seeing you now, I am filled with joy. You have saved our world, Lydia."

She wanted to hide under one of the benches in the room. "I really had nothing to do with it."

"Even still." Aria squeezed her hand again between hers

before releasing it. "I am so happy to see you. I heard about the death of your friend. I... am so very sorry. Both for his loss, your grief, and for how it happened."

She hated condolences. Hated them to the very core of her being. It wasn't that she didn't appreciate the sentiment; she really did. But she liked to mourn in private. Being reminded in public that her pain was a thing only dredged it back to the surface like sour milk. But that wasn't Aria's fault. "Thanks. I'm really going to miss him. He was my best friend."

Maverick paused, looking down at the ground for a long moment, his yellow eye flicking back and forth as he seemed to process all that she said. He looked back up at her, incredulous. "The prophecy. He killed the boy to protect you?"

"In some sick, stupid way, yes."

"But why? Why go to such lengths for you?"

Oh, fuck. *Fuck.* Damn it all, she really should have just said she didn't know. This was going to be awkward as hell. And potentially dangerous.

Aria beat her to an answer and slapped the back of her hand into Maverick's chest. "You are too old to be such a fool, Maverick. Can you not see? Although in some matters, I suppose you are still a whelp."

"See what?" Now the doctor looked defensive.

Aria smiled warmly at Lydia. "Aon cares for you, doesn't he?"

Maverick laughed darkly and shook his head. "You are wrong. Aon feels no such thing for any soul alive, nor has he ever."

"Would you have expected him to tend to a mortal girl in the manner he did?" Aria argued. "You yourself concluded he knew not what Lydia was meant to become, lest he would have dispatched her himself, and in short order. And here she stands, a free woman, outside his cage. He could have contained her and done what he could to prevent the prophecy. Why let her go?"

"I cannot fathom the man's madness. I do not know what he schemes." Maverick sighed. "Lydia. Is my wife's assertion true?"

"That Aon cares about me?" She paused for a long time and looked up at the black orb on its metal track in the orrery overhead.

"Go ahead, Lydia," Ziza prompted quietly. "You have no reason to fear them knowing the truth. All will know it in short order."

She looked back to the woman in blue curiously. She wondered how Ziza knew, but then she remembered. She was psychic. Well, that answered that. She was shit at keeping secrets, anyway. She looked back up at the orrery, finding shelter in not having to make eye contact. "Yeah. Aon's said as much. He could be lying, but I really don't think he is."

"What gives you such a conviction?" Maverick asked. "What makes you so certain he speaks the truth?"

Here goes nothing.

"He showed me his face."

There was a long silence. When she looked down from watching the orrery, Maverick had gone to sit back on the bench. Aria had joined him. The two looked shocked, to put it lightly. Ziza, though, was smiling once more. Lydia guessed that the woman smiled more in this meeting than she probably had in years.

"You jest," Maverick said, barely above a whisper. "He removed his mask for you?"

Lydia nodded.

"The warlock... *loves* you?"

Stuffing her hands into her pockets, she wished she could disappear like Q.

You could. But man, that'd be super weird right now.

Lydia snorted. Half at Q's comment and half at the stupid look on Maverick's face. "Again, that's what he said. I'm pretty sure he means it."

Maverick put his hand over his eyes as he leaned his head down. "And he murdered your friend to... protect you. What an ugly scenario for any involved. This is why I do not involve myself in politics. For this reason alone."

"The others will not believe her," Aria pointed out. "Kamira will not care what she says." She shook her head. "I do not think Edu will be convinced by much."

"No, worse still, consider this." Maverick lifted his head to look at Lydia. "Edu lost the woman he loved to Aon long ago. The King of Flames may seek to return the favor for hatred's sake alone."

Lydia groaned. Well, that was just *great*. Nobody told her that lovely bit of "family" history. "You're kidding me."

"It is very much the truth," Ziza interjected mildly.

There was a pregnant pause in the room for a long moment —one that Lydia didn't understand—before Maverick found the nerve to end it. "Be wary with this news around Edu. That is what I will impart with the most vehement earnestness. I cannot predict how he will react to your rise from the grave, your presence in our world as a dreamer, or now... this."

Lydia nodded. "Noted. I'm currently doing my best to avoid him altogether."

"How so?" Aria asked.

"I'm seeing the sights. Traveling Under and trying to get a sense for where I live now. That, and if I go 'home,' I know who'll come find me there."

"You two are reigning royals of Under. You cannot avoid him for much longer." Ziza had finished lighting the rows of candles and extinguished the long match, turning back toward them.

"I know. But I need a second to catch my breath."

"Then enjoy your grand tour." Maverick stood and helped his wife to stand. They really were a cute couple, in a messed-up-period-BBC-TV-drama kind of way. "We will go before word of your presence here travels."

"Will it?"

"I do not live here alone," the Oracle pointed out with all the passion of a brick.

"Then I should go. Thanks, Ziza, for answering a few questions."

"It is my duty. And, for you, my pleasure. Do come visit me again."

It was kind of like talking to an ice sculpture, but it wasn't unpleasant. "That sounds nice," she said with a genuine smile. She wondered what Ziza's story was—how she got to be the Oracle and all that. "Have a good night or—afternoon—or whatever. I really need to get a watch."

Maverick laughed quietly at that and unclipped his pocket watch and handed it to her. "I have many. Here."

Lydia smiled at the doctor and took it. It was a simple piece, clearly prioritizing function over form, but still elegant. "Always looking out for me, doc. Thanks."

Maverick bowed his head, a smile still on his usually stern features. "Anything for Mistress Lydia." He said it with such dry sarcasm it made her grin.

Lydia began to turn for the door. "May I have a word with you in private, before you go?" Aria asked her.

"Sure."

Twenty feet away and whispering in an alcove, Lydia was still certain the others could hear her. But it was good enough. Aria was holding onto both her hands now. It was something her great-grandmother used to do, and Lydia wondered how old Aria really was. Aria was looking up at her intensely, her visible yellow eye flickering in curiosity and a desperate kind of hope.

"You say the warlock professed his love to you. Is this really true?"

Lydia nodded.

"And how do you feel about him?"

Lydia cringed. "It's complicated." She'd said that a lot lately. "He killed Nick."

"Yes, but..."

"I don't know. I really don't."

"That you do not instantly voice your hatred speaks volumes." Suddenly, Aria hugged her.

Lydia froze, smiled, and then hugged the woman back. It was unexpected but not unwelcome.

Aria's words were ones of wisdom that spoke volumes. "Give it time."

"I guess I have plenty of that now."

Aria stepped back and smiled up at her knowingly. The woman was short—probably just around five feet. "That, we all do."

Movement caught her eye. A man in a blue suit was standing some ten feet away, looking at her wide-eyed, caught in awe and fear in equal measure. When she met his shocked expression, he scrambled in the other direction. A moment later, he returned and had two others with him, gawking at her from a distance.

She was going to draw a crowd *real* quick.

"I really should leave."

Aria smiled and patted her on the arm. "Go, then. See this world you have saved. And know that we are grateful."

Lydia said her goodbyes and smiled down at Aria and turned for the exit. The world was grateful. Now, hopefully, she lived long enough for it to count.

SIXTEEN

Stars.

Edu stood in the fields out behind his castle. The grass was long but barely reached his knees. The rain had finally ceased, and the smell of it was still thick in the air.

With the storm went the clouds.

One of his soldiers had come running into his bedroom, blathering like a madman. He had been wild-eyed in his panic, spewing something about the sky, insisting he come outside to see. So Edu had donned his britches and walked out to see what the man could possibly have been talking about.

There were no stars in the skies over Under. Not for fifteen hundred years.

Yet there they were.

Burning in their multitude, flickering and filling the sky. The stars surrounded the bright moons and filled in the empty void that had been present for so very long.

There was no question as to why the stars had returned.

"Well, put me on a popsicle stick and fuck me sideways, wouldja look at that!"

He turned his head to see Evie bouncing up to him through

the grass, a broad smile on her upturned face. She was looking up at the sky even as she bounded to his side and hugged his arm to her chest.

He smiled beneath the mask.

Slowly, but surely, she had found her way into his heart.

He reached up and ruffled her red curls underneath his massive hand. She giggled at the gesture, as it rocked her head from left to right.

"Oh, stop it!" Laughing, she swatted his hand away playfully before hugging his arm to her tighter. "This is because of Lydia?"

Edu nodded silently and let out a heavy sigh, turning his gaze back up to the stars. He should rejoice upon seeing the salvation of his world played out upon the skies above him. Yet it filled him with a kind of dread and anger all at once.

"I know it's complicated. But you should be happy. Under is saved! Look at that." She pointed up at the stars. "That's just beautiful."

Edu shook his head morosely. Yes, his world was saved, but at what cost? What would become of it now? To have it placed in the hands of Aon was a fate worse than death. Evie herself should understand that.

"I might not know her too well, but I know Lydia better than you do. I think she can handle herself. I wouldn't worry too badly."

Ylena was not around at the moment to translate for him. But it didn't seem to bother the redhead. She was learning to read his body language and seemed to intuit quickly from his mannerisms the meaning behind them. It was an impressive skill, and Edu was glad for it. He often found his inability to communicate left in him a deep and painful ache.

"Maybe you should go see her? Talk to her. I know she won't be happy to see you, but..."

Edu shook his head more firmly. The girl—the new

dreamer, he corrected himself—was a prisoner of Aon, and Edu would not pay whatever price the warlock would demand for such a thing.

"*My lord.*" Ylena's voice echoed in his mind. Their silent exchanges were not limited by distance. "*You are needed in the keep. There is news.*"

"Whoa!" Evie laughed as he scooped his arm around her and pressed her to his side. They disappeared in a roar of fire. When they reappeared on the other side, Evie was laughing and swatting at his chest. "How many times do I have to tell you, you big oaf? Warn me when you're going to do that! I—Oh!" She broke off at the realization that they were not alone in his throne room. Evie squeaked and ran from his side to go stand by a column. For a woman who was so often brazen, she was shy when put on stage.

Several figures stood assembled. Ylena stood beside his carved wooden throne. There were two others. Ah. That would be why Evelyn hid. A man dressed in all black with a black mask adorning half his face. Navaa, Aon's regent and second in command. With him stood another woman in black, whom Edu did not know. Edu did not care much to pay attention to the warlock's regiments.

"King Edu." Navaa bowed. The woman did the same. Those of the House of Shadows did not pay him much respect, and he instantly sensed danger. "I come with word from King Aon."

"Master Edu insists Aon could have come himself," Ylena said for him, "were he not a coward avoiding a fight."

Navaa's face twitched in anger, and it took great patience on the dark-skinned man's behalf to stomach the comment. "My master is busy with matters requiring his full attention."

Edu was glad for the mask, for it hid his eye roll. *I am sure he is.* Edu shrugged dismissively and walked to his throne and sank down into the wooden and regal chair. He gestured for Navaa to get on with it.

The woman at Navaa's side bristled visibly at Edu's disinterested and depreciative air. Edu could not have cared less for her thoughts. He wished them to deliver their message and leave as fast as they possibly could. Any wearing black within his halls was an unwelcome presence, especially as their factions stood on the brink of war. Anything they were to say was a waste of his time.

"The Queen of Dreams has been set free. Mistress Lydia is now released of Aon's care," Navaa announced.

Edu tilted his head to one side and leaned forward. Never mind. Now he was most certainly interested.

"Master Edu asks why he has done such a thing," Ylena said.

"The queen freed herself." Navaa shrugged.

Edu laughed sarcastically. It was one of the few sounds he could still make without owning a tongue. Edu shook his head.

"You are lying," said his empath.

Navaa narrowed his eyes. "I am doing no such thing. Master Aon lowered his guard to the lady at the wrong time. He was caught unaware."

"Master Edu insists you are still lying. Even if he has given you the perception of such an act, he allowed this to happen. Either you lie to Edu now or Aon has deceived you. No one catches Aon 'unaware.'"

Navaa was clearly becoming defensive. "It does not matter how the action transpired. The lady is free and no longer under my master's influence."

"Master Edu believes you are lying once more," Ylena said for him as he sank back into his chair. "She remains under his influence. But he knows on such matters you will not speak the truth even if you know it."

The chains may be gone, but the thread most certainly

remained. Aon had desired the power of the dreamers for thousands of years. He would not release her without some other scheme in mind. Sadly, Edu knew he had no hope of discovering it on his own. No one, in all their five thousand years of life, had ever outplayed the warlock. Defeated, yes, but not by tactics alone.

The question now remained, would he still bring a war to Aon's doorstep? Even with Lydia no longer his prisoner, it did not mean Aon was not plotting to use her to rule the world. There was a good reason why he and the sorcerer took turns in reigning as king while the other slept. They could not abide the other's mere existence otherwise.

Edu desired to fight the warlock for all he had done. For the manner in which the dreamer returned, he could never forgive him. Aon may have claimed ignorance in all that transpired, but there was far too much coincidence for Edu's liking. Aon would not have been so protective of the mortal child—so interested in her—if he did not know what she was intended to become. There was no other explanation for his behavior. Therefore, he had a careful hand to play in her rise as the Queen of Dreams, even if Edu's hand had stopped her heart.

If there was one thing Edu despised above all else, it was being played.

Why would he release her? Why would he let her go? It made no sense.

Yes, Evelyn, perhaps we shall go see Ms. Lydia, after all.

"If you have nothing else, Master Edu wishes you both to leave," Ylena said for him. He hadn't actually said anything of the sort, but she read his desire before he voiced it.

"There is one more matter he asked me to disclose to you." Navaa wore an odd smirk. "Aon is abdicating his throne to you as ruling King of Under. In light of recent matters, he feels it is inappropriate for him to remain so."

"What?" Ylena exclaimed, unable to hold back his outburst.

"As Aon most certainly will face charges for the crime he has committed, he feels he must step down until the issue is resolved."

Edu tilted his head. What crime? He certainly did not see keeping the Queen of Dreams as his chained pet an offense. What in the name of the Ancients was he playing at?

"What crime has he committed?"

"Murder, King Edu." Navaa was still smirking. It felt wrong for him to be delivering such news with such a haughty air. There was a game being played around him, and Edu knew he was too slow to see the cards for what they were. He would not know until the trap was sprung. "He killed the shifter pup who traveled here with Ms. Lydia. It was what inspired her to seek her freedom."

Inspired her to seek her freedom, he repeated to himself.

Edu remembered the boy. He had acted bravely in the face of defeat. He had Fallen to the House of Moons as a reasonably high-ranking shifter, if he was not mistaken. He remembered how keenly he had worried over Lydia and she for him. They were close friends.

Aon had murdered the boy to hurt her.

Edu was not surprised.

She must have denied the warlock use of her powers. She must have fought against him, and he, in his rage, took from her that for which she cared. It was a familiar story, one he had seen played out time and time again throughout their storied and ugly history.

Perhaps she was freed of his influence, after all. It was unlikely... but he had hope. That was, in all things, his fatal flaw. Yet, like a moth to a flame, he would always return.

"Go," Ylena commanded the two in black. They bowed and disappeared in swirls of black smoke.

Edu leaned back in his throne and debated the facts he now knew. Lydia must have fought against Aon when he had murdered her friend and, if Navaa was speaking the truth, freed herself.

But things were never what they seemed. There was more at work here than what the warlock's regent would have him believe. Aon desired the power of the dreamers for his own ends; he always had. To think his attempt to influence Lydia for his own means was over was impossible.

And with how Lydia looked at Aon? How she smiled at him, that day in the city square before Edu had taken her life? He knew that expression well. He had seen it many times in his thousands of years of life.

She cared for the warlock.

Either she was mentally unwell, or more likely, the warlock had manipulated her. Tricked her into feeling such a thing over a creature who had no merit to warrant it.

Edu sighed heavily and stood from his throne. He would not dismiss his armies who readied and trained in the fields outside his home. They very well might still be needed. Soon, he may need to march against Aon *or* Lydia. And if Edu's nightmare came true... he would have to march against both.

His only prayer was that Lydia had truly come to understand the magnitude of Aon's treacherous soul. And there was only one way to find out.

"Master Edu will take your advice, Ms. Evelyn," Ylena addressed Evie where she still hovered in the shadows. "He will go speak to Lydia."

* * *

Maybe this place wasn't so bad.

It was freaky, that was for sure. It was spooky, eerie, and creepy in just about everything it did. All the cities looked like a convoluted, twisted mess of architecture from all over the world and throughout time.

One city reminded Lydia of Colonial Williamsburg. Old houses and old everything, mixed in with a smattering of modern tools and electricity. Another town felt like what she might have imagined ancient India to have looked like. The smell of the food had been incredible. But she was too afraid to go and ask for some—and besides, she didn't have money. Or anything to barter, for that matter.

Suddenly, she realized she had no idea how anything in Under actually *worked.*

But everywhere she went, there were people. Masked, unmasked, creatures, and humanoid. It was fascinating to watch them go about their day. Laughing, fighting, and, well—living.

This wasn't just a world of horror and monsters. Oh, sure, she had come across a Hellhound eating a woman the day before, pulling meat from her bones like someone might chow into a chicken leg. There was death and pain here in large numbers. She knew what that felt like now. She knew that woman would get up tomorrow like nothing had happened.

She still wasn't sure if that made it okay or not. The jury was still out on that. That was what had sent Evie over the edge to try to commit more permanent murder, after all. Evie couldn't take dying again and again, over and over, without end.

But now they all had "her" monsters to hunt. There was that at least.

Shoving her hands into the pockets of her coat, she walked through the city of M'url. It was the same one Aon had taken her to. That night had been so much fun. She wasn't sure why she came here or why she wanted to see it again.

You're sentimental, that's why. Or lonely. I vote both.

"Shut up, Q," she muttered to the snake that was curled up inside the hood of her coat. "I'm not lonely."

She had kept the long coat with a hood so that she could

hide her face as best she could. Otherwise, she quickly discovered she couldn't get anywhere or do anything without being stopped.

Or causing outright panic.

When she'd shown her face in that old colonial city, people had screamed and run away from her. One man had fallen to the ground in prayer, arms outstretched on the dirt in front of him like she was some vengeful god. She had begged him to get up, and he had only wept and cried and begged for his life.

So she had done the only reasonable thing.

She had turned around and run like hell.

Now she tried to go unseen and dressed in nothing turquoise that might give her away. She had her hood pulled up tight over her head, trying to hide the marks on her face. Wearing that awful excuse for a mask wouldn't help matters, that was for damn sure. But nobody paid any attention to her now that she looked nondescript. She just tried not to make eye contact.

You miss him.

It was a statement, not a question. Stupid snake. "Aon killed Nick. In front of me. It doesn't matter."

You still miss him.

"Fine! Could you stop rubbing it in?" she snapped at the little thing coiled around her neck. She could see his wings glowing from the corner of her eye.

Yeah, I just wanted you to admit it.

"You're a dick."

A little head nudged her cheek, nuzzling her. **Yup. And you loooooooove me.**

Sighing heavily, she shoved her hands further into her coat. At least she felt safe, wandering the streets of a strange world by herself. Q still counted as part of her, so technically, she was alone.

It'd been quite a few days since Lyon had visited her, and

she had struck out into the world, exploring somewhere new and learning about the world that was now hers. She slept anywhere she could find a spot, often off in the woods and tucked somewhere as quiet or protected as possible.

She felt a little like she was on the run. But in a lot of ways, she was. Afraid to go home because of what she knew would find her there. Afraid to stay in one place for too long because of what might find her if she did.

At least this was giving her time to think.

Clever Priest, that was probably the other half of the reason for the advice he gave her. Wandering around strange cities and seeing the sights of Under had given her time to walk it out.

Nick hadn't deserved to die. He hadn't done anything wrong, except that he'd been friends with her. If she hadn't known him—if he hadn't mattered to her—he'd still be alive. Maybe even alive on Earth. If the Ancients had schemed to pull all this off, they might have taken him just so Aon could kill him.

She wouldn't put it past them.

She didn't know what to think about the big, weird, creepy elder-things that lived, chained up as prisoners, in that lake of blood. One thing she was sure of, though, was that they loved to mess with people. And they thought way far in advance. To play the Priest, to play her, Aon, Edu, and everyone—took a lot of careful planning.

While she wasn't sure if there really was a God back home, here, there was no question. She knew they weren't the most benign of ancient primordial creatures either. That book on mythology she had read told her about how the Ancients had tortured the original kings and queens. How they had done terrible things to them, and that was why they were finally overthrown.

Idly, she wondered how much that had a hand in making Aon and Edu the way they were. The other kings and queens were probably just as messed up as the two she'd met. She couldn't really recall their names off the top of her head—the three letter bizarre names were strange and hard to retain. It was funny that her short nickname kind of fell into that pattern, though. *I wonder if they planned that too.*

The thought that she'd never see her friend again put a rock into her throat that was hard to clear. She swallowed it down and tried to let it be. People died. It happened all the time. Tragedy was a thing that everybody had to put up with sooner or later. She wasn't unique in her suffering or her loss. People lost people. That was called life. On Earth or on Under.

But how many people had to watch the man who loved them kill their best friend?

Let alone the man she loved in return.

Stupidly enough, she was sure she wasn't alone in that. Someone had felt this pain before her. Somebody had this situation play out on the stage of their lives, even if it wasn't so spectacularly melodramatic with the roles being filled by a warlock and a werewolf. She tried not to laugh at the insanity of it all.

Q, infuriatingly, wasn't wrong. She missed Aon and the sound of his voice. She had come to adore his playful, witty teasing, his dark sense of humor and his touch. She missed how she felt when he held her and how surprisingly affectionate he could be. She wanted to listen to him tell another story or show off some stupid trick he could do.

But Aon had killed Nick.

Maybe the reasons behind it had been the right ones. Aon had done it so nobody else could and so Edu or anyone else couldn't use his life as blackmail to control her. Aon had also done it to finally break her of the fear that had controlled her. The fear that had made her want to stay in the safety of his home, even if she was his prisoner.

Well, it had worked.

There just was no getting away from the fallout of it. Aon

had murdered her best friend in cold blood. Sometimes, the intent behind the action mattered. But sometimes, it didn't. Sometimes, the act was bad enough that it didn't matter why it was done.

But God damn, she really did miss him.

And she just had to figure out where on the scale of "did the intention matter" this act fell.

Something dropped quietly to the stones behind her. Stopping in her tracks, she paused, but didn't turn around. For a moment, she had a Schrodinger's problem. If she turned around, it was a problem. Maybe if she kept walking, it would just go away.

"Well, well, well..."

Nope.

This cat let itself out of the box.

Shutting her eyes, Lydia let out a long sigh. "Go away, Kamira."

"That is hardly a proper greeting! And here I have come all this way to see you."

Rubbing her hands over her face, she resigned herself to the conversation that was about to happen. There was no avoiding it. Especially considering what little she knew of the woman, she wasn't going to be able to convince the shifter to walk away. "How are you married to Lyon? I really don't get it."

The woman behind her burst into laughter and walked around to stand in front of her. "He wonders the same quite frequently. I assure you, he had little to do with our relationship."

Lydia couldn't help but snort a small laugh and looked up at the shapeshifter with a faint smile. "You hunted him down like a wounded gazelle on the Serengeti, didn't you?"

"Oh, you have no idea." Kamira grinned, the streetlamps glinting in her green cat's eyes. "He didn't complain too much, though, I promise." She was dressed in a long, tattered, black cloak that hung around her otherwise nearly naked form. She pushed the hood off her head and reached out to do the same to Lydia.

Lydia flinched but then let her pull the hood of her black coat down. No point in hiding now.

"Oh, by the Ancients. It *is* true." Kamira stepped into her, far too close for her liking, and ran the fingertips of both of her hands along Lydia's face. She was tracing the turquoise marks. The woman was a good six inches taller than she was, and it was intimidating at best, even considering Lydia's new state of being.

After a moment of letting the woman get far too personal with her, Lydia carefully brushed her hands away from her. Kamira obediently took half a step back but not nearly far enough for Lydia. The shifter wasn't repulsive; she was just intense. She wasn't quite sure what to do with a woman coming on to her so damn strong.

Kamira was watching her with rapt attention as if memorizing everything about her. "You are a miracle."

"I had nothing to do with it." She said it before, she'd say it again, and she was sure she'd say it a few more times before everything settled out.

"Oh, I know. Yet the world is restored, all the same." The shifter pulled in a breath and let it out slowly. "I have slept on the beach for the first time in nearly two thousand years. I hunted prey that was not one of our kin." Kamira beamed, and the woman was nearly gushing with joy. "I cannot express to you how grateful I am. Whether you had any choice in the matter or not, the fact remains the same. *Thank you,* sister."

Before Lydia could do anything about it, Kamira took her head in her hands and kissed her. Full, on the lips, *kissed her.* Lydia let out a loud *"Mmmmfn!"* and pushed the woman away with both hands. "Holy fuck, Kamira!"

Kamira was cackling in laughter, clearly enjoying how

utterly put out she was. She was grinning from ear to ear. "Come, now, I had to taste you once before the warlock took you back. He is so utterly selfish."

"Don't do that again."

"Very well, my queen." Kamira's bow was capped with an overdramatic flourish of her arms. "I shall heed your demands."

"Oh, knock it off." Lydia couldn't help but smirk. The woman was wildfire, but she was endearing in her own right. They all kind of were. Except maybe Otoi. "You're full of shit."

"Your friend used that phrase to describe me quite frequently. You modern children and your odd turns of phrase. You must teach me what they all mean." Kamira pulled her cloak closer over her and sniffed the air. "We have drawn attention."

"Let's walk and talk. Or you can go away." Lydia turned to keep walking the way she had originally been headed. "I vote you go away. But I don't think you'll listen."

Kamira fell in step next to her. "Don't be coy."

"I'm not being coy. I'm being annoyed. I don't want a crowd." Lydia pulled her hood back up over her head and shoved her hands inside her pockets. "I hate being on stage."

"Shame, then, that you are now a queen."

"Tell me about it."

"I do not know how to."

Lydia blinked and realized Kamira had taken her literally. She snickered and sighed. Talking to people that old was going to take some getting used to. "It's a phrase. It means, 'I agree with you.'"

"You could have simply said that instead."

"Language has fallen a long way since you were on Earth."

"Of that, there is no question." Kamira chuckled. "So, why are you avoiding everyone? You have flitted from place to place, running about, never tarrying in the same location long. It is quite hard to hunt someone who can move through space as a royal may do. It has been a challenge, but... why? Why run?"

"I'm not running. I'm exploring."

"You have slept in the trees. In alleyways and on the roofs of buildings. You are running. More importantly, you are hiding."

Lydia scratched the back of her neck. "Kamira, I don't want to have this conversation."

"I think," Kamira began, clearly readying herself for a profound statement, "you and I will have to become well acquainted. One, you are a queen, and two, a friend to my husband. Therefore, what I shall say next is something you should be aware of before we go much further in our relationship."

"What?" Lydia asked with no small semblance of dread.

"I do not *ever* give up."

Lydia groaned and looked up at the stars and moons overhead, silently asking whoever was listening why she had to put up with this crap. "What was your question again?"

"Why are you running? From whom are you hiding? Are you afraid Aon will find you?"

"No. Aon's not after me. He'll leave me alone until I tell him I'm ready, trust me." Honestly, she wasn't. Aon was smart enough and respectful enough to give her space after what he had done. "I'm afraid of Edu."

Kamira let out a thoughtful noise as she twirled one of her long dreadlocks between her fingers. "You fear what Edu may do when he finds you. But not Aon? Interesting."

"I don't want to see either of them right now."

"For different reasons, I assume. One killed your friend. The other killed you."

Blunt but succinct. She'd give Kamira that much. "In short? Sure. I'm also not sure if Edu is going to try to kill me harder a second time. I don't particularly want to find out."

Kamira hummed and looked up at the night sky. It was

clear, and the stars were on full display. "I barely knew this world before Aon's Great War began. I was only around four hundred years old when it started."

Lydia snorted. "Yeah, a regular spring chicken."

"Feh!" Kamira laughed. "You mortals. Time passes differently when you are this old. In those days, we were numerous in those who were two, three thousand years, even at that time. Most of them died during the war."

"How many died?"

"Many, many millions. Countless. We were cut in half, even before Aon destroyed a whole House in his wrath."

Lydia paused and let out a long breath. Half the world, and a whole House. Everyone had talked about how costly Aon's war had been, but she hadn't really known the numbers until now. It was fascinating how one death—like Nick—was a tragedy. But millions of deaths became so enormous in scope to understand, it became meaningless. Her mind couldn't wrap around a world being that deeply maimed.

Maybe Aon really was a monster.

If only she knew why he had done it. Why he had killed Qta. Maybe that would help everything make more sense.

But, sometimes, the intent behind an action didn't matter. Sometimes, no matter how hard you wanted to do things for the right reasons, the methods were still so wrong there was no defending it. Millions of lives...

Kamira broke Lydia out of her thoughts. "I barely remember what this world was like before the void came for us. I have not seen the stars in fifteen hundred years, Lydia. Edu remembers the stars. He was ancient when I arrived. He was older than our most long-lived Earthen civilizations, even then. Perhaps to him, this is not such a miracle. Perhaps to him, dignity and revenge are all that matter. I do not know. He and I are friends, but we are not... eh, what is your word for it? Near?"

"Close."

"That one."

Lydia found herself smiling despite herself. The woman was funny in her own, far-too-assertive way. "Where are you from originally, Kamira?"

"Me? Why?"

"I'm curious." And Lydia desperately needed to change the subject away from Aon's bloody past.

Kamira shrugged. "Tartessos."

"I have no clue where the hell that is." Lydia laughed. "I liked history but not that much."

"I think you creatures call it Spain now or some such nonsense. South, by the ocean. Oh, how I have missed the ocean!"

"Yeah, you said." Lydia smiled. That was what it meant to people to have their world back. It was becoming increasingly hard to hate her new role in this world when she saw the joy it brought them. "If Edu doesn't fuck it up, you can keep sleeping on them."

Kamira's happiness switched to weariness, and she sighed. "Yes. The Red King. I will do what I can. None of the other Houses will support him, if he tries to destroy you. I can promise you that."

"You so sure? You all decided to have me killed once already."

"Twice," Kamira said with a sneer. Lydia stammered in shock, but Kamira interrupted. "Never mind, never mind. It does not matter."

Sure, it didn't! Twice? *Son of a bitch, these assholes were out to get me.* "You were all shitting your pants about a sad little mortal girl, weren't you?"

"Yes, indeed, we were." Kamira snickered before letting out a whoosh of air in a sigh. "I have conferred with the others. I am the only one who might even think to stand with Edu. And seeing you now, seeing the stars, and this world restored? I cannot. Edu will be on his own, if he comes to harm you."

"That's great. But will you help me?"

"I do not think you will need our help." Kamira smirked at her knowingly. "You will have your warlock at your side, will you not?" Kamira leaned into her like a gossip at the prom. "I can smell him on you."

"Gah!" Lydia pushed her away from her. "That's disgusting. I don't smell like him!"

Kamira howled in laugher and slung an arm around Lydia's shoulder, hugging her into the shifter's side forcefully. Lydia nearly staggered and fell with the force of the embrace. "Oh, you are so shy! Of course, you do. Do not forget what I am. I can smell a great deal of things."

"Don't tell me. I really don't need to know. And that's still disgusting." She made a face. Kamira was grinning as she held Lydia to her like they were the best of friends. Lydia had no idea what to do except just go along with it.

"Do you mean to deny you have not lain with the warlock? And several times, I think? Do you mean to tell me that was not a trace of him on your lips I tasted when I kissed you?" Kamira looked down at her gleefully. "It was not so bad, I find. Fascinating."

Lydia shoved Kamira off her and growled in frustration. The woman was impossible. "Fuck off, Kamira."

"That, I believe, was not a no."

Lydia put a hand over her eyes. "I hate you."

"No, you don't." Kamira was snickering and grinning again. "And that was still not a denial."

"What do you want from me?"

"I want to know the lay of the land. There are heady politics at work, and I despise nothing more in this world than such games. You wander this world, lost in your grief for Nicholas, but I see in you no anger at the man responsible for his death."

"Are you trying to say I'm not pissed Nick is dead?" She shot a glare at the shapeshifter, who seemed entirely unfazed by the insult.

"Of course, you are. But I do not see you, the creature who decked Otoi with a tray for daring to speak out of turn, raging against the man who did the deed." Kamira's face darkened in anger. "I am beside myself that the boy is dead. He was my pup. My newest child to my pack. I would storm Aon's home and strangle him with my bare hands if I could. But I am not a queen. You are. And yet you mourn in peace. Why?"

"Kamira, please."

"He was mine. He belonged to my House. But I cannot pursue payment for his death. You can, and yet, you have not. I *demand* to know why."

"I don't think I answer to you." Lydia shot Kamira an angry glare. "I don't think I have to explain shit to you, you freak."

Kamira grinned wide, a predatory expression. "So quickly she learns. I've watched you. I've seen that little glowing creature that follows you about."

There goes my sick entrance, I guess.

Kamira continued, blissfully unaware of Q's comment inside her head. "I think you could defeat me in a fight, should it come to it. But," Kamira straightened her shoulders, "I have not come for that. I came to see the new Queen of Dreams. To tell her I am sorry for my part in her death. I only involved myself to spare Nicholas, and it did no good in the end."

Once more, it turned out that Aon hadn't been lying. Edu had come for Nick, and Kamira had shot him down and offered her own help in exchange. Lydia sighed sadly. "I know. It's... it's okay. I've forgiven everyone else. I might as well forgive you too."

"That is noble of you. I do not deserve your pardon, but I will take it thankfully."

"Will you leave me alone in exchange?"

"No."

Lydia let out a tired laugh. "You're the fucking worst, Kamira."

"If you asked my husband, I think he would beg exactly the opposite."

It took a half second for the joke to register. But when it did, she looked over at the shifter woman with a shocked expression before bursting out in laughter. Kamira joined her in the peal before the two of them faded into an amiable silence for a few moments.

"May I call you Lydia?"

"Don't call me 'queen' or 'mistress' or any other bullshit, so yeah. That or Lyd. Nick called me that."

"I will call you Lyd, then. In his honor." Kamira smiled faintly. "He had promise. He was a good man. He whined... oh, by the Ancients, that boy could *whine*."

Lydia chuckled, agreeing. Grief plucked at the wound in her heart, drawing fresh blood.

Kamira continued to speak, her voice softer, seeing the pained expression on her face. "But he was a good man. A good shifter. He would have led a pack of his own in time. And he was voracious in his need to protect you. You were his packmate to him. His family."

"He died because of me." There were the tears again, and Lydia did everything in her power to bite them back.

"Yes. He did. I will not issue platitudes at you to say otherwise. But he died because of his family. Because of someone he saw as his own. Any of us would pray to die with honor in such a way. He will be remembered."

Lydia was silent for a long, long time, looking down as they walked. The cobblestones were beautiful in their uneven, long-worn pattern. Rubbed smooth by what must be a thousand years or more of people passing by. They were the proof of all the time that had passed. Tiny, individual monuments to a hundred million footsteps.

Kamira had asked why she wasn't angry.

"I'm in love with Aon."

Silence hung between them like the world itself was holding its breath. Kamira made no noise as she walked; not even her dozens of bits of jewelry jingled as she moved. The only sound was Lydia's boots on the stones that glinted, still damp from the recent rain, in the moonlight.

Lydia took a breath. "He was given a prophecy, the day I came back from the dead. Ziza said a king would rise to destroy me and a friend would be my undoing. Aon didn't kill Nick to hurt me. He killed Nick to protect me. The man I love murdered my best friend to save me from the words of some glorified, undead puddle monsters."

Kamira was silent.

"Tell me how I'm supposed to feel about that, Kamira. Give me advice on that, and I'll take it."

It was the first time she confessed her feelings out loud. It felt good. Cathartic, in a way. "I'm angry at him. I'm furious. I want to scream and break things. I want to bash his head into the stones until he's goo. He made me watch as he murdered Nick. I had to kneel there, helpless, as he died. All because I was too afraid to stop Aon. I could have. But I didn't think he would go that far. I didn't think he'd hurt me that badly."

Lydia was on a rant, one she had been building up for a solid week now. "I wanted to feel safe. I wanted to feel like everything was going to be okay. All I want—more than anything—is for everyone to leave me the hell alone for a hot second. Ever since I came to this stupid world, people have been trying to kill me, scare me, hunt me, fuck me, or all the above! And just—*just*—when I felt like I was getting my legs under me, Edu killed me. I died. I died, *for real*. Not this fake *fucking* bullshit you people go through every goddamn day. I know the difference now. It's not the same.

"Then I wake up on the shores of that stupid pond, and now I have to deal with *this* shit. Anywhere else and you assholes would have thrown me a parade. But not Under! Oh, no. Aon tortures me to get me to fight back, but I'm too afraid to try. I'd rather let him gut me like a fish than to step out into this world. Why? Because of Lyon betraying me. Because of Edu killing me. Because this world has wanted nothing but to make me suffer since day one. I could put up with that. I could put up with Stabby McDouchebag and his 'lessons in pain.' But then... Nick. Then he killed Nick. And that was too goddamn far.

"So now, I'm hiding. Yes. I am. I admit it. Because Edu is probably going to kill me again. Why? Because 'reasons,' I don't know. Because he wants to piss Aon off. And screw what I want, because I clearly don't get a say in any of this. So good for you, Kamira. You got to sleep on the *fucking beach*!"

Lydia's angry monologue finally died off, and she let out a long whoosh of air from her lungs. She was shaking with the adrenaline-fueled rant she had just unleashed on the woman who was still walking beside her. Kamira was watching her, wide-eyed, stunned by the tirade.

"Fuck." Lydia finally said, far quieter than her tone had been a moment prior. "Sorry. It's been a hell of a few months."

"I think perhaps that speech was not meant for me," Kamira said thoughtfully after a long moment of silence. "I think perhaps you should repeat that for Edu. It is at him that you should rail."

"What good will it do? He'll just set me on fire."

"Edu likely thinks you are a puppet of the warlock. That you love him, I find... impossible. But miracles have abounded as of late. A mortal girl rejected from the pond, who then dies and rises as the queen of a dead House? Who am I to say that you do not mean your words?" Kamira smiled at her gently, and it was the first time her expression wasn't vaguely threatening. "I am happy for him. He is—for once in his long, pathetic, and desolate life—lucky."

"Please don't tell anyone what I said."

"Does the warlock know?"

Lydia shook her head. "Too much was happening all at once. It didn't feel right to tell him."

Kamira let out a small hum. "Wise. I will tell no one, least of all my husband. It would be a spare second before he burst into Aon's home to relay the news like an overeager puppy. Your secret is safe with me."

"Thanks."

Kamira shrugged. "As for the rest of your predicament? I say do not forgive Aon until you are ready. If that means tomorrow, or if it means never, that is up to you. Neither is the correct answer unless you wish it to be. You will not betray Nick's memory with forgiveness. Aon will pay for that crime soon enough."

"What do you mean?"

"There will be a trial. Aon has abdicated his role as ruling king to Edu in light of his crime. We must all sit in judgement of the man and decide his punishment."

Threaten me with a good time. "Do I have to? Never mind, never mind," she interrupted Kamira before she could speak. "Queen. Right. Got it." Lydia let out a groan and ended it with a weary sigh. "When?"

"When you and Edu may sit in the same room without violence. If that ever comes to pass. Which brings me to my other piece of advice—go home. Go to the temple, build your world. Face the King of Flames. You say you were nothing but a frightened mortal girl? I saw a woman so hopelessly out of her league, helpless against everything that surrounded her, with the gall to stand on her own feet. Be so again. Tell Edu where he may go sheath his sword, if you must. He will respect that."

Lydia looked off thoughtfully, debating Kamira's words. The shifter was making a lot of very good points. "What if I lose?"

"Then this whole adventure was for naught. But at least," Kamira smirked, "I got to sleep once more on the 'fucking beach.'"

Lydia laughed and couldn't help but enjoy her sharp humor. Lydia had been on the run for a week. She couldn't keep this up. She had been avoiding Edu since the moment she came back to life. If she didn't let this happen, Edu would find her eventually, anyway.

"I really don't want to die a second time."

"Then don't."

"I'll do this. If," Lydia took in a deep breath, held it for a second, and let it out, "you won't try to kiss me again."

A flash of white teeth in a wicked grin. "I make no promises."

SEVENTEEN

It had been a week since Lydia left the Temple of Dreams, and it looked like it had been busy while she was gone.

Magic was frickin' *weird*.

Standing at the edge of the huge reflecting pool, she looked around her "home." It still felt weird and foreign to think of it that way. But it seemed it was working hard to try to make it feel more familiar. If she couldn't go home to Boston, maybe some of Boston could come to her.

The architecture had officially gotten a little bit... messed up.

Wrought iron railings jutted up from the ground and twisted with the monolithic stone blocks. Brown brick mixed with vines. It was still a jungle, with leafy shrubs and fronds growing over polished stone and steel as if it had always been there. Everything was far too angular—warped with sharp-edged spirals. Instead of stacked stone monolithic columns, ionic Greek-styled ones that resembled those on the front of the Museum of Fine Arts, rose from the dirt instead.

Makin' yourself at home.

"I guess." Shaking her head, she stared at her surroundings in confusion. "It's not like I'm trying."

Dreamer.

Sitting on the edge of the stone block that ringed the reflecting pool, she shrugged. The pool still had a lot of the Aztec-esque influence, which she liked. But it now far more resembled the pond out by the Opera House instead. Even the buildings that ringed the pool looked more familiar than they had before. But it was somehow trying to be both part of what Qta once was and what Lydia was now, all at once.

I mean, it makes sense. You are about as Aztec as bratwurst.

Snorting in laughter at Q's joke, she watched as he swirled up overhead to dive into the pool with a splash. It still looked very deep, judging by how quickly the glow from his wings disappeared beneath the waves.

She was still wearing a few layers from exploring Under, and it felt far too hot in the thick of the jungle. Looking down at her arms, she *willed* herself to be wearing something different. She was still getting used to using her magic. Her clothing changed in the blink of an eye. Cargo pants, a tank top, and screw it—it was a jungle—no shoes. She shifted to sit with her feet over the edge of the block into the pond and stuck one of her feet in the water. The water was cooler than the air. It felt nice.

Aren't you afraid something's going to chomp your toes?

"Nah." It was true; she wasn't. She had met quite a few of her dreamed-up monsters over the past week, and they all seemed to adore her. She felt like Doctor Dolittle from hell. "Nothing in there's going to bite me. Except you, maybe."

Q's glowing wings appeared beneath the level of the water, and he slithered up onto her foot, looking up at her, holding onto her calf with his wings.

Meh, maybe later.

Suddenly, Lydia realized something. A sound that had been there since she came back. But so small, so normal, that she overlooked it. Crickets. Chirping insects were singing their song to each other all around her. She smiled.

More things she had apparently brought back, just by living. "I get it, I get it..." It was another reminder of why this happened to her. Why she had to suffer through all that she did. Too bad she didn't trust the fact that her misery was over. Really, she had the sinking sensation it was only just beginning.

Reaching down, she picked up her necklace and looked down at the little blinking false insect in the glass chrysalis. The memory of that day in the marketplace stung for two reasons.

One, because it had been the day she died.

Two, because right up until that point, she had been happy. She had been with Aon, and things had just started to be okay. He had been so offended at the merchant's insinuation that the little ball of magic in the glass chrysalis had been somehow sentient or had moods. No matter how hard she tried, she couldn't keep her mind from straying back to the topic of the warlock. "Pretty soon, I bet your real-life counterparts will come back," she said to the chrysalis quietly. "I really hope they do."

Poof! They just did. Look.

Turning her gaze up from the chrysalis and away from her looming thoughts, she gasped. More than just the stars were reflected in the surface of the water. There were a thousand more points of light than before. But these were blinking like fireflies, arcing through the air in their heedless pattern of colors.

Unlike fireflies, these insects came in every color. Even, just like the false critter in her necklace, an impossible black.

"I just did that?"

You did. Q crawled up her legs, using his claws to dig into her cargo pants like a cat to get there. Sitting in her lap, he watched one of the bugs swing close to him, and he snapped at the bug, playfully trying to eat it. **You wanted them back. And so? Poof. They're back.**

"If I had any confidence that I was going to survive the next few months—if not few hours—of my life, I'd be much happier about this." In awe, she watched the beautiful dancing array of insects as they spread out from the pond and into the jungle. "You really think that Edu isn't going to try and kill me again?"

I have no idea. I'd like to think he isn't that stupid. Well, he isn't. But he really might be that angry at Aon. And—Q disappeared in a blink of an eye just as a roar of fire from behind her illuminated the stones around her. There was a warmth at her back that dissipated as quickly as it had come. **Speaking of. I think we're about to find out.**

Fear and dread were old friends to her now.

Turning, she saw the source of the flame. Edu, in full armor, standing about twenty feet away from her. He must have appeared in a rush of fire that left the grass around his feet singed and burned black.

Lydia remembered how scared she had been of him the first time she had seen him on the streets of Boston. His armor reflected the light of the moons, accentuating the long horns and the arching carapace-like spines. He was still a nightmare to her, but now for very different reasons. He was no longer impossible. She knew he existed and knew what this world was capable of. That night on the street of Boston, he had been a creature from outside reality. Now he was more terrifying to her in a very, very different way.

Now she knew exactly what kind of horror he could bring her.

The memory of him burning out her heart made her nauseated. But she tried to look brave as she swiveled around and stepped off the stone to face the man. He was in full armor, carrying that massive, wicked sword of his. He had come for a fight, and she was unarmed and in a tank top and barefoot.

Whatever.

Don't you wish you looked queenlier now?

Not the time, Q.

Ylena stood at Edu's side, her hands folded neatly in front of her. "Master Edu greets you, Mistress Lydia."

She did her best to sound assertive. "Go away, Edu. Just turn around and leave. You're not welcome here."

Edu tilted his head to the side and back slightly. "Master Edu takes no offense at your sentiment. It is understandable, considering what happened when you and he last met."

"Oh, you mean when you fucking *killed* me?" She didn't even try to keep the anger out of her voice. "Go away, Edu. I don't want to see you, and I certainly don't want to stand here and talk to you. Especially not when you're decked out for a fight."

"He fears you have little choice in the matter. He has come to discern whether you are a threat to Under."

"Screw you. You've already made up your damn mind, and we both know it. You've wanted me dead since day one. You only want to talk to me to see if you have a good excuse to kill me a second time, that's all. Don't lie to me."

"Master Edu insists he has not made up his mind."

"Right. Sure. Well, I'm not going to give you anything to clear your conscience. If you're here for a fight, then just get on with it."

"If it comes to it, he does not think there will be much of a fight." Edu tilted his head the other way, eyeing her, clearly deciding she wasn't a threat.

She might not be, but Q had yet to play his hand. "Uh-huh." She sighed and rubbed a hand over her face. "So, what do I have to do to get you to leave me alone?"

"Do you serve the warlock?"

"Again, with that bullshit line of reasoning. 'Do you serve the warlock?'" Lydia mocked Ylena's tone as she repeated the question. "No. I don't. I don't, and I never have. Not then, and certainly not now. But that wasn't good enough for you last time, before you burned out my heart, was it? You aren't going to believe me, so why waste time and ask the question?"

Oh, man, you're feisty when you're angry. I love it.

"Master Edu wonders, then, why you spent time willingly in his presence while you were mortal. You were not his shrinking, weeping prisoner."

Lydia wouldn't deny it. She could have refused to be anywhere near Aon. But she had been fascinated with him and drawn to him like a moth to a flame. But Edu didn't need to know that part. She had plenty of other good reasons to turn it around on him. "Because, unlike some people around here, he wasn't a complete asshole to me. He treated me with as much respect as he was capable of. He didn't lock me in a cell, try to bone me the first chance he got, or then decide to kill me."

Edu was silent—or rather, Ylena was—for a long moment. "Master Edu does not feel the need to apologize for his actions. With the information he had then, he would have repeated his decisions. But he understands why you feel slighted by him."

"Slighted? Slighted!" Laughing, she pointed at him before she went to continue her argument. It was then that she realized she was holding a dagger. It had a carved gold handle and a black obsidian blade. Somewhere she remembered obsidian could be sharper than steel. When she got it, how she got it, she didn't know. Maybe she summoned it in her anger. Either way, she pointed it at him now. "Is that what you call what you did? Aon didn't make me into the Queen of Dreams. *You* did. You're to blame for me and this whole mess. Go home and leave me be."

"You still insist that Aon had no knowledge of what you would become. Master Edu finds this impossible to believe.

Why would he have looked after you so intently, if you did not benefit him in some way?"

"Maybe, just maybe, because he isn't the complete bastard you think he is. Oh, he has his moments, don't get me wrong. Trust me." Shaking her head, she gripped the handle of the knife tightly. It was comforting, even if it was a stupid weapon against a man with a broadsword. "But of the two of you? He has the better manners, by far."

"You do not understand what you say."

"When I woke up like this, I was terrified to use my power because of what *you* would do to me. In an attempt to get me to spread my proverbial wings, he autopsied me alive. He killed my best friend and made me watch, Edu. Don't you think I know what he's capable of?"

"He destroyed over half the lives that lived in this world. He doomed it to the void. He has, for the past five thousand years, been nothing but a bane to all those who would call this place home. Aon is, and shall ever be, irredeemable in all things he does."

"Then what do you want me to say?" Lydia shouted. "What could I possibly say to convince you? You aren't here to listen to me, clearly. I don't believe Aon knew anything about what was going to happen to me."

"Then why did he dote on you? Why not keep you in the same manner he keeps all his other 'guests?' Tortured and tormented?"

Because Aon loved her. But she couldn't say those words to him. She couldn't do that to the warlock—she couldn't embarrass him like that. Besides, Edu would never believe her. Worse yet, if Edu *did* believe her, he might kill her just to hurt Aon. "Because he was bored. I don't know!"

"You lie. What transpired in his estate when you were mortal? What plots did he hatch with you?"

"Plots?" Lydia snickered. "Do you know what I did while I

was there? I wandered his house. I asked him stupid questions. I watched him take notes. I put back his goddamn books in his library. Maybe he enjoyed having some company who didn't instantly assume the worst about him."

"You slept with him."

"Go to hell, tin can." That was her new favorite nickname for Edu, she decided. "That is none of your goddamn business. And coming from you, that's rich. I thought sex here wasn't a big deal?"

"You do not deny it?"

"No, because I'm not ashamed of it. Yes. We've slept together. News of the century, story at eleven. Are you happy now?"

"Willingly?"

That made her laugh. "That's rich. Says the guy who propositioned me mid-orgy from his personal fuck-stage? You have absolutely no business judging either of us on the subject."

Edu watched her for a long time, unmoving. "You defend his honor. Why?"

"I am not defending his honor, ass-wipe. I'm defending mine."

"No. You argue that Edu has wronged you, yet the warlock has not. He has held you prisoner in a cage since you returned from the dead. He murdered your friend. Yet you see fit to argue on his behalf. Why do you not despise him for what he has done?"

"You murdered me, Edu. You don't get to play righteous right now."

Edu tilted his head slightly to the side. "Master Edu observes that you are dodging the question. Do you denounce the warlock for all that he has done?"

Lydia gripped the handle of the blade in her hand tighter. "I don't serve him. I'm not his slave, and I'm not his mindless puppet. I never have been."

"Master Edu insists you answer the question. Do you condemn him for his murder of Nicholas?"

"Are you asking me to condemn you for the same crime, Edu?"

"You were mortal. It is different."

Lydia paced away a step, laughing at the ludicrous argument. "The only way it's different is that you committed the deed. Even if I had stupid marks or a mask at the time, you would have still killed me if you thought the warlock 'plotted' something. That's what you're doing now. You've come here to kill me because you hate him. No other reason."

"Master Edu asks once more why you do not share his sentiment in hating the man."

"Because I don't!" She whirled toward Edu. Something strange happened then. It was as though she were touching the side of an electrical generator. Like she had been plugged into a wall socket, but... without the pain. It just kind of tingled. Looking down at her hand, a strange turquoise electricity was snapping between the tip of the blade and her fingers. It coiled up around her wrist.

Marks, turquoise and thin, surged on the surface of her arms, fading in and out. Apparently, when she was mad, she could summon lightning now. Fun.

"Then either Nicholas was not valuable to you or you have no soul of your own."

"Fuck you, Edu!" The words left her in a scream as the electricity arced further up both her arms. "Nick was my best friend. I'm furious at Aon for murdering him. I had to watch Nick die! But I know why Aon did it. And because of that, I can't hate him."

"Whatever he said was a lie, and—"

"Ziza says otherwise!"

Ylena broke off, and Edu's posture stiffened. "You went to see her?"

"Aon told me about a prophecy Ziza gave him. I had to go see if it was true. Do you know why Nick died, Edu? Do you know why Aon did it? So you couldn't use him against me, like you already tried to do the night you killed me. In his sick mind, he was doing it to protect me—from *you!*"

Edu twitched as if she had slapped him. He stood there for a long moment, and even Ylena looked surprised. "Repeat the prophecy."

"That a king will rise to destroy me and a friend will be my undoing. And here we are. Step one, check. And Edu? The only person who has tried to manipulate me so far has been you. Aon never tried to use Nick against me. You did."

Edu shook his head. "You are blind to his crimes. You cannot see what he has done to your mind. He has warped you, twisted you, molded you to his desires. It is clear you cannot be saved."

Edu hefted his sword and pointed the tip at Lydia. She swallowed reflexively. This man was five thousand years old and the best fighter in Under. Even if she had Q and weird powers now, she knew this wasn't going to go well.

"I don't want to fight you, Edu." Namely, because she was going to lose.

"Then do not. Accept what he must do."

"Killing me dooms the world again. Don't you care?"

"No. Better the void than what Aon would make of this world as the King of All. For thousands of years, he has coveted the power you wield. Now you have given it to him. Shame. Edu hoped you were stronger than this."

"I'm not brainwashed, you metal-clad moron!"

"Master Edu begs to differ."

Growling, she looked up at the stars. "Just because I don't hate him for what he did, you think I'm his puppet. Well, you know what, Edu? I don't hate you for murdering me either. I get why you did it. I'm angry at you, just as I'm angry at Aon for killing Nick. Both of you are just epic shitheads doing the wrong things for the right reasons."

"While Master Edu hopes you speak the truth, it begs one more question. Why did Aon release you?"

"He killed Nick. I got angry, and I took him down. Then I left. He didn't let me go."

"Were you in chains?"

She paused. "No."

"Aon has the power to contain you, if he wished it. He could have kept you his prize in a cage. Yet he let you go. Why?"

She knew the answer. Fuck if she was going to tell him. "Go ask him yourself. I don't know."

"What reason did he give you?"

She shrugged. "He didn't. I didn't know he could. I don't know how any of this bullshit works."

Edu tilted his head again. "You rose a queen, yet you are still ignorant of this world and its ways?"

"Yup. Well, mostly."

"Mostly?"

"Mostly." She whistled.

Q suddenly rose from the ground—from within the earth —coming up from the dirt like a ghost might move through the floor of a house. He was huge, some seventy feet long, as he loomed up over Edu and Ylena. Both staggered backward, startled at the unexpected creature. His turquoise wings were glowing and casting odd, ghastly light on everything around him.

"Boo, motherfuckers."

"This is Q. He's me. He's everything I should be, but... I was dead. Asking a dead girl to take on all that is more than I could handle without going insane. So I made him instead."

"Hey, Machoman. Hey, Blinky," Q sarcastically greeted Edu and Ylena. **"If you wanna tango, you'll be dancing with me."**

Edu gripped the hilt of his sword tight enough that his armor audibly creaked. He raised it and took a defensive stance, looking up at the massive winged snake as Q sat there, reared up, the claws of his wings digging into the dirt in front of him.

"This is not possible."

"She doesn't look so helpless now, does she?"

"More trickery," Ylena hissed through her teeth. Edu was getting emotional, and the barrier between him and his psychic interpreter was breaking down. "More of the warlock's games at work."

"I'm a what, now? I am one hundred percent, bona-fide me, Chump. Aon couldn't even start to think up something as magnificent as this."

"No. A queen, with barely any power to show for it, save for a monster such as you? You are a figment of his magic. You are how he controls her."

"Yuh-huh, 'kay, sure. Man, you're uppity. Maybe you need to get laid more—oh, wait."

"Enough of this. You are a perversion of the warlock. Both of you. This cannot stand!" Edu's blade burst into flame.

Lydia had never been in a fight before.

Now, it seemed, that was going to change.

EIGHTEEN

There was much that seemed awry to Edu. So many portions of the equation did not add up as he talked to Lydia, the risen Queen of Dreams. The mortal girl, rejected by the Ancients, murdered by him, and then... brought back as this.

When he found her, she argued, spirited and passionate with him. Edu had held a hard line to push the edges of her reasoning. To see if she was a façade of a woman, pretending to be whole. He needled and pushed and insisted he did not believe her words, to edge her into the madness she had suffered.

Either due to her rise or due to Aon, he did not know. But Edu had not expected to find a sane girl. No one could have born the burden of such power without losing themselves in the exchange. It could not be possible.

What he had found had been worse than what he could have imagined. He had expected Lydia to either be Aon's mindless puppet or a shattered creature, devoid of any attachment to reality. Instead, he found a woman who believed she was still whole—free of the corruptive spread of the warlock's influence.

And one who somehow, for some inexplicable reason, did not despise Aon as she should.

That was reason enough to be suspicious. Aon had held her captive as a queen. For what reasons, Edu could not fathom. She claimed it was to "protect" her, but that was a sham. For what possible inspiration could Aon have to shelter the girl?

Lydia said there was a prophecy, given to Aon, that had inspired him to kill her friend. He would have written it off immediately as a lie but that the girl had been clever enough to confirm it for herself with the Oracle.

Is it possible he cares for the girl? Edu dismissed the thought as quickly as it had come. Aon felt no such thing for anyone. The only remaining choice was that there was foul play at work. He could just not yet see the game for what it was.

Stranger than her inability to hate Aon, he could not sense in Lydia the magnitude of magic and influence that he should. It was as though she were muted somehow. At first, Edu believed perhaps Aon's twisted plan hand gone awry. That he was able to bestow upon her only a fraction of what she should contain.

That was, until the creature had risen from the dirt to fight him.

The glowing-winged, ghastly snake that had loomed up before him like a phantom was *impossible.* In that creature, Edu could finally feel the hum of power that always followed a king or queen. This thing defied the laws of Under in every way Edu understood. There was only one explanation—Aon was to blame.

The warlock was to blame for all of this. The girl's arrival, her rejection from the Pool of the Ancients the first time, and now her unnatural state. Even Lydia's death at his hands was merely a chess move by the warlock. A careful ploy to let the girl project her blame onto Edu, instead of harboring hatred toward the man himself.

All to control her. Manipulate her. Wield her for his own ends.

Edu was certain.

It was for that reason that he decided she could not survive. Damn the world once more to the void as it may, he did not care.

Aon wished to become the King of All.

Edu would rather die.

* * *

Well, this sucked.

And now she was probably going to die.

Again.

For real.

Again.

Lydia and Q were holding their own—technically her own, she supposed—but she wasn't ready to go toe-to-toe with Under's oldest and most skilled warrior. Edu wasn't as stupid as Aon made him out to be. He quickly figured out that Q couldn't die and was fighting through the winged snake to get to her.

Q was doing damage but not enough to keep Edu down. Edu, meanwhile, hacked the snake in half several times in succession. Each time his sword cleaved Q in two, the snake would fall to the ground, thrashing and screeching, only to dissolve into smoke and reappear a moment later, furious.

If Edu was bleeding, it was impossible to tell through his armor. All Lydia knew was that every time Q went down, Edu would come straight for her, intending to take her head right off. There would be no gentle death this time. This wasn't euthanasia—this was war.

It was amazing what adrenaline could do. Lydia was hitting back at Edu with everything she didn't know she had in her.

Lightning. Daggers she could summon and throw with accuracy she certainly hadn't owned before. Hell, at one point, she summoned a spear that stuck into his armor. She'd been proud of herself for a hot second, until she realized she hadn't done any actual damage.

Edu blocked one dagger with his blade and took another to the arm. The obsidian pierced through his armor and into his flesh, but he didn't even make a noise of pain. It was as though the knife wasn't even there, for as little as it bothered him.

The fight dragged on for what felt like hours. In all honesty, it was probably only minutes. Rocks were shattered, earth was scorched. Lydia was bleeding from a cut on her side when Edu got too close and made a narrow pass with his sword. Time felt like it moved slower as the three of them tangled. Her, her monstrous snake, and Edu.

She suspected it from the beginning, but it was starting to become painfully clear...

Edu was going to win.

She was going to die.

Again.

Her heart was racing, and she was sweating. She ached, and she might have a cracked rib from when Edu had thrown her into one of the boulders that ringed the reflecting pool. She was limping, bruised, battered, and bleeding.

Edu pinned Q to the dirt with his sword, driving it through his midsection and deep into the ground. Q thrashed and let out a high-pitched screech, writhing in agony and trying to get loose. But her snake couldn't pull himself free.

"Let me *up!*"

She could only back away—too tired to fight any longer— too scared of what was going to happen, as Edu stalked toward her. He didn't need his sword to end her life. They both knew it.

"Master Edu regrets your fate, Lydia. He did then, he does

now. You do not deserve what the warlock did to you," Ylena said from where she stood nearby, having passively watched the fight like it had been a tennis match.

Between gasps of air, she still took shelter in her defiance of the man. "You're the one trying to kill me for the second time, Edu... not him."

"He warped you, corrupted you, used his ill-gotten powers to create what you now are. Master Edu wishes you could see that he is righteous in this act."

"That's a lie, Edu. This is all the work of your stupid puddle monsters. They sent me out a mortal. They sent me out a second time like this. Not Aon. He had nothing to do with any of this shit-show, save trying to protect me."

"And that is the cruelest joke of all of this, that you believe such blatant falsehoods." Edu was only a few steps away from her now.

She turned to run, seeing no shame in taking off for the woods. In a flash, Edu was in front of her, cutting her off at the pass. With a sweep of his arm, he knocked her to the ground hard. The fall was painful, stunning her for a precious second.

And one half second too long.

A gauntleted fist twisted in her hair, and she was wrenched back up to standing.

"You will die on your feet. You have fought bravely, and fought well for your age and lack of training. Master Edu will give you this honor."

She couldn't even scream, couldn't even find the strength or time to shout or argue as Edu summoned his own dagger to his hand. As the blade came down toward her throat, something impacted Edu hard enough to hurtle him sideways violently with extreme inertia.

She stood there, stunned and untouched, feeling like the vase of flowers on a table left behind by the yanked-out sheet in the famous parlor trick.

She was shaking. Trembling like a leaf in the wind. She pressed her hand to her side where the wound was, but it was already healing. If she survived long enough, it'd be gone in an hour.

Q was still struggling to free himself from under Edu's sword. He was making progress, but it was slow going. That left one question; what had hit Edu?

"So ready are we to doom the world back to the void? Although you always were a jealous one. Did you want to know what it felt like to destroy the world as well, old friend?"

Aon.

The warlock had appeared, standing some fifteen feet away. What had hit Edu had been a runaway train of black fire. It had bowled the King of Flames into a building, and he was now pulling himself out of the rubble. That seemed to have really hurt him. His left arm was hanging limp at his side. He grabbed it with his right hand and snapped his shoulder back into his socket with a sickening *crunch*.

"You came to save your pet," Ylena hissed angrily, the line between her and Edu running thin again.

"I simply came to assist the Queen of Dreams. I came to ensure our world does not greet oblivion for a second time," Aon corrected casually, as if he were noting someone's misuse of grammar. "But I see how someone of your feeble mind may confuse the two."

Edu snarled and held out his hand. His sword wrenched free of the ground and flew to greet his palm. Q snarled and darted to Lydia, curling around her protectively, looming over her and hissing loudly at the King of Flames.

"Leave, Aon," Ylena demanded.

"No. Not until you vow to go from this place and never return. Not until you leave Ms. Lydia be and see the truth in that I had nothing to do with her rise." Aon was idly fixing his cufflinks as if Edu's angry advance toward him was nothing to worry about. It was probably a normal afternoon for them.

"So that you may stay? So that you may use her for your own ends?"

"What ends may that be?" Aon scoffed.

Lydia decided she was going to stay out of this fight for now. She was hurt and exhausted—and so was Q. She put her hand on her snake's side, petting him, silently thanking him and comforting herself.

"To become the King of All," Ylena replied. "To rule this world by yourself, as you have always wanted."

"We have known each other for five thousand years, Edu, and you understand me so painfully little." Aon sighed dramatically and took a tone as though he were talking to a petulant child. "If I wished to rule this world by myself, I would have murdered you in your sleep fifteen hundred years ago, when our world was doomed, regardless."

Edu hesitated.

Aon chuckled cruelly. "That thought never once occurred to you, did it? Of course not. Then riddle me this. You and I both know I could have kept Lydia in my cage if I desired it. I did not. I released her. I am only here to protect her. And once you are gone and the threat resolved, I shall leave her to her own ends. What good does that do me? What piece on the chessboard does that gain me?"

"You wish her to continue to operate under the false belief she is of her own mind," Ylena replied, but "her" conviction seemed to be wavering. The comment about Aon killing Edu in his sleep had struck home. It was a damn good point that Lydia had never thought about before.

"Ah-hah. Well, she is not living happily within my estate, licking my boots. She is not my pet queen. I have not wed her in the dark of night and made her my bride. She is not my slave nor my servant. I believe, if I am not mistaken, if I asked her to do anything at this point in time, she would tell me precisely where I may put this clawed gauntlet of mine. Isn't that so?" Aon's black mask turned toward her.

She jolted as she was now the center of attention once more. "I want you both to leave me the absolute *fuck* alone."

He gestured at her as if she were proof. "See? What good does that do me? I could have broken her mind to my will if I wished it. You know I could have."

"Lies," Ylena snarled. "She is your puppet, nonetheless, Aon. The moment Master Edu departs, she will invite you to her bedchambers."

"Well, a man can hope... but no. I think not." The warlock shrugged. "To protect her, I destroyed what little friendship she felt toward me. I will not leave here until you vow to me, on the pain of your own willing execution, that you will no longer seek her death."

"Then Master Edu recommends you should pull up a chair."

Pinching the bridge of her nose, she wanted to scream or cry. Wished a horde of monsters to rise from the dirt to chase them both off. But she knew not even on her best day could she take on both Edu *and* Aon. And she was too worn out and too tired to do anything of the sort. "I need you both to leave. Please." She decided to try the nice route. It was the only one she had left.

"I wish I could, my dear," Aon said to her gently, pressing his leather-gloved hand to his chest. "I do not wish to intrude upon you, but I will not let him kill you once more."

"Master Edu recommends a duel to the death, Aon," Ylena said loftily. "Fight him until either you or he lies dead. Once and for all, as it has always been fated to be."

"You really are quite the perfect specimen of a moron!" Aon laughed. "For the past fifteen hundred years, I have sought to restore this world to its proper balance. Killing you would pitch it into disarray once more. No, you enormous idiot, I will do no such thing."

"Then this is war." Edu raised his sword to point the tip of it at Aon. "For Edu will not rest until this corruption of yours is put to rest."

"And break the treaty?"

"You broke the treaty when you murdered the shifter boy," Ylena insisted. "It was null when you held Lydia prisoner."

"Ah, if I may quibble specifics." Aon raised a clawed finger. "She was not my prisoner. The door was closed but hardly locked. She could have freed herself the moment she felt the desire to do so. And, I maintain, she did."

"But you do not argue you shattered the peace treaty between you when you murdered her friend?"

"Of course not."

"Quibble all you like. This is still war between us," Ylena responded. The line between her and Edu had seemingly fully dissolved.

"She is not my corruption. I had nothing to do with her rise. You had a heavier hand than mine. I merely buried her. You killed her. The Ancients gave her this gift."

"Prove what you speak is the truth!"

"Gladly. And how am I to prove it to you, precisely? My words have done you no good. Hers the same. By what method can I convince you, then? Shall I raise the Ancients themselves and ask?" He snorted derisively.

She felt like she had quite literally zero to do with what was unfolding. This was less about her and much more about a grudge match five thousand years in the making. "Can I just go to bed and leave you two numbskulls to sort this out?" Both Edu and Aon ignored her and kept arguing.

Edu shook his head, and pointed a finger at Aon. "Perhaps you are right. You cannot convince him. Edu has decided the only way to rid this world of your corruption once and for all is to rid it of the source. You."

"Then what do you even ask me for?" Aon laughed once more, dark and vicious. "Another war? You wish to halve the population of this cursed realm once again?" Aon's tone carried a familiar, malicious air. The warlock was rising to the challenge now. He was clearly too tempted by the promise of mayhem and pain.

"It seems to be the only way either of us will stand down. For I will not leave before your corruption is cleaned of this place." Edu stepped toward Aon threateningly.

"And how, pray tell, brother mine, has Aon managed to coerce the Ancients into granting such a gift? No. I think once more, your anger and hatred has gotten the better of you."

A fourth voice broke into the fray, one Lydia did not recognize. It was clear as a bell, and soft, yet it cut through the argument like the ice that formed on the top of snow. Razor sharp and clear. It came from nowhere. It was almost whispering, it was so soft.

The unexpected interjection froze Edu and Aon both in their tracks.

"What a shame. When I woke, I felt such joy. I thought I never would see this world again. Yet I came to bask in the rapture of our Gods, and I find my brethren bicker all the same. We have salvation, and yet we balance on the brink of destruction once more."

Looking up to find the source, she watched as something materialized over her.

It was a swirl of white light. The glowing, twisting orb tightened and then burst like a nova around it. The bright rays forced her to turn her head away and lift her arm to cover her eyes.

When the light cleared, a man was hovering in mid-air. No, that wasn't a man.

That was an *angel*.

A full-fledged, honest-to-God, white-winged angel was suspended in the air overhead, his wings spread. As her eyes focused on the sudden influx of light, she realized his wings weren't truly white, no more than an opal was. They were every color all at once, flashing together in such an array of shades that it appeared to merge them all.

The man was gorgeous and awe-inspiring. He made her feel small. Tiny and insignificant. He was a creature of pure glory. The angel was wearing a swath of pure white fabric that wrapped over his chest and around his waist, belted in a thick band of gold. His chest was inked with white markings on a bronzed and tanned surface, as were his arms. He was thin, angular, and narrow-hipped.

He landed on the ground with bare feet, and his opalescent, shimmering, and translucent wings folded behind him. It was only then that she realized he wore a full mask of white porcelain. It looked, much more than Aon or Edu, like an actual face. It was breathtakingly beautiful. All of him looked angular, masculine and yet completely androgynous at the same time. He was too gorgeous to be real, too perfect to be possible. He was a marble sculpture by Michelangelo or one of the other great masters.

It made the angel unsettling at best. But at least with his wings folded behind himself he was a little less imposing. He wore jewelry around his wrists, his waist, his neck. They were thin gold chains, wrapped and coiled around him and dangling from his arms.

Lydia finally shut her mouth.

Aon and Edu were still both staring at the angel in stunned silence. The creature in question turned to her, and Lydia took a step back into Q's coil reflexively. She watched as the angel unfurled a single wing and bowed, folding the glowing appendage in front of his body as if it were another arm. He had long, platinum blond hair, and it fell along his porcelain face as he posed dramatically toward her. "My lady, my Queen of Dreams... it is my most absolute and honored pleasure to meet you."

Lydia didn't respond until Q jabbed her in the back with the end of his tail. "I—uh—I'm sorry, I'm... still catching up. Who're you?"

The porcelain mask tilted up to look at her, black holes for eyes as she could not see what was underneath. "My apologies. I am Rxa, the King of Blood. And I believe I have arrived just in time."

A LETTER FROM KATHRYN

Dear reader,

I want to say a huge thank you for choosing to read *Queen of Dreams*. If you did enjoy it, and want to keep up to date with all my latest releases, just sign up at the following link. Your email address will never be shared and you can unsubscribe at any time.

www.secondskybooks.com/kathryn-ann-kingsley

I hope you loved *Queen of Dreams* and if you did I would be very grateful if you could write a review. I'd love to hear what you think, and it makes such a difference helping new readers to discover one of my books for the first time.

I love hearing from my readers – you can get in touch through social media or my website.

Thanks,

Kathryn Ann Kingsley

www.kathrynkingsley.com

X x.com/vodriel

instagram.com/kathrynannkingsley

PUBLISHING TEAM

Turning a manuscript into a book requires the efforts of many people. The publishing team at Bookouture would like to acknowledge everyone who contributed to this publication.

Commercial
Lauren Morrissette
Hannah Richmond
Imogen Allport

Cover design
BRoseDesignz

Data and analysis
Mark Alder
Mohamed Bussuri

Editorial
Jack Renninson
Melissa Tran

Proofreader
Catherine Lenderi

Marketing
Alex Crow

Melanie Price
Occy Carr
Cíara Rosney
Martyna Młynarska

Operations and distribution
Marina Valles
Stephanie Straub

Production
Hannah Snetsinger
Mandy Kullar
Jen Shannon
Ria Clare

Publicity
Kim Nash
Noelle Holten
Jess Readett
Sarah Hardy

Rights and contracts
Peta Nightingale
Richard King
Saidah Graham